Jane Lane was born Elaine K [...]
was published when she was ju [...]
the pen-name of Jane Lane to reflect the historical [...]
of her books, Lane being the maiden name of her
grandmother, a descendant of the Herefordshire branch of
Lanes who sheltered King Charles II after his defeat at
Worcester. A versatile and dynamic author, Jane Lane has
written over forty works of fiction, biography and history
as well as children's books.

BY THE SAME AUTHOR
ALL PUBLISHED BY HOUSE OF STRATUS

JANE LANE

A Summer Storm

HOUSE OF
STRATUS

This edition published in 2002 by House of Stratus, an imprint of House of Stratus Ltd, Thirsk Industrial Park, York Road, Thirsk, North Yorkshire, YO7 3BX, UK.
Also at: House of Stratus Inc., 2 Neptune Road, Poughkeepsie, NY 12601, USA.

www.houseofstratus.com

Typeset, printed and bound by House of Stratus.

A catalogue record for this book is available from the British Library and the Library of Congress.

ISBN 0-7551-0829-9

To Elaine Weston
A small thank-you for a great friendship

Contents

Chapter One

Thunder in the Air

(i)

Richard stood at the lectern, hands behind him, an attitude learned in earliest childhood; one should touch the pages of a book as little as possible lest one left a smudge. He was not reading, for he knew the Romance of King Meliadus by heart. There were times when he gazed for pure joy in the skill with which the artist had mixed his pigments, powdered chalk and eggshell, crushed lapis lazuli, the precious gold leaf burnished with a pencil of haematite. But today he played a favourite game, identifying the characters with persons of his own real world.

At present only the scene was set: a forest, that natural habitat of all knight-errants, 'holt woods of hoar oaks full huge, a hundred together'. Through it, followed by his faithful squire, rode the hero in search of adventure; in the distance, at a cross-roads, lurked a caitiff-knight. Richard hesitated over the identity of this villain; usually he picked one or other of his three uncles, Sir John de Ghent, Sir Edmund de Langley, or Sir Thomas de Woodstock. But this morning he had fallen foul of a member of his Council,

1

Sir William de Montacute, Earl of Salisbury, and he cast Sir William for the odious role.

The great capital H at the beginning of the text served as a window; over its horizontal leaned the heroine, wistfully awaiting the outcome of the contest which would be portrayed in stages along the bottom margins. She was today and always the Princess Anne of Bohemia, daughter and sister of two Holy Roman Emperors, in a few months to be his bride. The hero was, of course, himself, Sir Richard de Bordeaux.

First making sure his hands were clean, he delicately turned a page.

Ah! The lances were out, couched low. Sparks flew from shields in the shock of the cope. In the first course both used the body-stroke, in the second aiming high against the helm. Then the caitiff's horse refused. ' "For love of the high order of knighthood," cried Sir Epinogris (alias Sir Richard), "let us avoid our horses and fight on foot." Either gave other many great strokes, tracing and traversing, rasing and foining, and hurtling together as it were two wild boars.'

He glanced at the top margin. Yes, there she was again, the heroine, this time on a castle battlements, holding her tiny dog, the only companion of her captivity. To add pathos, the artist had hung upon the wall her psaltery, its strings rudely broken.

He had just reached the climax of the tale, when the hero smote the villain grovelling upon the earth, and bestrode him for to pull off the helm from his head, when the sordid outer world intruded. Sir Richard de Bordeaux turned reluctantly into King Richard II, aged thirteen, who must listen to his Lord Chancellor's account of a debate in Parliament.

Sir Simon Sudbury made those little mumbling movements with his lips which betrayed nervousness. As Archbishop of

Canterbury he was all that could be desired, pious, upright and learned. But when, in the spring of this year, 1380, the Great Seal had been thrust upon him, he had known that he was out of his depth, and since then his distaste for his new office had increased.

First there was the necessity for another session of Parliament, when he had rashly promised not to recall the members this year. They had been disgruntled enough in the summer, asked to provide funds for yet another military expedition to France under Sir Thomas de Woodstock, Earl of Buckingham. Having achieved precisely nothing except the pillaging and burning of French countryside, Buckingham was now demanding reinforcements, which meant the raising of yet more money. And next there was the fact that Westminster must be avoided for the reassembling of Parliament, and this for a very ominous reason.

Just recently, a rich Genoese merchant had been murdered in London, and if the verdict went against the assassins in the forthcoming trial, there might be riots. So Master William Walworth, elected Mayor on the feast of SS Simon and Jude, had warned the Continuous Council who, during the King's minority, ruled the realm. Ever since the late King Edward III laid claim to the French throne, he had encouraged Genoese, Flemings and Lombards to settle in London, giving them extraordinary privileges and thus tempting their compatriots to fight on his side. The result was an intense hatred of foreigners in the City; rightly or wrongly, every Londoner believed that these aliens sucked the wealth from England, using the cheap labour of their countrymen and concealing trade secrets.

Therefore was it decided that Parliament should assemble here in Northampton, though it was not the

season of the year for travelling, and a particularly wet
autumn had brought widespread floods. For the same
reason, provisions were in short supply. But today, all such
inconveniences as cramped lodgings and scarce food had
become mere trifles to Lord Chancellor Sudbury.

'Lord Treasurer prays me to offer you his excuses, sire,'
he murmured, as he bent over the young King's hand. 'He
has taken to his bed with an ague, and sends my Lord Prior
here in his place.'

Richard smiled absently in greeting. Half of him was still
engaged in mortal combat at a cross-roads.

'Tu autem Domine miserere nobis!' moaned the
Chancellor, gripping the ends of his lambswool pall. 'Never
did I pronounce that formula more fervently than when
I ended my address to the Nether House this morning. I
know not how my tongue was able to articulate the dire
sum, £160,000! And yet, as I told the knights and burgesses,
it is the very least required. I have been forced to borrow on
all sides, even pledging your Highness' jewels to Master
Mayor, and still there is three months' pay owing to the
Lord of Buckingham's army, while as for reinforcements –!'
He raised his hands to heaven in a gesture of hopelessness.

'Yet the Nether House promised to do their best,' the
Sub-Treasurer encouraged him. Sir Robert Hales, Prior of
the Knights Hospitallers, was worldly and ambitious.
Strongly suspecting that Bishop Brantington's ague was an
excuse to resign the treasurership in these difficult times,
he hoped to be nominated in the Bishop's room.

'It is true,' admitted Sudbury. 'Yet not seeing how so
great a sum was to be raised, they requested by their fore-
speaker that some from the Upper House be assigned to
counsel them. After long debate, they have chosen a poll-
tax; it being in the interest of every soul in the realm to
prosecute the war with France.'

4

Richard's handsome head jerked up like a horse's against the curb, and his fair skin flushed.

'It is their own interest that concerns them,' he snorted. 'Had they chosen the ordinary course of voting tenths and fifteenths on landholders in the country and householders in the towns, they would have been obliged to put their hands into their purses. But a poll-tax will hit the poor commons who have no one in either House to speak for them.'

The two officials were silent, while Hales, concealing a smile, glanced at the gorgeous manuscript open on the desk. His highness had been stuffing his head as usual with an outdated chivalry, in which the chief obligation of knighthood was towards the poor and the oppressed.

'You say it is in the interest of every soul in the realm to prosecute the French war; I say it is not,' continued Richard, now harping on another of his favourite strings. 'For the past thirty years, all we have exported to France is men and arrows; all we have imported is loot and ransom money. What chivalry is there in such a war as this? What allies would my grandfather have found unless he offered them huge bribes? The only war I would willingly undertake is that against the Infidel, in which King Philippe of France was about to engage when my grandfather sent him a defence. Jesu! if I could but go upon crusade like the first King Richard of England!'

His sharp anger had died as quickly as it arose, and his imagination took charge again. In the white surcoat and red cross of the crusader, he was fighting Saracens, recapturing the holy places, throwing down the crescent and silencing heathen horns.

Sudbury's voice droned on beside him, quavering with nerves. As Bishop of London, he had been ordered to preach throughout his diocese the justice of Edward III's claim to the French throne when war was renewed in 1369. As it was by that time extremely unpopular with those who were taxed to maintain it, Sudbury had become heartily disliked, and this poll-tax would scarcely endear him to the commons.

'It is to be similar to those imposed in 1377 and 1379, except that instead of one groat, every person above the age of fifteen, save only beggars, must pay three. I fear it will add to the general discontentment,' sighed Sudbury, 'but at least it is to be graduated, great landowners paying as much as £6, so that in those districts where they reside, the strong will aid the weak, and the poor man will have but one or two groats to find for himself and his wife, instead of a whole shilling.'

He paused for comments, but Richard, in the thick of a most complicated struggle with Saracens, had not been attending. He said earnestly:

'Pray see that those jewels of mine pledged to Master Mayor are redeemed. Among them are some I intend to have reset for the Princess Anne before our wedding in June.'

(ii)

William Walworth, Mayor of London, was a man of many parts. He was a 'mariner', undertaking at a price to protect English shipping from pirates; a merchant who exported and imported such diverse merchandise as millstones, quicklime, sturgeon and pearls; and a money-lender, accepting as security a silver girdle, a gold mazer or a jewelled baselard. His clients ranged from bishops to squires, and in a special strong-box he retained at the moment some of King Richard's jewels, pledged to him by the Continuous Council.

6

But the mistery to which he had been apprenticed at the age of fourteen was that of fishmongering; and it was in his capacity as Renter Warden of the Guild of Stock-fishmongers that he sat in solemn conference with his brethren on this winter day of 1380.

Their hall, in Stock-fishmongers Row which ran from Thames Street to the quay of Edgate, was a modest one, though the guild was among the richest in London, for the devout abstained on Wednesdays and Saturdays besides Fridays, while during Lent the sale of red and white herrings was enormous. With the Master presiding, flanked by the two wardens, the liverymen had gathered today to discuss the pageant they would stage to greet the Princess Anne on her entry into London next June. On one thing only were they unanimous; their pageant was going to outdo all the rest, even that of the Goldsmiths.

They had already decided on four gilded sturgeon carried on four horses, four salmon of silver, similarly borne, followed by forty-six liverymen arrayed as knights and riding upon what ordinary folk called pike, but among the craft they were 'luces-of-the-sea'. The question remained, what should they have for the grand set-piece? The Master wanted Neptune drawn by dolphins, that fish which was the emblem of both the Salt- and the Stock-fishmongers, with mermaids and tritons; a liveryman daringly suggested Venus rising from the sea, but was vague as to her proper entourage. Both ideas met with vigorous opposition from Master Walworth, on the grounds that heathen gods and goddesses were unseemly in a spectacle put on to welcome a Christian bride.

'Wot's wrong, may I ask,' demanded Master Walworth, 'with our 'oly patron, St Peter, in 'is barque?'

It was objected that they had used this pageant many times before, and that the citizens would expect something new; but Walworth waved aside such arguments. Since his election as mayor last October he had become extremely dictatorial; his strong London accent was partly a pose, as was his appalling French when he was invited to Court. On the one hand he was the poor little parish boy, the industrious apprentice who had made good; on the other he was the greatest personage in London. He loved to recall how a former mayor had feasted in one day King Edward of England, King John of France, King David of Scots, and the King of Cyprus. And he let no man forget that at least for a twelvemonth he reigned supreme in the City, and at his court at Guildhall had power to sentence even aldermen if he found them guilty of some offence.

It was fortunate that at this point the Steward announced dinner, and over their meat and ale the brethren's ruffled feathers subsided. Talk turned upon the poll-tax, and someone remarked that Bishop Brantington was wise when he resigned the treasurership; a shrewd man, he knew there was trouble brewing. Already there were angry mutterings against his successor, Prior Hales, who with the Chancellor was blamed for laying on poor folks' backs an intolerable burden.

'Mark my words,' said the Master darkly, 'this tax'll prove the spark to set alight the stubble. Ever since the Pestilence of '49 we've had unrest both in town and country, and it'll take but this to make the lower sort fall a-rioting.'

'There'll be no rioting while I'm major, Master,' said Walworth sharply. 'I knows me dooty, which is to keep our lord King's peace in this 'ere City, and any 'prentice or journeyman wot breaks it will 'ave me to reckon with. I ain't proud, mind you; I ain't forgot wot it was like to sleep among the fish-'eads under me master's counter, and no one can't accuse me of being 'arsh with the poor.'

This was true. On taking office last October he had at once issued an ordinance to assist the poor of London, whereby bakers must bake special bread at a farthing a loaf, and brewers must brew ale at a farthing a pint (for he deemed ale as necessary for sustenance as bread). He had laid down stiff penalties for those who refused to give change for a farthing; and he had set a personal example of charity by ordaining that every boat of his that brought fish to Billingsgate must put aside one maund as alms.

'I warned the Council,' pontificated Walworth, 'that Parliament 'ad best not meet 'ere in London last month, for I considered it me dooty to make 'em safe rather than sorry. But when John Kirkeby was condemned to 'ang for the murder of the Genoese, was there stirs? Any wretch wot thought to make 'em knew that Will Walworth was a-waiting for 'im with the stretch-neck and the lash; ay, 'e knew there was one at Guild'all now that wouldn't never stand no nonsense. I'll wager any of you, brothers, five gold angels there'll be no rioting in this City while I'm mayor.'

He was extremely affronted by the number of his brethren eager to accept his bet.

(iii)

Joan, Princess of Wales, was at her dower-house, the manor of Berkhamsted, expecting a visit from the King, her son, whose fourteenth birthday had been celebrated with the usual pomp on the feast of Epiphany, 6 January. She sat in what she still called her bower, an old-fashioned term but pleasantly romantic, surrounded by her chamber-beasts, two yapping little dogs, a monkey dressed as one of her pages, and a popinjay in a cage which punctuated the spiritual talk of her confessor with an occasional high-pitched screech.

Sitting bolt upright in his white tunic, hands clasped beneath his scapular, Brother Dominic was denouncing feminine fashions, in particular the long train and the kirtle which was moulded to the bust and bared the shoulders.

'Ladies dragging their long tails after them even into church, where they make both priest and people drink of the dust they sweep after them! As for a kirtle cut low at the neck, it is like nothing so much at the hole in a privy.'

Really he had the most caustic tongue, and she wondered, not for the first time, why she did not replace him as her confessor with a secular priest, always inclined to be mild. But it was fashionable to confess to the friars, and no doubt Brother Dominic was a very holy man.

'You must please to remember, my child, that the too great attention paid to adornment by the wife of Uriah, combing her hair at an open window, aroused the lust of King David. How different was Judith who, while she decked herself in gay garments to trick the Assyrians, after her exploit eschewed such vanities, and shunned the light of the sun, though she was young and fair.'

That last was a very unkind hit; the Princess was fifty-two and corpulent. And she knew precisely whither it was leading; Brother Dominic was about to urge her once again to become a consecrated widow, taking a vow of perpetual chastity before her bishop, lest being so weak and carnal, she was tempted to marry a fourth husband. She shuddered; such a vow entailed not only early rising and the wearing of a hair shift on Fridays, but a most unbecoming dress.

'I sometimes wonder,' mused the Princess, forestalling him, 'if it is not my duty to marry again. My sweet young son lacks a father.'

'The King will soon have a wife,' Brother Dominic crisply reminded her. 'As for marrying again, it is not a question of whether you should, but whether you could. Your once famous beauty is waning every hour, as your mirror ought to inform you, seeing how much time you waste looking into it.'

Here the popinjay screeched, as though in agreement.

'I intend making a pilgrimage to the shrines of Kent,' remarked the Princess placatingly, 'once the roads are open after the winter.'

But Brother Dominic was not impressed.

'Nowadays all too many pilgrims go merely for the sake of novelty and gadding abroad. But for you, my daughter, I would suggest as an excellent penance a visit to the shrine of Notre Dame de Rochemadour, where no woman who has used wine to colour her hair is allowed inside unless she cuts it off.' This was said with a deliberate look at the Princess' elaborately arranged coiffure, which he knew she dyed regularly in an effort to remain what she was called in youth, the Fair Maid of Kent.

When Brother Dominic had gone, she put her feet up on the cushioned banquette. He was so rude and harsh that she felt quite exhausted, and she must compose herself before dining in company with her two grown-up sons, Thomas, Earl of Kent, and Sir John Holland. They were out hawking, and she would have to listen to every wearisome detail of their sport, just as she had been obliged to pretend interest in their father's description of siege or foray. Thomas of the Blind Eye the French had christened him, in reference to his wife's goings-on when he was Governor of Creyk in Normandy. Strange, mused the Princess, fondling one of the little dogs that had leapt upon her lap, how mad in love I was with low-born Thomas; and now I cannot even remember what he looked like.

She could have made a splendid marriage, niece of King Edward, adopted daughter of Queen Philippa after the execution of her father when she was two. But as she liked to say, her heart always ruled her head; first it betrayed her into a secret mating with Thomas Holland, a mere steward,

11

and then, when Thomas was fighting Infidels in the Empire, into an equally secret marriage with his master, Sir William de Montacute, Earl of Salisbury. What a delicious scandal there had been when her uncle, King Edward, discovered the bigamy! The trouble with me, decided the Princess, is that I was never able to say no to a personable man.

But then she flushed. There had been no chance of saying no to her third husband, for it was she who had done the wooing.

Her vanity still smarted from the scene, enacted here in this very chamber at Berkhamsted, when, her marriage with Salisbury annulled by the Pope, and Thomas Holland newly dead, her infatuation and his indifference had driven her to actually propose to her cousin, Edward, Prince of Wales. And had he proved worth the cost of such humiliation? Oh, she had revelled in her new status as the wife of England's heir, and in the extravagant court they kept at Bordeaux; but it had not taken her long to realize that though fiery as a soldier, as a man the Prince was cold. Why had she not noticed that his eyes were as fixed and expressionless as those of a bird of prey, that he laughed seldom, smiled never, and had not an emotion in his heart except for what he deemed the righteous cause of conquering France?

She did her best to forget his last years here at Berkhamsted, ravaged by disease, at feud with his father, quarrelling with his brothers, brooding over those great days when he was master of a third of France, haunted by the stain he had cast upon his honour when, in cold blood, he had slaughtered three thousand men, women and children at Limoges. By the time of his premature death at forty-five, he was hated and despised, he who had been the idol of the English people.

12

Well, thank God their son Richard had not inherited either his coldness or his looks. Richard took after the distaff side, resembling his beautiful great-grandmother, Isabella of France, his gentle, saintly grandmother, Queen Philippa, and, supremely, his mother. He had the thick, dark yellow hair, the pale skin and the deep blue eyes of her who had been called the Fair Maid of Kent. Perhaps it was a mercy that her elder son by the Prince had died at six years old, for little Edward was the living image of his father. On the other hand, she sometimes feared that Richard had inherited in too intense a degree her own romantic temperament. He chose to live in a world which did not now exist, and which was inhabited by damsels in distress and by knights pledged to the most impossible code of chivalry.

After dinner she received the King's Outer Marshal, whose duty it was to hang up his master's escutcheon on the gate of those houses where he chose to stay. King Richard, the Marshal told her, having with him a large retinue, would not incommode his mother, but would lodge at the Trinitarian monastery just outside the town. The Princess smiled indulgently; dear Richard had always favoured the Trinitarians, founded by a French hermit who established his first monastery by a little lonely fountain where a white hart came to drink. It was in honour of this St John of Matha that Richard had chosen for his personal badge a white hart couchant, crowned and chained.

All the same, the Princess was a trifle disappointed. Almost certainly the Earl of Salisbury would be with her son, and it was still piquant to reside under the same roof with an ex-husband. Of course the Pope had annulled their marriage when it was discovered that she was the legal wife of Thomas Holland; but the fact remained that she and Sir William de Montacute had been at bed and board together, and she was confident that the loss of her had broken his heart. That he had remarried with what some thought indecent haste after the annulment, she explained on the score of his avarice. The Countess of Salisbury was dull and plain, but she had an enormous fortune.

Poor man, how he must miss the fiery quarrels and the passionate reconciliations he had enjoyed with the Fair Maid of Kent.

(iv)

Splashing and lurching along the winter roads came King Richard's train.

First jolted carts containing his trussing-beds and other furniture, then another with that of his chapel, antiphoners, grails, altar-cloths, one set of best vestments and one of second best, with a cope. Escorting it were yeomen of the vestry, singing-men and boys, a riding-chaplain, and two canons, the fringe of tails on their almuces bedraggled by the wet. The band of minstrels followed, their instruments loaded on pack-beasts; then ten of the thirty sergeants-at-arms with their maces, under the command of the Inner Marshal whose duty it was to guard any temporary abode. The chamber knights preceded the squires; archers of the guard rode immediately in front of the King's horse; the Chancellor-Archbishop and other members of the Council followed him; and behind all, like gulls after a plough, a crowd of beggars and petitioners appeared from nowhere.

Richard unhooded to the statue of St Rhadegunda, patron of the Trinitarians, who blessed him from a niche in the gatehouse of the monastery, and dismounted to greet the Prior and monks, ranged in procession to receive him.

Outwardly he was gay and gracious, but his conscience was uneasy lest he had hurt his mother by staying here rather than with her. The code of chivalry by which he

14

tried to rule his conduct demanded the most delicate consideration for women. But ever since he had been brought from Bordeaux at the age of four, there were certain of the royal residences he would always avoid if he could.

Windsor Castle was one. There he had sickened at the sight of his grandfather, King Edward III, senile, dribbling at the nose, old hands pawing the strumpet on whom he had bestowed his dead wife's jewels, the bold, painted, gaudily dressed Dame Alice Perrers. There he had listened to his uncles, tall as giants, talking interminably of the French war, boasting, not of their prowess in the field, but of the number of hostages they had captured, the amount of ransom they were demanding for each.

But haunted worst of all for Richard was the manor of Berkhamsted, his home till he became King at the age of ten. A ghost stalked it, the wraith of his father, swollen with dropsy, bitter of tongue, terrifying the child with warnings to beware of his uncles, especially of Sir John de Ghent, for they coveted the throne. And there was something that frightened him even more, something shameful his father had done when he stormed a place called Limoges. Richard's tutor, Sir Simon Burley, who had been present, steadily refused to speak of it, thus only deepening the boy's impression of horror. He guessed that it was in Sir Simon's mind when he urged his pupil to control his rare fits of implacable anger; for it was in cold, not in hot, blood that the Prince of Wales had massacred the inhabitants of Limoges.

It was not only a ghost which made Richard shun the manor of Berkhamsted on the present occasion; his extremely fastidious temperament caused him uneasiness in the company of his mother. A precocious child, he had picked up very early the gossip about the Princess of Wales and her sordid matrimonial entanglements before he was born. Sometimes he wondered fearfully whether she were not an enchantress. She was not unlike the picture of the four evil queens in one of his books, who, finding Sir Launcelot asleep under an apple-tree, would have cast love spells upon him but for the timely appearance of a damsel. Be that as it might, he knew instinctively that his mother's love for him was shallow. Throughout his childhood he had never known the tender affection of any woman except for that of his old nurse, Mundina, now wife of his Master Tailor, Walter Raufe.

But soon there would be Anne, his Daughter of the Caesars as he proudly styled her. He had never seen her likeness, yet he knew her, for she was the heroine of all his romantic legends. Let her name be Felice or Isolde or La Fiere, she was always the same, slender as a lily, white as the hawthorn, constant, debonair, courageous and *sage*. This coming June she would step out of the illuminations into his arms, and they would live happily ever after.

It was typical of Richard to insist that the highlight of their wedding celebrations must be a tournament, he who disliked war but doted on its bloodless mimicry in the lists. He had sent heralds to proclaim this tournament throughout his dominions, inviting 'gentlemen without' to a *joute à plaisance* with 'gentlemen within' at Smithfield on 14 June, the day after Corpus Christi. Equally typical was it that he should depart from the usual custom of running a third course with the battle-axe, a weapon he deemed barbaric. Only the lance and the sword were fit for knights.

During his stay at Berkhamsted he arranged a rehearsal. His mother must deputize for the future Queen and present the prizes, and his chamber squires, armed with parchment lances stiffened with buckram, and wooden shields, for the combatant knights. It would afford these young men valuable practice in the sport essential to their rank. Even the monks, in soutane and scapular of white serge, with a blue and red cross upon the breast, must leave their studies or their illuminating and pretend to be squires and pages. As for the Princess' women, there was not one, however elderly, but must lead through the priory gate by a silver chain an acting knight in his tilting harness. Sitting with his mother in a window of the Scriptorium, Richard longed to be down there in the lists, but his high conception of his regality denied him the pleasure of jousting; he must be judge, not combatant.

'Has it not occurred to you, fair son,' enquired the Princess, shivering with cold on this bleak winter day, 'that your bride may have no interest in such rough sport?'

'Rough sport, madam?' echoed Richard, both hurt and shocked. 'Is she not the granddaughter of that most perfect knight, blind King John of Bohemia?'

On his other side, the Earl of Salisbury gave a small grunt of disgust. The only incident in the whole of the French wars ever to arouse this lad's interest was that of blind King John who, when the day was lost to the French at Crécy, bade his attendants tie their reins to his that they might guide him whither he could strike one blow for his ally, King Philippe, before he fell.

'It would be well to remember,' pursued the Princess, 'that the Lady Anne is older than you. By but three months, it is true, but a maid of fourteen is very much more mature than a lad of the same age.'

She was bitterly jealous of her future daughter-in-law, and lost no opportunity of disparaging her. For so many years, she herself had been first lady of the land, and soon she must give place to this unknown German girl. What made it worse was that Richard absurdly fancied himself in love with a complete stranger; such romanticizing, his mother tried to impress on him, could only lead to disillusionment when they met.

The tournament commenced, and Richard, craning from the window, revelled in a colourful scene of which he never tired, the heralds in their tabards, the harpers waiting to record notable feats, the minstrels thumping nakers or blowing lustily upon horns, the fantastic pasteboard helms of the combatants which, seen from above, made it appear that lions, greyhounds, bears and unicorns were jousting, so high were these crests. From the moment when heralds proclaimed the *laissez-aller*, Richard carefully kept the score, so many points for splintering a lance, so many for unhorsing. He thrilled with pride in these chamber squires of his, the youthful companions chosen by his tutor to take the place of the brothers he lacked.

There was no doubt in his mind who was the best jouster among the 'gentlemen within' today, though it would be for his mother to pronounce the verdict. Ralph Standyche might be a somewhat solemn, even stolid youth, yet how professionally did he shake his lance when first it was placed in his hand by his pretended squire, how well he had mastered that trick of bending forward suddenly at the moment of the cope, and after each course how skilfully he recovered his mount and pranced back to his side of the lists.

'Hold!' presently cried the King. 'That was a foul stroke. Had not your lance been bated, Sir Knight, you would have run your challenger through the thigh.'

The culprit excused himself by declaring that it was due solely to the restiveness of his horse, but Richard was adamant.

'You know it is against the law of arms to strike below the girdle. I judge that you have tilted dishonourably and must withdraw from the lists. Do you not agree with me, Sir William?' he added, turning to the Earl of Salisbury.

'I fear I was not attending, sire,' replied the other shortly. 'My thoughts are occupied with real, not mimic, war. If Sir John de Ghent has his way, we must send an expedition against the new King of Castile, whose throne he claims in right of his wife. I much misdoubt whether your Highness' poll-tax will raise sufficient for both this and the reinforcements demanded by the Earl of Buckingham.'

'It is not my poll-tax,' sharply countered Richard. He disliked Salisbury, not only because that earl had figured in his mother's amorous escapades, but because he resembled Sir Kay in the Arthurian legends, who was contemptuous of chivalry. 'It was imposed by Parliament, and it may cause dangerous disaffection when it is collected in the spring.'

'The Gascons grumbled at the hearth-tax imposed by the Prince when we held our court at Bordeaux,' remarked his mother. 'The commons of every country murmur, but they pay.'

'Madam, I swear to you,' cried Richard passionately, 'that had I my years I never would have consented to the poll-tax. Not only does it oppress the weak, but it is levied to maintain an unjust war.'

'*Unjust?*' spluttered the outraged Salisbury.

'I do and ever have deemed it so,' persisted Richard, his blood well up, and even the delights of the tournament forgotten while he rode a favourite hobby-horse. 'Though my grandfather perfomed *hommage de bouche et des mains* to King Philippe for his French possessions, thus acknowledging himself a vassal, he quartered the fleur-de-lys upon his shield, claiming the throne through a woman, which is against the law of France. God warned him of the injustice of his cause, first by a stupendous thunderstorm which killed six thousand of his men in one day, and again by months of adverse winds which prevented him from sailing on another expedition, so that at last he confessed, "God is for the French".'

He paused for breath, and added more calmly:

'Better, it seems to me, to make alliances with the Scots and the Irish and thus attend to the arts of peace within our own realm, than to pour out men and treasure in a bad cause. When I have years, I shall visit Ireland, wherein no King of England has set foot for two centuries.'

The heralds' cry of '*A lostel! A lostel!*' proclaimed the end of the tournament, and the combatants unhelmed before coming to make their obeisance to the King and Princess. The latter formally addressed young Ralph Standyche.

'Sir Knight, these gentlewomen thank you for your disport and great labour that you have performed this day in their presence. And the said gentlewomen award you this diamond, and send you much joy and worship of your lady.'

The house being but small, Lord Salisbury was obliged to share a chamber with one of his Council colleagues, Sir Richard de Fitzalan, Earl of Arundel. Thither the two men went to array themselves for supper, and while their squires were dressing them, they discussed the French war, the chief topic of all their conversations.

The prospects should be brighter now that Charles le Sage was dead, and the new King of France a boy twelve. On the other hand, the King of Navarre had 'turned French' once again, which was a sad blow; and the Duke of Brittany, who had promised to pay for English arms in his own private war against his overlord, so far had not contributed a franc, and there was a nasty rumour that he too was 'turning French'.

'We would have done well, to my way of thinking,' remarked Salisbury, when the squires had been dismissed, 'to send the King with his uncle of Buckingham on this last expedition. It is high time he was blooded.'

A man of fifty-two, Salisbury had long outgrown the ardour which had caused him to slip home from France and marry unwittingly another man's wife. Except for one outstanding feat of arms, when he commanded the rearguard at Poitiers, he had distinguished himself only by his perspicacity in buying notable prisoners cheap from the squires who had captured them, and in the number of rich estates he had acquired by way of ransom. Lord Arundel had not even one feat of arms to his credit; he was sluggish and comfort-loving, and it was largely due to his negligence that the English had lost St Malo in the previous winter.

'You forget,' he sneered, in answer to Salisbury's observation, 'that his Highness deems it an unjust cause. Our Richard bears no resemblance to his father or his grandfather, those twin thunderbolts of war. By the rood! I begin to doubt his courage; he will not even joust. The only fights in which he will engage are between the pages of a book.'

'Aye,' agreed Salisbury, stroking his grizzled beard. 'I have pleaded with him many a time to cease reading romances. They are mere poems, I have pointed out to him, fit only for ladies and gleemen; but he heeds me not. His tutor is to blame. Sir Simon Burley reared him to have his head either in the clouds or buried in some legend.'

But the mention of Burley brought them back to the all-absorbing topic of the French war. Sir Simon had been sent to negotiate a royal marriage the principal object of which was to tempt the Emperor over to England's side in the conflict. While many barons and knights of the Empire had fought upon that side for pay, the Princess Anne's father, who had died last St Andrew's Day, persisted in 'standing neuter'. The burning question was, therefore, whether her brother, the new Emperor Wenceslaus, might be lured into a military alliance.

At supper in the Prior's chamber that evening, it chanced to be Ralph Standyche's turn to carve his master's meat. It was a duty in which he had little practice, for Richard detested flesh sent whole to the table, preferring minced meat eaten with a spoon. But tonight the Prior had provided a leche-lombard, that spiced sausage which required the most delicate carving if it were to be in the wafer-thin slices acceptable to the King. A long fringed napkin over his shoulder, which served the purpose of white gloves when he offered a dish, Ralph was holding the leche-lombard with two fingers and a thumb while he carefully wielded the knife with his other hand, when Richard unexpectedly addressed him.

'You did not tilt as a Poursuivant d'Amours, fair squire. Have you no lady?'

'So please you, sire, I have. My father betrothed me when we were children to the daughter of Sir John Newton, Constable of your Highness' castle of Rochester.'

'Yet you do not wear her favour when you joust? Oh fie for shame!'

Ralph flushed with embarrassment. A very down-to-earth young man, he had no use for all this romanticism, and he detested the artificial style in which he was expected to reply:

'Alack, sire, my lady has not bestowed her favour on me.'

'That must be remedied,' decided Richard. 'Sir Robert Knolles, I have given you leave of absence to view the progress of the chantry chapel you are building on the new bridge at Rochester. You shall take Squire Standyche with you to obtain his lady's favour.'

The man he addressed was a hard-bitten old soldier, of mean parentage, as sour as a sloe. He had so distinguished

himself in razing towns and castles in France that the
gable-ends of overthrown houses were called Knolles'
Mitres. Much esteemed by the late Prince of Wales, he had
been given the captaincy of all the Household knights and
squires. Richard shrank from him; he seemed to smell of
blood and fire, and his manners were those of the camp.
He had black teeth which he could not help, and black
nails which he could. This afternoon during the
tournament, Richard had caught him yawning, without so
much as a hand before his mouth.

Before giving the signal to his band of minstrels to
entertain the company with song and poem, the King
looked round upon his Councillors.

'Fair, sweet lords,' said he, with a touch of malice, 'I fear
you found the tilting tedious, itching as you do for more
than mimic war. Perhaps our own commons will oblige
you by rising in rebellion against the poll-tax.'

There were dutiful smiles; but Chancellor Sudbury
crossed himself. For he remembered the proverb that there
is many a true word spoken in jest.

(v)

It was still a mystery to Ralph Standyche why he should
have been chosen as one of King Richard's chamber
squires.

At Poitiers his father had been created a knight-
banneret, most honourable of ranks below that of baron,
and bestowed only on the field of battle. Among other
privileges, it gave Sir Thomas Standyche the right to offer
congratulations to a new king at his coronation; and
accordingly he had sent his elder son with a modest gift, a
delicately enamelled clasp to fasten a dagger to the back of
the pouch. The child King received it with his usual grace,
and Ralph was preparing to return home to Kent, when he

was informed by Sir Simon Burley that it was his Highness' pleasure to take him into the royal service.

'The forty chamber squires are to be of sundry counties,' Sir Simon explained, 'that they may be representative of the whole realm, and it happens that so far none has been chosen for Kent.'

He did not disclose the real reason why he had advised Richard to appoint one who had not served the customary apprenticeship as page. As tutor, he felt it his duty to pick some sober and steady young men who might counteract the influence of most of Richard's companions, in particular that of his bosom friend, Sir Robert de Vere, Earl of Oxford, nicknamed by the King 'Sir Dinadan', the merriest jester and maddest talker of the Table Round.

Ralph by no means relished the honour. Country born and bred, his ambition reached no higher than learning to manage his father's modest estate when the time came for him to inherit it. Though he would be a churl indeed who could resist the royal lad's charm, Ralph found life at Court affected and tiresome. The long evenings after Vespers, spent in dancing, harping and the recitation of legends, appeared to him a waste of time, as did the hours when he must stand as still as a stone, ready to fetch and carry or hold a torch nearer.

Riding to Rochester in the company of Sir Robert Knolles, he parted from that sour old *condottiere* when they reached the town, and Ralph made his own way to the castle. Courtesy demanded that he left his baselard, his only weapon, with the porter in the gatehouse; this done, he dismounted in the bailey, and found his future father-in-law in angry altercation with a sharp-faced, under-sized man who, from the axe, adze, square and spokeshave lying in a bag at his feet, was plainly a carpenter. When Ralph had kissed Sir John Newton and said a word or two of greeting, the irate knight burst out:

'You come timely, son, seeing you are a squire in our lord King's service and can testify that this rogue breaks the law in his demands. I would engage him to repair my mews at three groats a day, and he had the impudence not only to demand double but, if you please, wine and fresh meat into the bargain.'

'Take it or leave it, Sir Knight,' said the man with a shrug. 'You will not get a more skilled carpenter than Jack Straw in the whole of Kent or Essex, and if you choose to leave it, I know many will give me what I ask.'

In answer, Sir John quoted from the Statute of Labourers, renewed several times since it was passed by a parliament of 1349, whereby it was made illegal for any labourer to demand, or any employer to offer, a wage higher than that fixed before the Pestilence of that dreadful year. Jack Straw shrugged again, said pertly that if Sir John thought he could get labour at three groats a day, let him try, and shouldering his tools, went off without unhooding.

'By'r Lady, I know not what this realm is coming to!' groaned Newton. 'The rogue speaks true enough, confound him, for I have tried other travelling carpenters, and those in the town likewise, and it seems they have banded themselves into conventicles, all demanding this illegal wage. But you are impatient to salute Barbara, I have no doubt, and will find her in the kitchen.'

Ralph stood in the doorway, half hidden by the smoke and steam, admiring his betrothed before she was aware of his presence. Thank God she was not in the least like the heroines of King Richard's beloved legends, who seemed to spend their time either gathering flowers to make themselves a chaplet, or getting captured by caitiff-knights. Barbara gathered flowers for use in cookery or medicine, and any caitiff rash enough to lay a hand on her would receive a whack from her distaff.

A study, fresh-faced maid, she stood like a general commanding his troops, every now and then making that familiar gesture of tossing her one long plait sheathed in ribbons. At one of the several fires a scullion held the bellows ready to increase the heat under a cauldron on its iron tripod if she saw fit; but she was not so intent on this to be unaware when the pepper-quern stopped grinding.

'Give it two turns more,' she directed. 'Sir Knight likes his sauce well peppered.'

Glancing over her shoulder at a lad who was chopping herbs upon the dressing-board, she saw Ralph. As she went to him, she paused to admonish another kitchen-boy who, his face shielded from the heat by an old wet straw target, was turning a spit on which a dozen plovers were roasting. He must baste them again from the pan on the fire beneath. She touched with a finger-tip a jelly in passing to see if it were set, and remained slightly distrait, explaining that she had a new cook-maid whom she was instructing how to skim a kettle of salt fish.

'The jade will neglect it as soon as my back is turned.'

Far from being hurt by her housewifely abstraction, Ralph thoroughly approved of it. She was his counterpart. As seriously and efficiently as he would rule over his father's manor when the time came, she would reign over kitchen, stillroom, bake-house and dairy. It was typical of their relationship that Ralph had brought her as a gift an ounce of sewing-silk; he had no money to waste on gewgaws, and she had no taste for them.

At dinner, he exclaimed with pleasure as he took one of the plovers from the spit on which they were served, and set it on his trencher of stale bread. It was some time since he had enjoyed such fare, for the King expected his squires to share his taste for made-up dishes eaten with a spoon. The poll-tax being mentioned, Ralph reported that he had encountered on his journey some of the collectors, appointed by the Barons of Exchequer, setting out upon their duties.

'They are to deal with the constables of hundreds and the mayor and bailiffs of towns, to see that in each place as many shillings are paid as there are folk above fifteen years of age. There were mighty sour looks cast at them as they rode, and in one village a dead cat was thrown.'

Ralph left early next morning, for it was both his duty and his pleasure to spend part of his leave of absence in visiting his father and younger brother Hubert at Easter Hall.

He had come within the walls of Maidstone on his way thither before he remembered that it was market-day. Deeming it not worth while now to make a detour, he was soon wedged into a stream of pack-horses, country wives with a lamb laid over the saddle, others on foot with a basket of eggs in each hand and one of apples balanced on the head, morris dancers prancing with a jingle of the little bells sewn on their hose, wicker carts drawn by a dog-team, and the usual quack doctors offering a pennyworth of the powder, found in the ruins of Troy, which gave Helen her beauty, or a bit of red cloth such as had erased the smallpox scars from the King of Aragon.

You will end up in the pillory, my friends, with your nostrums hung round your neck, thought Ralph. But when he came to pass the pillory, he found it already occupied, and surrounded by such a press of folk that he was obliged to draw rein.

It was, of course, always a favourite spectacle, for appropriate punishments were meted out in it, and it was fun to watch a pie-baker who had sold 'venison' pasties made from inferior beef, being obliged by the beadle to eat them all. But this crowd was curiously silent and attentive, and the person whose head and hands protruded through the holes in Maidstone's pillory was of an unusual type.

His face, framed in a grubby white hood, with its red liripipe wound round his neck, was oddly disturbing, the staring eyes giving a hint of madness. He was uttering what appeared to be a sermon, in a sustained bellow which seemed to have upon his hearers an effect positively hypnotic, and Ralph, wedged in, perforce became one of them. At first what the man roared out was familiar enough to him; he had heard such diatribes against pride and avarice in high places from the friars, both Dominican and Franciscan, many a time at the churchyard cross after Mass. But this man did not wear the habit of either order; nor, in painting a horrifying picture of Dives in hell, did he proceed on orthodox lines to bid his hearers be content with their rustic poverty, since riches were so many traps. Instead, he identified Dives with present-day manorial lords, both ecclesiastical and lay, sheriffs, bailiffs, stewards, lawyers, and any man in a position of authority.

Ralph was sickened by him. Some of the friars were bad enough, for in denouncing those who trusted in riches or power, they unwittingly instilled a spirit of rebellion, the fact that it was only the abuse of such things that was sinful being apt to pass unnoticed. But this man was preaching rank sedition, and that at a time when throughout the realm there was serious unrest. He excelled in the popular pulpit art of pulling faces, making crude jests, singing little catchy jingles which stuck in the mind, playing upon words and pleasing these Kentish folk by talking in their dialect. Groans of pleasurable horror greeted his tale of a steward condemned for eternity to cutting his tongue into little pieces with a razor and throwing the bits back into his mouth. A butcher's 'prentice near Ralph remarked:

'Sir John Ball saith troth. All stewards be vexious to the poor.'

'Aye,' agreed an ale-vendor, leaning over the counter of his booth, 'and he be a learned man. He was quoting from St Bernard a while since, who said that if 'twere possible for the rich to have their deserts, you'd see the world's jails full of 'em.'

Ralph was uneasy when at length he was able to thrust a passage through the crowd and proceed upon his way. He had heard of Sir John Ball, nicknamed by sober folk the Mad Priest of Kent. Though Ball had no licence from his Ordinary to preach, he had roamed the countryside for the past twenty years in the manner of an Old Testament prophet, and had seen the inside of more than one ecclesiastical prison for his seditious sermons. With the national temperature raised by this new poll-tax, such a firebrand might prove dangerous indeed.

Before he reached his home that day, Ralph was destined to encounter the third man of a trio, at present obscure, with whose names the whole realm would ring ere he was six months older.

The roads, which would be thronged once spring returned, were almost empty, and Ralph picked his way with what speed he might along the half-flooded causeway. For not only was it unsafe for any lone traveller to be abroad after dark, but he was liable to be arrested, however innocent, once curfew had sounded. He came to a stretch where the local landlord had not complied with the law to clear his ground of undergrowth for the space of half a bowshot on either side of the highway, to prevent thieves lurking there. Keeping a watchful eye upon these bushes, Ralph rounded a bend, and saw approaching him a solitary pedestrian.

The man walked with something of a swagger, and had been singing aloud a bawdy song, but at once became silent when he spied Ralph. A wintry sunset shone upon his face, and Ralph thought he had never seen one so brutal. His eyes were as green and as cruel as a cat's, his body lean but thickly muscled, and the hood, pushed back upon his shoulders, exposed the lack of his right ear. Ralph slipped a hand on the dagger beneath his cloak, suspecting that this wayfarer might be in league with cut-purses lurking in the undergrowth; but then he noticed that the stranger carried in both hands a crude wooden cross painted red.

So he was a felon who, having taken sanctuary in some church, after forty days had 'abjured the realm' in front of witnesses, and was now on his way to the nearest port where, until he found passage to perpetual exile, he must go up to his knees into the sea every day as an earnest of his intention to keep his vow. The cross he carried made him safe from arrest, and despite his evil face, Ralph felt a pang of pity for him.

'God speed you, poor man,' he said as they came abreast. The green eyes wandered over him in so deliberate a manner that he added wryly: 'By St George, you will know me again if ever we meet.'

The bend had intervened between Ralph and the fugitive when the latter, muttering a ferocious oath, flung his cross into the bushes and plunged into the thick woods beyond. Better become an outlaw, though such, like wolves, could be killed with impunity, than wallow in the hold of some filthy ship to banishment. If I can't contrive to elude the constables and live on game, my name's not Wat Tyler, thought the man with the cruel green eyes.

(vi)

It was dusk when Ralph reached his destination, but a half moon lit the familiar scene, the small Saxon church in its graveyard, the common from which a goose-girl was driving home her hissing flock, the wattle and daub houses of the villeins, each with its virgate of arable divided from its neighbour by balks of turf. Sir Thomas Standyche's was a modest manor, a knight's fee, possessing only four hides of land including the demesne; for the rank of banneret was honourable rather than lucrative. The manor house, buried in trees, lay beyond the village, and peeping at Ralph through the leafless boughs rose the domed turret of the louvre, its side openings emitting plumes of smoke from the central fire in the hall below.

Crossing a dry ditch where the moat had been, he blew the horn beside the gatehouse, and when the porter had admitted him, dismounted in the little forecourt with its dovecot and well. As he passed through the entrance into the screens, his father's lame step sounded in the hall, and a moment later he was clasped in a warm embrace.

Sir Thomas was but forty-two, though he looked far older. A thigh wound he had got at Poitiers eighteen years before still pained him, especially in wet weather; and he had never recovered from the grief of losing his wife and eldest son in a mild recurrence of the Pestilence in 1369. The domestic side of his household had been ruled since then by his sister, Dame Agatha; afflicted by an imaginary disease known as 'my malady', she was accustomed to take to her bed at frequent intervals, with the consequence that her maids were slack and the house had a sluttish air.

During supper in the hall, Ralph began to suspect an increased melancholy behind his father's determined cheerfulness, and that its cause lay in his younger brother. Sir Thomas and his wife had reared their children in accordance with an old maxim, 'Courtesy came from heaven when Gabriel greeted Our Lady, and in it are included all the virtues, as all vices in rudeness.' It might be that Hubert was too young at his mother's death to profit by such teaching. At all events he went out of his way at supper tonight to be offensive.

Accustomed for the past four years to the Norman-French spoken by the nobility, Ralph was talking in that tongue about some function at Court when his brother interrupted.

'If you wish me to understand you, you will have to speak the language of churls. I know no more French than my left heel.'

Sir Thomas intervened pacifically. The monks, said he, were coming more and more to teach boys to construe their Latin into English, for they learnt grammar more quickly thus than in the French which had been universal before the late King declared war against France.

'I am obliged to you for defending me, sir,' said Hubert, with a sort of pitiful sarcasm. He wiped his knife on the cloth instead of on his bread trencher, and made to throw the latter to his dog.

'Fie, son, you know very well your trencher must go into the alms-basket,' his father rebuked him mildly.

Glancing from one to the other, Ralph suspected hidden fires. In his opinion, his father had always been too soft with Hubert, who was apt to be headstrong and perverse, but never until this occasion had he known the lad to behave so outrageously. Sir Thomas said grace, and led the way into the dais-chamber behind the high-board, growing cheerful again as he pointed out to Ralph the improvements he had made here since last the elder son was at home.

When he inherited Easter Hall, it had consisted merely of the great hall, open to the roof, and still the heart of the house, the dais-chamber and the domestic offices. Above the chamber he built a solar, as being lighter for his wife at her needlework, approached by a flight of outside steps, and in both these rooms he had put a chimney, of which he was immensely proud. But now what did Ralph think of the newly glazed windows? Dame Agatha kept complaining that either she must freeze or close the shutters and go blind, so he had glazed the windows to please her, though that entailed taking away the outside grille which protected them from thieves. And his carpenter had made for her this table-dormant, so that she would not have a board set up on trestles to hold her work-box.

Ralph duly admired, privately comparing the heavy spiced cakes baked by his aunt and eaten with muscadine, with the light ones of Barbara's baking which he had enjoyed last evening at Rochester. Noting how his brother had deliberately sat down upon the window-seat, away from the fireside bench, he tried to coax Hubert into a better humour by describing the junketings at Court on Twelfth Night.

'We had the usual pageant of the Magi, but this year they rode into the hall on strange beasts, the likeness of which our lord King discovered in a bestiary presented to him. St Joseph marvelled how they came in thirteen days from their far country, and said they, "Sir, we got us, everyone, dromedaries to ride upon, for swifter beasts there be none, one I have, you shall see." These dromedaries were of course men concealed under painted cloths, and they made us all merry by the manner in which they pranced and neighed and flicked their tails.'

'I well remember the pageants in the village here when I was a boy before the Great Pestilence,' mused Sir Thomas.

He shuddered, oppressed by horrors which still haunted his dreams. At the impressionable age of ten, he had known a year in which half the population of England died; he had seen the corpses of his own parents rot because there was no one left to bury them, and men so famished that they turned to cannibalism.

'Aye,' he went on prosily, stroking the pet hawk which went everywhere with him on his wrist, 'England has never been the same since that year. Some said openly that Christ and His saints were asleep, so frightful and unheard of was the pest. It broke every bond of attachment asunder; villeins fled from their lords to escape it, husbands from their wives; there were no laws in force, and the vilest crimes went unpunished. It begot restlessness and greed; there being such extreme shortage of labour, lords tempted away their neighbours' villeins by offering a money wage, and the villeins themselves began to clamour to compound their customary work on the demesne for rent.'

'It was a blessing in disguise,' remarked Hubert from the window-seat, 'if it made men wish to throw off slavery.'

'My villeins are not slaves,' indignantly retorted his father. 'They are serfs bound to the land, but so long as they work three days a week on the demesne, the land in turn is bound to them. They perform service which has been the custom of this manor from time beyond counting, and in return they have security of tenure, a share in the waste and woods I hold, and protection from wild beasts and robbers.'

'They are slaves nonetheless if they cannot quit the manor,' persisted Hubert. 'Master Parson was preaching only last Sunday that all Christians, lord and villein alike, are from one father, Adam, and thus all should be equal.'

'He said that all were equal in their souls before God,' corrected Sir Thomas. 'Certes, boy, the veriest simpleton can see they are not otherwise equal, for some are tall, some short, some comely, some plain, some wise, some foolish. You confuse sound doctrine with that preached by sundry of the friars who are become inciters to sedition.' He turned to Ralph. 'This new reeve elected by the villeins from among themselves is, I fear, a trouble-maker. He came to me on St Agnes' Day upon the matter of boon-work when ploughing starts. Says he, they would have beef and mutton on boon-days, whereas it has ever been the custom of this manor to give them pigeons and bacon. Our Lady pity us, for these are troublesome times.'

When he had led his sons in night prayers before the image in the little oratory contrived in the thickness of the chamber wall, and given them his blessing, they collected a bed-sack each from the coffer and retired to their sleeping-chamber above the bake-house. While he undressed and slung his clothes on the wall-perches, Ralph was silent, rehearsing in his mind a small lecture on filial respect and good manners generally. Hubert needed correction, and if their father was too indulgent to administer it, the elder brother must. He was just about to begin, when Hubert, already on the bench upon which he had thrown his bed-sack, fell to boasting of how popular he was with the villeins because he sympathized with their grievances.

'Adam the reeve was talking to me in the hovel where the cows are calving, and says he, when the collectors of this poll-tax come, they'll get no money from my pouch. Because there is only Sir Thomas to help poor men with it, each living soul at Easter Green must pay two groats, which is a wicked burden laid on the backs of those who labour with their hands.'

'Said he this in front of the cowherd?' sharply demanded Ralph.

'He did, and why should he not? The poll concerns all. And the cowherd said he had not two groats to pay, and he wished he were of the landless men such as tilers and thatchers who wax fat and kicking, selling their labour to the highest bidder. And says the reeve, the whole manorial system ought to be abolished. Why should I, says he, pay the merchet when I marry my daughter, or why should my son pay the heriot when I die? Why must I fold my sheep on the demesne, when I need their dung for my own virgate? And why should there be warrens and fishponds on the demesne? Conies and carp should be free to all.'

'You treacherous young hound!' fumed Ralph. 'How dare you listen to such murmurings against our father!'

'I can't stop them, nor would I if I could. I agree with those who would have villeinage away. Oh, it is all very well for you who live daintily at Court, having your nightly livery of ale, and a servant to wait on you, and fresh meat daily, and a fat wage. There should be neither rich nor poor, noble nor villein, and only one lord in the land, our lord King. So saith Sir John Ball.'

'Whom I saw today in the pillory at Maidstone. Now you listen to me, boy; I will not stomach – '

But Hubert interrupted by springing off the bench and snatching up his bed-sack. The younger lad's pleasant face was distorted with some emotion the nature of which his brother could not understand.

'I'll go sleep in the hall with the servants,' he snarled, 'for who am I to bed with the King's chamber squire?'

As he crossed the room he sang defiantly:

'John the Miller has ground small, small, small,
The King's Son of heaven shall pay for all, all, all.
Beware or ye be woe, know your friend from your foe,
Have enough and cry Ho!'

'What senseless jingle is that?' demanded Ralph.

'The bearward was singing it at the village cross last time he came, and he had it from Sir John Ball. It's a good marching song, aye, and beware when you see men march to it, for they'll be going to take vengeance on those who keep them slaves. Sleep well, brother – till then,' jeered Hubert, making a dramatic exit.

(vii)

By the end of February, the collectors had paid in their receipts, and those of the Continuous Council who were in London met to study them. They assembled in the offices of the Custos Rotulorum in Chancellor's Lane between Holborn and Fleet Street, for this house was a repository for records, and they wished to compare the present returns with those of the poll-tax imposed in 1379.

The morning was so dark that candles had been sent for. Vicious volleys of hail peppered the closed shutters, gusts set moving the three tassels attached to each string of the Chancellor's broad-brimmed hat, and the rolls of manuscript had to be kept down by paper-weights. This dour aspect of the outer world was reflected in the faces round the board, for scrutiny of the returns had convinced the Council of widespread fraud. They were asked to believe that the adult population of the realm had shrunk in two years from 1,355,201, to 896,481, though the kingdom had not been visited by pestilence, famine or foreign invasion. It was monstrously incredible.

'The enormous predominance of males in the population of the country parts is in itself suspicious,' said Sir Hugh Segrave, Sub-Treasurer, 'for it is a fact that in rural communities females tend to be in excess. In a very small number of hundreds are recorded the females one would expect; in the rest there are no widowed mothers, unmarried daughters and other such dependants; there are only husbands and wives. And why? Because a man pays for himself and his wife together.'

He glanced at the Chancellor for comments, but Sudbury only made that nervous mumbling with his lips. During the past few weeks it had grown plain that he and his colleague Hales had become the focus for popular fury, though it was Parliament that had imposed the poll-tax, and Hales had not then been Treasurer. Both had been hissed at on the highway recently, and on the gate of his priory at Clerkenwell, Hales had found chalked, 'Death to Hobbe the Robber'.

'What has happened is clear,' continued Segrave. 'With peasant cunning these clowns have practised a form of evasion which might have deceived us had it not been so widespread. By wheedling or threatening the constable of their hundred, they have got him to suppress the existence of those dependants liable to the impost; nor is it unlikely that some of the collectors themselves have been party to this fraud. The question is, what must be done?'

Instead of applying their minds to so practical a problem, the Council vied with one another in apportioning blame and inveighing against the commons generally. The peasants were disaffected and unruly, otherwise they would not have dared so to cheat the Exchequer. For thirty years past, ever since the Great Pestilence, there had been unrest, accelerated by the disasters of the French war which had begun to take the place of triumphs a decade after that calamity. The best cure for these rebellious churls would be to ship them overseas to man the English garrisons, but alas those garrisons were now all too few. Lord Salisbury's voice was heard above the rest, indulging his hate of Sir John de Ghent, Duke of Lancaster, whose ineptitude as a commander he blamed for the loss of the English possessions in France. Seeing that no one else was ready with a suggestion, Segrave answered his own query.

'In my opinion, a writ should be issued in the name of our lord King to the Barons of Exchequer, declaring that we have ample evidence of shameless negligence and corruption on the part of some constables and collectors, and directing them to appoint a fresh body of commissioners. These must travel round the shires, compare the list of inhabitants in the returns with the actual population, compel payment from those who have evaded the impost, and imprison such as would presume to resist.'

Sudbury uttered a little groan, and began nervously to twist his episcopal ring over the finger of his glove.

'But already there is so much unrest, Sir Hugh. Might not such harsh measures provoke stirs?'

'They have not the wit to unite,' scoffed Sir John Legge, one of the King's sergeants-at-arms.

Segrave turned to him with some eagerness.

'I believe it was you, Sir John, who was chiefly responsible for persuading your fellows in the Nether House to choose the poll-tax at Northampton. Would you undertake to find men to serve on this new commission?'

'Sir, willingly.'

'I cannot but warn you that their task will be odious, even that they may be in actual peril. For so wholesale a fraud as has been practised argues that the commons are become reckless, and may well be prepared to resist by force.'

When the gathering broke up, Sudbury drew his friend the Treasurer aside by an unsteady hand laid on his sleeve.

'There is news from Canterbury that likes me not,' he faltered. 'My officers there have felt themselves obliged to arrest John Ball once more.' He grew weakly indignant. ' "Sir" John Ball I will not style him, for he is no longer God's knight, having deserted his parish both at York and Colchester. He has ever preached a gospel according to himself, and now at Canterbury-cross he was bidding folk withhold tithes if they were poorer than their parson.

Whereupon my officers put him in ward, from which, he swears, twenty thousand saints will shortly release him.'

Hales laughed heartily.

'So false a prophet will languish long in jail,' said he, 'if he pins his hopes of release upon a rustic rabble.'

(viii)

Paschal-tide fell late that year. After the rigours of Lent, and in the midst of the busy season of lambing and ploughing, folk of the hundred of Easter Green were in no haste to return home after Matins and Mass on Sunday. Many of them had trudged miles to church, fasting so that they might receive the Sacrament; the rest of the day was lawfully given to recreation, and in the church porch they found a foretaste of it in the shape of a chapman, his pack open on the bench to display his tempting little wares.

'Be off with you, knave!' a churchwarden indignantly admonished him. 'Take your baubles to the village green and traffic not on consecrated ground.'

The chapman whined, complaining of the heaviness of his pack and the length of the way he had travelled, while his sharp eyes scanned the congregation. They would not have sought him on the village green, but their attention was easily caught by the latten candlesticks, the bright pewter pots, the pins, laces and tabors laid out upon the bench. Already the blacksmith's wife was fingering a hood lined with what the pedlar swore was coney, though it looked suspiciously like cat.

Hubert Standyche lingered with the rest, partly out of defiance. He knew his father disapproved of chapmen, who had an evil reputation for petty thieving and for spreading false news.

'What d'ye lack, fair squire?' wheedled the pedlar. 'A silk headkerchief for your lady? A purse and belt? A musical pipe? All good-cheap such as you will not see in Maidstone.'

Hubert bought the purse and belt, and walking through the churchyard, idly examined them. To his surprise there was a scrap of folded paper tucked inside the purse, and his astonishment grew as he read what was written in a clerkly hand:

'Sir John Ball greeteth you all well, and doth you to understand that he hath rungen your bell. Now right and might, will and skill. Now God haste you in everything. Time it is that Our Lady help you, with Jesu her Son, and the Son with the Father, to make in the name of the Holy Trinity a good end to what has been begun. Amen, amen, for charity amen.'

He puzzled so long over this cryptic jingle that the rest of the congregation, chivvied by the wardens, had left the churchyard before he moved. But sitting with his back against the wall was the chapman, his pack rebound across and across with rope, while he munched a dinner of bread and cheese. Hubert marched up to him and demanded:

'Did you know this paper was in the purse you sold me?'

The pedlar louted with his head in a servile manner, but his eyes were wary. He could not read, he said; someone must have slipped this paper into the purse while his back was turned for a moment. Convinced that he was lying, Hubert said provocatively:

'Whoever wrote it was a forger. Sir John Ball lies in ward.'

'But not straitly kept, Master Squire. It's a clerks' prison, d'ye see, and Sir John being in priest's orders, he is free to write and take the air and receive his friends. So I have heard; but what should a poor man like me have to do with such high matters?'

41

All this evasion only increased Hubert's interest.

'Say what you will,' he insisted, 'I now believe Sir John Ball made you his messenger. Therefore answer me, what does it mean, "a good end to what has been begun"?'

The pedlar shrugged, filled his mouth with bread and cheese, and mumbled inarticulately that he did not rightly know, adding as it were an afterthought that he had heard Sir John Ball would encourage folk to refuse this wicked poll-tax. Hubert felt a thrill of excitement. Squatting down on his haunches, he whispered:

'And will they?'

The pedlar's calling had accustomed him to sum up men, and it was pretty plain to him that this young spark was not on the side of 'them' in the government. But to make quite sure, he whispered in his turn:

'Are you of the company of John the Miller? Are you one of us?'

One of us – a magic phrase! Hitherto Hubert had been as it were upon the outside of the circle, listening while villeins grumbled, picking up mysterious catchwords from his friend the reeve. But now he had the chance to become an initiate; it was easy to convince himself that the bit of paper in the purse was a direct invitation. His rapt expression satisfied the pedlar, who turned confidential.

'I've lately been in Essex, squire, and in an alehouse there I met with one Jack Straw, a master carpenter. Says he before all the company, when the new collectors reach these parts, they'll get not money but a beating. For the commons everywhere, says he, are resolved not to pay a penny more than that already extorted from 'em. And mark my words, squire, Jack Straw saith troth. For these collectors bring with 'em no soldiers, but only three clerks and a couple of sergeants-at-arms.'

Riding homeward to dinner. Hubert was at war with his conscience. He ought to report such seditious talk to his father, who would inform the bailiff of his hundred. Yet why? If the Council were rash enough to try to extort more poll-tax, they should not send forth their collectors with a compelling power so weak. Besides, he was entirely on the side of the commons; or so he liked to think. The truth of it was that his idealism and his generous impulses had not until now discovered a cause to espouse, and in poor men's grievances, which he did not fully understand, he found one ready made.

He had his own, and being a lonely boy he was apt to play the dangerous game of brooding on them. Providence had been most unfair in bringing Ralph into the world before himself; by law, their father's estates must descend to the eldest son, though Sir Thomas could leave his cattle and household goods to the younger. Then there was Ralph's amazing good fortune in being taken into the service of the King, a stroke of luck he seemed not to appreciate, for on his rare visits home he showed no enthusiasm for life at Court. If only he, Hubert, had been sent with their father's modest gift at the coronation, King Richard would have picked a chamber squire far more worthy.

At school he had been Ralph's superior right from the time when he could reel off the alphabet to its triumphant conclusion, 'X, Y, Z and Ampersand!' He could outride Ralph and outshoot him with the long-bow; given the chance, he could have sung a romance to the harp, played the accompaniment to a dance on lyre or dulcimer, aye, and jousted as well as he. Yet here he was, little better than an unpaid servant on his father's dull manor. Last year when he was fourteen, he had plagued his father to send him to Oxford or Cambridge; but no, he must learn the management of the estate while Ralph was absent at Court, though he had no prospect of inheriting.

Hubert came purposely late to dinner, and made an offensive noise drinking his potage. His father's silent disapproval pleased him; though capable of strong affection, he despised Sir Thomas for spoiling him on the one hand, and for keeping him chained at home upon the other. But then he remembered that scrap of paper in his new purse, and all his ill humour vanished.

He would pass on its message to Adam the reeve, who could read, for he had been destined for the Church and had risen as high as acolyte in the minor orders before deciding that the priesthood was not for him. Adam would be deeply impressed to find that Squire Hubert had received a personal invitation from the famous Sir John Ball to 'make a good end to what has been begun'.

In what that good end consisted, Hubert was still vague; but he knew there were stirring times ahead, and that he would play a major role in them.

Chapter Two

Lord of Misrule

(i)

The forest echoed with sounds of a stag hunt, thud of hoofs, crashing of undergrowth, bay of hounds, and the mote, a single call blown long or short upon horns. The voice of the huntsman could be heard addressing his pack with affection and encouragement: 'So ho, *mes amis*, see him!... Ho! Ho! Back there!... Hark, the brave Beaumont gives tongue!' Flat on his belly in a ditch, Wat Tyler cursed, his one ear pricked to distinguish the horn-notes, a hand fidgeting with the sharpened stick which served him for dagger.

'Yon was the rechase,' whispered a youth who crouched near him. 'They've lost and will look elsewhere.'

But it was not until the forest had resumed its early summer silence that Wat moved. He had learned caution both as soldier and highway robber; and since he had broken his vow to quit the realm after leaving sanctuary, he could be killed with as much impunity as the stag these huntsmen had just lost. 'Deservedly,' ran the maxim, 'ought they to perish without law who refuse to live according to law.'

Though this skulking in pathless woods and fens was tedious, Wat made the best of it until something better came his way. During the spring he had gathered round him a band of other outlaws, mostly villeins who either had absconded from their manors without licence, or who, having cheated the first collectors of the poll-tax, had gone into hiding when the Council appointed others. Wat despised them, their petty fraud, their futile grumbles, their bovine wits, while they on their part had grown both to respect and fear Wat Tyler. He fascinated them by his stories of foreign parts; he had crossed the terrible sea many a time, while to them the next county was *terra incognita*. And he cowed them by his complete ruthlessness. He had chastised within an inch of his life a fellow outlaw who hinted that Wat's ear was lost, not at the battle of Navarette, but in the pillory.

Spitting in the direction of the departed hunt, Wat sat down with his back against a tree, and began skilfully to fashion some arrows for the bow he had made for himself. It was a wretched thing, he grumbled; and never losing a chance to impress his simple comrades, he informed them that all the best bow-staves came from abroad, English yew not supplying pieces sufficiently long without knots. His weapons had been confiscated when he reached the peace-stool and found sanctuary, and he mourned the loss of a handsome baselard, picked up at Montclar before that town was given to the flames.

'Dieu! The Prince was nearly roasted in his bed that night, and henceforth slept in his tent at a prudent distance. Yet take it all in all, there never was a weapon invented to beat the long-bow, as the *monsieurs* discovered to their cost when for the first time death overtook them at two hundred yards.'

The youth who had crouched beside him in the ditch asked what prince he spoke of. Just turned fifteen, his father had concealed his existence from the tax-collectors, and now that they were coming round again had bidden him hide. Wat gave him a playful cuff.

'God's bones, what a question! The Prince of Wales, *mon enfant,* he whom the *monsieurs* dubbed le Prince Noir because of his famous black armour. He was little older than you when his father blooded him at Crécy, and he proved a chip off the old block. I can see him now when we stormed Limoges; he was then too sick to ride and we drew him in a four-wheeled chariot through the town, spearing by his orders every living soul we met, and howling with joy at the thought of spoil to come.'

The lad eyed him fearfully. Wat Tyler spoke of the slaughter of unarmed civilians as though it were a mere matter of swatting flies. But the youth cheered up when Wat remarked it was time they thought of dinner. He was expert at snaring game; and if they were still skulking here in the autumn when herds of swine were sent to fatten on acorns, he promised them roast pork.

'But today we'll dine on fowl,' said he, springing up with a lightness surprising in so heavily muscled a man. 'It being now the season when hawks are mewed, we can take our pick of their prey till Lammas. What will you, *mes camarades?* Bittern, heron, river-mallard, or d'ye fancy a dish of larks?'

They never tired of seeing him bring down a bird on the wing, though that, he boasted, was nothing; he could notch with a shaft every crevice in a man-at-arms' harness. While their meal was cooking today, he went off into one of his tirades against the commanders of the English armies in France, speaking as though he were intimate with these great ones. Of all the sons of the late King Edward, in his opinion not one except the Prince had military talent; but it was against Sir John de Ghent, Duke of Lancaster, that he was most bitter, and even his rustic companions knew something of Gent's reputation.

His private life stank, for he was living openly with his daughters' governess, Dame Katherine Swynford; he was held responsible for the two previous impositions of a poll-tax; the whispers that he aimed for the crown seemed confirmed by the fact that on the Prince his brother's death-bed, the dying man successfully pressed for the coronation of little Richard directly the latter's grandfather died, for fear that Ghent might make himself king. And lately there was a rumour that, claiming the throne of Castile in right of his wife, he was pestering the council for men and arms to wrest it by force from Don John. Thus, purely to further Ghent's private ambition, England might be taxed for yet another war.

'I was with the expedition to besiege St Malo in '78,' said Wat, tearing at the tough meat he had shot. 'Parbleu! I knew more of soldiering when I was a raw recruit than Ghent, Cambridge and Arundel put together. They shipped sixty thousand men to Calais, and they shipped sixty thousand back again to Dover without having struck a blow.' He spat contemptuously. 'But I'll tell you what they brought home in their own ships, these famous commanders; rich prisoners to be held for ransom. That's all they understand of war – hark!'

The loss of an ear had not impaired his hearing, and he had caught the sound of a footstep far off in the forest. Signalling his companions to keep quiet, he drew his makeshift dagger from his belt and was worming forward as silent as a serpent, when a voice was heard singing that jingle which had become a sort of password to all malcontents of late, the meaningless but blood-stirring song about John the Miller.

The man who approached turned out to be an old acquaintance of Wat's; they had sat in the stocks together when this Abel Ker, a vintner, was convicted of selling unwholesome wine. That was in Erith, Ker's native town, but it was from Dartford that he brought his news.

'Essex may have started the good work, but Kent has not lagged behind,' he gloated. 'I'll tell you when I've broken my fast.'

From other skulkers in the forest, Wat had already heard snatches of the doings in Essex last month. The affair had begun with a petty riot when one of the new commissioners attempted to revise the poll-tax returns, the men of three villages banding together to drive him out of their neighbourhood. The Council in London replied by sending down Sir Robert Belknap, Lord Chief Justice, to try the rioters before a jury, and this, Ker related, had resulted in the first bloodshed. As soon as the Lord Chief Justice opened his commission, he and his clerks were set upon by a multitude who whipped out concealed knives. The clerks they stabbed to death, the judge they let go, but not before they had burned his documents and forced him to swear on the Mass-book not to hold another session.

On hearing this tale, Wat's comrades swore there could be no turning back now; blood had been shed, and it would prove the signal for a general rising, in which they were resolved to have their share. But Wat remained sceptical; it was one of the busiest seasons of the year in the country parts, with sheep to be washed and sheared, and the hay to be mown. These rustics might grumble, cheat the government by making false returns of the poll-tax, and even indulge in isolated riots, but most of them would slink off soon enough to their husbandry. In any case, no government could ignore the maltreatment of judge and the killing of his clerks; swift vengeance would overtake the murderers, and that would be the end of it.

'You have not yet heard me out,' protested Ker, and plunged again into his story.

The day before yesterday, he himself had led a small armed band against the monastery of Lesness, where by threats they had forced the Abbot to release his villeins from their manorial service, and then had burnt his manor-rolls. Ker's hearers betrayed a new interest; so it was not only against the poll-tax that men were rioting; here was a definite declaration of war against the feudal system. When a man inherited his father's virgate, he had to appear at the manor-court and take an oath of fealty to his lord, all this being written down in the roll and a copy given to the new tenant.

From Lesness, continued Ker, he and his band had taken boat across the Thames to confer with rioters in the villages about Barking, and here a London butcher, visiting his grazing land, told them that certain influential men in the City were ready to open its gates to them if they marched thither. He was a master butcher, insisted Ker, a man of wealth and a warden of his guild.

'But he is not Master Mayor,' scoffed Wat, 'who has power to call out the citizens of every ward to the number of seven thousand, well armed, if there is an attempt against the City.'

Ker refused to be discouraged; he and all his associates were emboldened by the ease with which they had defied the authorities so far, and he had not yet completed his tale.

'I came back yesterday,' said he, 'with a hundred friends from Essex, and entering Dartford we called on the townsfolk to join us, which many did, and we drove another judge out of the gates, pelting him right heartily. And now we could march on Rochester Castle, to release a villein, one John Belling, who absconded from the service of Sir Simon Burley, the King's tutor, and was captured at Gravesend. But we need a leader, one who has seen war and can teach us how to fight.'

Wat gnawed his nails for a while in silence. He was flattered by the implication of that last remark, but he retained his native caution.

'You speak of entering a strong castle,' he jeered, 'as if it were a cow-hovel. D'ye think the Constable will not resist? Have you gyns to batter the walls? D'ye so much as know what gyns are? Or have you miners skilled in sapping?'

'Some from the iron-works of Kent have joined us,' Ker said eagerly, 'and whether they can sap or not, their picks make deadly weapons, as do the knives wherewith each man cuts his meat, not to speak of farm tools. Jack Straw says it can be done, and would have come himself to captain it, but that he has the men of Essex to command.'

'And who may Jack Straw be?' demanded Wat, instantly jealous.

'The Essex men have chose him for their captain, for he's one that's stood out boldly for high wages, and knows the countryside, seeing he's a travelling carpenter.'

Wat laughed contemptuously.

'And will deal many a fatal blow with his adze, I warrant him!'

But his comrades did not join in his mirth. They were deeply impressed by the tale Abel Ker had told them; they were sick of skulking and itched for some action. Wat made up his mind. A quick-witted, self-reliant rogue, he knew himself born to command; with his ruthlessness and his real knowledge of war, it was possible that he could lick this rabble of angry rustics into the shape of an army. At least there was the chance of plunder again, the rich loot which had been as common as blackberries during his French campaigns.

'When it's dark, *mes amis*,' he said softly, 'Abel shall guide us to his headquarters. And then, *en avant* to Rochester!'

(ii)

At the high-board in the hall of Rochester Castle, Sir John Newton sat at dinner with his daughter, his two young sons, and an uninvited guest, the Mayor of the town. Sir John was peevish; at meals he liked his minstrels to play in order to drown the unseemly clatter made by the men-at-arms not on duty, who ate at trestles along the sides of the hall. But Master Mayor was in haste; he could not stay for private conversation in the dais-chamber afterwards, and so Sir John must listen to his jeremiads over meat.

'My bailiffs are divided as to what measures we should take in case these rogues come hither, as it is like they will, a horde of them being now but fourteen miles from us at Dartford. Jesu pity us! Rumour has it that they are several thousand strong.'

'Pooh, a rabble of husbandmen!' scoffed Sir John, who was knuckle-deep in a barnyard mallard, excellently cooked. He chewed for a while, then flung the bones to his dogs beneath the table. 'Close your gates, Master Mayor, call forth those citizens who are bound to keep arms in their dwellings, and I warrant you'll see this scum take to their heels.'

'But there is as much discontent in the town as in the country, Sir Knight,' quavered the Mayor. 'Not only does this poll-tax affect all equally, but we have journeymen and others banding together to demand higher wages than those fixed by law. Moreover, where there is mischief afoot, our townsmen of the lower sort are ever swift to join in it.'

He paused to take a gulp of wine from the cup his young hostess had just replenished.

'Far be it from me to speak evil of dignitaries, yet I cannot but marvel why after such breaking of the King's peace as there has been in Essex, and now these past few days in Kent likewise, the Council does not act with vigour.

To defy the Lord Chief Justice upon his lawful occasions, to murder his clerks – '

The alarum-bell on the castle keep interrupted him, and almost simultaneously a billman rushed through the screens at the lower end of the hall, gasping as he ran that a mob numbering several thousand had been seen approaching the castle.

Sir John Newton was a man who liked his ease, and having served in but one French campaign, he had prevailed on his patron, Sir John de Ghent, to get him appointed castellan of a royal fortress. While he would have preferred one well away from the coast, he had led a very peaceful existence here since 1377, when the French, landing in the Isle of Wight, burnt Portsmouth and attempted to do the same to Dover. During that scare, all garrisons in the south had been increased; but since then, more and more soldiers were withdrawn for expeditions to France, and Sir John now had but a skeleton force of old men past their work and youths who had never seen fighting.

It at once became apparent that he was not to be relied on in a crisis like the present one. Should he, or should he not, light the beacon on top of the keep? he demanded of the world in general. On the one hand the townsfolk might hasten to his aid when they saw this signal; but on the other, after what Master Mayor had been saying, they might throw in their lot with the insurgents.

Here the Captain of the Guard broke in, respectful but firm. The very first essential was to raise the drawbridge, lower the portcullises, and close the gates, but these things could not be done without an order from the Constable.

'I was at that very instant about to issue such commands,' Sir John said pettishly. 'Barbara, and you, my sons, retire into the keep and take the womenfolk with you.'

'Let the rogues enter, and they'll find my distaff can do more than spin,' said the sturdy Barbara. 'And keeps, sir, can be traps rather than places of security, so Ralph tells me.'

'What does that young spark know about it?' retorted her father. 'Do as I bid you, girl, and you, armourer, get me into my harness.'

This was always a long ritual, and today Sir John made it lengthier because he would not stand still. In fustian tunic with gussets of mail, and hose padded at the knees, he kept disappearing on various futile errands, his armourer following him about with his little anvil, nails, hammer and pincers. Wherever Newton went, he was met with tales of woe. One of the portcullises was stuck, its chains, long unoiled, refusing to work the counterpoise weights. There were no pavises in the armoury to protect the cross-bowmen, who therefore hesitated to man the parapet-walk. There were several ancient 'gyns', trebuckets and mangonellas, but not one member of the garrison had ever been taught how to fire them. Stones and hot lime could be poured through the machicolation on to the heads of the attackers, but it would take time to collect such missiles, and already the enemy had reached the edge of the outer ditch.

That they were led by someone with military experience quickly became apparent. Every man in the bailey scattered in panic as an object came whistling over the battlements, landed on the flagstones and burst into flames. Sir John's order to bring water from the well was brusquely countermanded by the Captain of the Guard; it was Greek-fire, said he, shot from a catapult, and only earth or sand would extinguish it.

A yell from the parapet brought Sir John puffing up the steps, followed by the Captain who, viewing the scene below, shook his head gravely. The insurgents had longbows in plenty, and under cover of a volley from these, they would fling into the ditch (which unfortunately was a dry one) vast quantities of faggots and brushwood, thus enabling them to reach the foot of the walls. If they had scaling-ladders, grunted the Captain, the garrison would be overwhelmed.

'I beg you, Sir Knight, to parley,' whimpered the Mayor. 'Pray think of your innocent daughter and your two young sons.'

For very shame, Newton refused; but when he was told that a party of the mob, armed with pickaxes, had actually crossed the ditch and were beginning to sap at a point where the wall was weakest, he felt he had no choice. At last standing still long enough for various pieces of plate to be screwed on to his harness, he grasped his pennoned lance to give him additional dignity, and clanking up to the postern, ordered that narrow gate to be opened for him.

He had anticipated a reverent hush at the sight of him thus accoutred: few of this rabble could have seen a knight in full armour before. But the silence that greeted his appearance was not, he sensed dolefully, one of awe; it was imposed by a bark of command from a man, plainly their leader, who stood arms akimbo at their head. Old soldier was written all over him; his long-bow protruded over his shoulder like a single wing, and the salute he gave the Constable was smart and military.

'You've had a taste of what my boys can do, Sir Knight, shouted Wat Tyler, 'but I warn you 'twill be but the first course of a bloody banquet if you resist 'em. They have no quarrel with you nor with any of your garrison. We're all loyal subjects of our lord King Richard, and all we've come for is to demand the release of one John Belling, a villein wrongfully imprisoned here. Give him up, and I swear by

St Sebastian, patron saint of archers, that we'll retire peaceably.'

Sir John could scarcely suppress a gasp of relief, and sent at once to have the prisoner brought out by way of the postern. Wat was gleefully astounded. So far, it was true, the authorities had shown themselves weak; but that the constable of royal castle, who was responsible for the safe-keeping of any prisoner immured therein, should so tamely hand one over to a mob of insurgents, was almost past belief. Newton was about to retire through the postern again, when Wat hailed him.

'Fie for shame, Sir Knight! These lads of mine have marched far and have empty bellies. I must tell you that the watchword they have chosen is "King Richard and the commons", and were our lord King here in person, I'll wager he would not grudge loyal liegemen meat and drink.' And then, as Newton hesitated, he added with menace: 'I'd be loth to force your gates with a battering-ram, for then I could not answer for the lives of your garrison.'

Before Sir John could make up his mind, his garrison had made up theirs. The drawbridge was lowered, the one workable portcullis raised, and the gates thrown open, all in double-quick time. Like stampeding oxen, the whole horde rushed through, scattering towards kitchen, buttery and cellars. Wat, meanwhile, taking the knight's hand with odious familiarity, remarked that as captain of the King's true commons, it was fit he ate at the high-board in the hall, where doubtless dinner was still upon the table.

'You shall be my carver, Sir Knight. And have your sons sent for; I need pages to pour my wine.'

An outbreak of raucous laughter, followed by a howl of pain, brought him off the dais in an instant and out of the hall. Presently returning, he related how some unmannerly whore-sons among his men had got into the keep and attempted to take liberties with a young lady.

'But God's bones, sir, this spinster seemed well able to defend her virtue. She has given one of my lads a bloody coxcomb with her distaff, and she has armed her maids with the spikes of great candlesticks. Parbleu! I love a wench of spirit.'

All this while the unfortunate Constable had seemed to himself to be in the grip of nightmare, entirely unable to resist or even to protest. It was not that he was a coward, merely that the whole incident was outside his experience; in his brief taste of war he had been on the attacking side, surrounded by a vast host of fellow knights. But when Wat, having finished his meal, said that now they must be gone, and that Sir John and his two young sons must prepare to accompany them, the knight recovered at least his power of speech. He was still grasping his lance and, so far as his hampering armour would allow, gesticulated with it as he spluttered that men would hang for these outrages, that it was treason to enter by force a royal castle, and that as for himself he was resolved not to budge one step from his trust. Wat let him rage himself into a state bordering on apoplexy, and then, shrugging his shoulders, remarked;

'Why, as for budging, you must please yourself, Sir Knight, but to be frog-marched along the highway sits ill with the dignity of your rank. Dieu! You have served in France and know it's the rule to take hostages. You there!' he shouted to some of his men who were lounging near the screens. 'Go strip the armoury, but you may leave the cross-bows, the clumsiest weapons ever made. God's bones, I can discharge six arrows while your arbalester is still winding up his string. You have my permission to unharness, Sir Knight, if you please; to ride in all that armour would be very fatiguing.' And then, thrusting his face close to

Newton's, he snarled: 'Stay stubborn, and I'll cut your sons into collops with my own hands, by God's throat I will!'

Putting a protective arm round his two boys, Newton bowed to the inevitable. But at least, he said stiffly, he had the right to know whither he was being carried. Wat clapped him on the shoulder and said he was now behaving like a sensible man.

'As a hostage, you have *not* the right to know, but I'll tell you. We march to Canterbury, with much business to attend to on our route. These honest lads of mine hold the Chancellor-Archbishop responsible for the wicked poll-tax, and though he is not at Canterbury at present, his palace is,' said Wat, screwing up one green eye in a wink.

(iii)

Sir Thomas Standyche stood at the foot of a ladder in his hall, directing his steward in taking down from the rafters the banner he had won at Poitiers. For eighteen years it had hung there, gathering dust and soot. Regardless of the soiling of his hands, he stroked the frail silk, inspecting with pride the jagged cuts made by the Prince himself when he hacked off the forks to turn a knight-bachelor's flag into that of a knight-banneret.

The hall itself looked strange, denuded of the arms and harness ordinarily hung on pegs round the walls, and now distributed among the able-bodied on his manor. Every day for the past week, he himself had donned the mailed hauberk and hose he had worn at Poitiers; some of the metal rings, sewn by one edge only, had come loose, exposing the leather foundation, and Dame Agatha professed herself too sick to mend them. The banner rolled under his arm, he was about to take it outside for a careful shaking, when running footsteps sounded from behind the screens and Hubert burst in, his face radiant.

'The commons have captured Rochester Castle! It was rendered to them without a blow!'

His father stared at him.

'What lying rumour-monger told you that?'

'It is no lie, sir. The Constable and both his sons have joined the commons, and march with them to Canterbury.'

The knight snorted with contempt. His old friend, Sir John Newton, was no hero, but that he should so tarnish his honour as to surrender the King's castle to rebels was not to be credited, much less that he would actually join them. But as Sir Thomas left the hall, his heart was sick; Hubert had always been wilful and restless, yet that did not excuse his favouring the cause of men who were guilty not only of riotous assemblies but of more than one murder.

It seemed to Sir Thomas of late that he was back in the year of the Great Pestilence. Now as then, his world was full of the sound of lamentation, as wives and mothers came weeping to his door, telling how their menfolk had run off to join the rebels. They could not manage the work on their virgates single-handed, let alone on the demesne; and if their men did not return in time for reaping, they would have no bread next year. With touching trust they begged him to recall these runaways, he who was their natural lord and protector. Already, as in that terrible year of 1349, hay was rotting in the fields, sheep remained unshorn; the kine, untended, broke into the demesne, and weeds invaded the growing oats and barley.

Sir Thomas was as bewildered as the women who came to him for aid. He could understand the discontent caused by the poll-tax, but from what he heard, it seemed that this impost had but sparked off a rebellion against a whole way of life. A very simple, old-fashioned gentleman, he deemed the English feudal system the best in the world, binding together all classes, from the King who was overlord of the entire realm, to the villein who was secure upon his strip of land so long as he performed certain customary services. Undoubtedly there were harsh and unjust lords, human nature being what it was, but that did not make the system evil. It was but an enlargement of the family, the first unit of society; he knew each man, woman and child upon his manor, and if there was strife among them, or they failed in their duties, he dealt with the trouble at his manor-court, where he was acquainted with the local conditions, as the sheriffs, at their courts called Views of Frankpledge, were not.

Of course they grumbled; that too was human nature. But until this time they had seemed as attached to their virgates as trees are rooted in the forest. They, like himself, were natives; they had been settled on this land as long as had his family.

But there was something else incomprehensible to Sir Thomas. Why did not the Continuous Council act? It was now a full week since the first outbreak of violence in Essex, and still he heard no word of calling out the *posse comitatus*. Perhaps it was feared that in Kent and Essex this local militia might prove disaffected; doubtless orders would have been sent to the shire-reeves to summon the country forces in parts of England untainted by this strange new poison of revolt. Yet he remained uneasy. He knew nothing of great affairs except for what Ralph told him on rare visits, and from his elder son he had got an impression of a Council far too numerous, jealous of each other, chiefly concerned to prosecute a war which promised plunder and huge ransoms.

If only he could get word to Ralph and learn what measures were being taken by the authorities, he would feel more easy in his mind. But the countryside was so disturbed, and London so far off, it was not to be expected that they could communicate. Besides, the King's court was peripatetic, seldom staying in one royal manor longer than a month, and he had no idea where Ralph might be.

Well, at least his own duty was clear. He held his land on condition that he supplied a set number of men, fit for military service, if required by his supreme overlord, the King. He would not be able to make up that number, since so many of his villeins had absconded; but he must arm and drill those who remained, together with his household servants, and be ready to march them under his banner directly orders came to him. His lame leg might prove a handicap in fight, but his sword-arm would not have forgot its cunning.

Meanwhile he must take into account the possibility of an attack upon his manor, though so far as he could learn, it was not directly in the path of the insurgents. The fate of those who were in that path varied; his friend Sir Nicholas Herring, attempting resistance, had had his house razed to the ground and barely escaped with his life. Others he knew had suffered no worse than the driving off of their livestock and the looting of their valuables; some of these were poor parish priests and village craftsmen, which made the whole thing even more in-explicable. Others again had fled, leaving their dinners on the table, and then there was a chase organized, the wretched fugitive tracked over heath and fen with the calls used in hunting.

His own precautions were simple. He sent away Dame Agatha to a cousin in the Midlands, doled out among his servants and remaining villeins the quilted gambesons, bascinets, shields and spears from his walls, drilled them in the base-court daily, and buried his strong-box containing his bonds and manor-roll in the woods. Bitterly he regretted now the glazing of the windows in solar and dais-chamber of which he had been so proud, for thus he had deprived them of their old protective outside grille.

His loneliness was extreme. Except at dinner and supper, he seldom saw Hubert, and he hesitated to discuss the situation with this son who took the rebels' part. He knew perfectly well that he was largely to blame for Hubert's wilfulness; he had spared the rod because from infanthood his youngest-born had been his darling, with all his faults so much more lovable than the docile but rather chilly Ralph. In the dais-chamber after supper, the solitary knight strove to keep his troubles at bay by playing at tables with his steward. But he could not concentrate on the game, and the formula became monotonous:

'It is time you turned the tables on me, Sir Knight.'

Desperate for counsel, he rode over on an impulse to the Benedictine monastery secluded in a dale some ten miles distant, where his sons had been taught their grammar, rhetoric and logic. The Abbot was absent, he was told when he alighted in the gatehouse, but Father Prior would certainly receive him after Tierce. He walked in the cloister-court, called the Paradise, and listened to the chanting in the great church; how thin it was nowadays, he thought sadly. When he was a boy, that huge cruciform temple had seemed to rock like a ship with the thunder of psalmody, as the Precentor on the right side, and the Succentor on the left, led each his half of the choir. But the Pestilence had reduced the community to a mere handful, and their numbers had never been made up again.

The Prior invited him to dine, and over the meal waxed eloquent about the house's troubles. Only this morning, said he, the Seneschal, a layman in minor orders who collected the abbey rents, had brought him a long list of grooms, millers, swineherds and fewterers who had absconded. This because these artificers not only demanded an unlawfully high wage, but to work only two days in the week, if you please. Doubtless they had run off to join Wat Tyler, the biggest rogue unhung.

'I believe he was a felon ere ever he went a-soldiering; you know the late King's custom of filling up his ranks by emptying the jails before one of his expeditions to France. Certainly there was a hue and cry for this rogue last winter on account of highway robbery, but I'm told he contrived to reach the peace-stool in some church.'

As for advice, the Prior had none to give, unless Sir Thomas cared to follow Father Abbot's example: his superior, said he, lowering his voice, had gone a-visiting his other houses in parts which so far were trouble-free. More depressed than ever, Sir Thomas rode homewards; he had nearly reached Easter Hall when he received a severe shock.

Beside the road there stood an alehouse, a wretched bothy; its ale-stack, a pole with a bunch of leaves on the end, was so long that it threatened to pull the hut down. Like all such places, it had an evil reputation, kept by a crone who hired out her daughters in an upper room while she served tinkers, wandering jugglers and unthrifty peasants below. She was not above slipping white opium into their ale and robbing them while they slept.

And it was into this den, by the back door, that a familiar figure slipped as Sir Thomas passed by.

So this was where Hubert picked up false news and seditious jingles! His father took one foot out of the stirrup, then put it back again. If he ordered Hubert out, the boy might refuse and cause a scene, intolerable to be witnessed by the company gathered there. But what could have come over him, brought up as he had been on pictures of the Prodigal Son living riotously in just such an alehouse as this? The ox and the ass drink only when thirsty; in these homely words did Parson warn his flock against intemperance. And they would be throwing the dice in there, a pastime Sir Thomas held in peculiar horror because the Roman soldiers had gambled thus for Christ's seamless robe.

But no; Hubert would not come here either to drink or dice. Statute after statute had been passed against the false news, leading to slander and sedition, talked in such dens. It was this more dangerous stimulant the lad sought.

Hubert came home late to supper, neglected to apologize, sketched a sign of the cross, and began to scrape the marrow from a bone set before him, making an unnecessary noise with his spoon. Without waiting to speak till he was spoken to, he announced that he had met a wandering gleeman, who was waiting in the screens to know whether he might entertain them while they ate.

It was clean against Sir Thomas' code to refuse hospitality to any stranger who came to his door, and he sent a servant to bring this minstrel to the high-board, though strongly suspecting that Hubert had met him in the alehouse, and that his songs would be either filthy or profane. His latter apprehension proved unfounded; sitting on the floor, half reciting and half singing to his harp, this gleeman gave them the legend of Robin Hood, who had become increasingly popular of late as a hero who robbed the rich to give to the poor. Sir Thomas noticed how avidly Hubert drank in every word.

> 'These bishops and archbishops
> Ye shall them beat and bind,
> The High Sheriff of Nottingham
> Him hold ye in your mind.
> But look ye do no husband harm
> That tilleth with his plough... '

In the dais-chamber afterwards, Sir Thomas steeled himself for a straight talk with his son. He began abruptly:

'I saw you sneak into an alehouse by the back door today.'

Hubert lifted his chin in defiance.

'I was in good company, sir. There was a Grey Friar came in with his alms-bag, and he being of the listers who may wander where they list, had been of late in London where, says he, there is to be a grand tournament in honour of the King's marriage. There will be huge sums squandered on such empty show, says he, while the poor are mulcted by this poll-tax.'

'He did not neglect, I warrant him, to sell you letters of fraternity whereby, at a price, you will have a share in the merits of his order. These friars flout the rule of their holy founder, who most strictly forbade them to ask money alms but only the necessities of life. Moreover many of them are become as busy sowers of sedition as our chapmen.'

'They are food friends to the poor,' retorted Hubert, 'as is Sir John Ball, wrongfully imprisoned because he preached fearlessly against pride and greed in the rich. He says that lords, both clerical and lay, are grown so avaricious that they grieve more over the loss of a little gold than if they had lost God through mortal sin. And as for the manorial lords, says he, they think that because they allow men to live upon their lands and defend them against wolves and robbers, they have a right to fleece them at their pleasure.'

Hubert fished inside his pouch and brought out a dirty scrap of paper, smoothing the crease with as much reverence as though the thing were a holy relic. He read aloud emotionally:

'Now reigneth Pride in price,
And Covetise is holden wise,
And Lechery withouten shame,
And Gluttony withouten blame,
Envy reigneth with treason,
And Sloth is take in great season.'

'If Sir John Ball wrote that gibberish,' grunted the knight, 'he did ill to omit Anger from the Seven Deadly Sins. Moreover, my son, Envy is liker to be found in the poor than in the rich.'

'Yet will I ask you this, sir,' challenged Hubert, bright-eyed. 'If the cause for which the commons have risen is an ill one, why have the Council taken no measures to repress them?'

Since this was precisely the question which tormented Sir Thomas, he was silent. A great longing rose in him to take the boy into his arms, to appeal to his warm heart, to remind him of those dear days when, after supper in this chamber, his mother sat at her needlework while he and his brothers played their merry games of frog-in-the-middle or hot-cockles; anything to contact the real Hubert, whose affection was but overlaid by the natural urge of his years to assert himself. But fathers did not so address their erring sons, and he let the moment pass.

Next day, 9 June, was Trinity Sunday, and Sir Thomas put on his best garb for Matins and Mass in his parish church. He shouted for Hubert to accompany him, and getting no response, rode on ahead. Parson, plainly in an attempt to wean his flock from the prevailing discontentment, preached on holy poverty.

'Husbandmen and craftsmen may be called with the clergy God's knights, proved not in the lists but by snow and frost, hunger and weariness. The poor man in his hut, wealthy in conscience, leaps more quickly to heaven than from the lofty palaces of kings. God allowed His own mother and His apostles to be poor in this world, when He could have made them rich had He listed.'

But sensing that his congregation remained unmoved, Parson sighed, and concluded as usual with a snatch of simple verse:

'Love we God, and He us all,
That was born in an ox-stall.'

After Mass, Sir Thomas went to pray at the tomb of his wife and eldest son in the chapel of the little chantry he had founded; his hand was unsteady as he lit another taper on the hearse above their grave. Cowardly though he knew it was, he longed for the time when he would lie here beside them, with that old banner, which soon he might have to carry into civil war, hung over his effigy. Last night some stragglers from the main body of insurgents had paid his manor a visit, draining his fishponds, releasing his hawks from the mews, and hanging up a rabbit on a pole at his gate as a sign that the game laws ought to be abolished. He was fortunate, he supposed, to have escaped so lightly. Since these rioters had stained their hands with murder, they would be reckless.

A blow far crueller than any he had suffered so far fell on him when he returned to Easter Hall. Hubert was nowhere to be found, but in the chamber, kept in place beneath a candlestick, was a note for his father, pitiful in its childish pomposity. No Christian, wrote Hubert, should be a bondsman to any save God and his prince; this was the cause for which the commons had risen, and since he believed in its justice, he had gone to join them.

(iv)

Thought he dared not think of his father, not look back at his home, Hubert insisted to himself that he was in the highest of spirits and that his conscience was at ease. At last he was his own master; in his pouch were eight groats saved from the money his father gave him; and the gleeman's song of last night rang stirringly through his head. He, too, was to join a band of brave outlaws; and to prove that he was as pious as Robin Hood, he heard Mass at the first church he passed.

His destination was Canterbury, for he had learnt at the alehouse that the Kentish insurgents had gone thither to release Sir John Ball. Because it was a pilgrim route, thronged at this season, he went by bridle-paths; but even here in the forest he overtook a pilgrim, who was leading a lame horse. It was but courtesy to stop and enquire if at the next village he could send a farrier to the rescue; this elicited from his chance acquaintance a long and very glib recital of his woes. His only son had the falling-sickness and he had been on many pilgrimages overseas to pray for his recovery; but lately he had heard that St Mildred the Virgin at Canterbury was the patron of those afflicted with the disease of his son.

Though romantic, Hubert was no fool, and he began to feel suspicious. It was true that this man wore the shaggy grey gown, representing St John the Baptist's garment of camel-hair, the large round hat slung on his shoulders and the equally big rosary-beads at his girdle, which formed the usual garb of pilgrims on horseback. But though he said he had hired his horse at Southwark, Hubert noticed that the animal was not branded in a prominent manner as a deterrent to the unscrupulous to quit the road and appropriate the mount. When the man went on to say that he was newly returned from Compostella, and offered for sale a relic which he swore was a nail-paring of St James himself, Hubert demanded with heat:

'If you have been to Compostella, why do you not wear the scallop-shell on your scrip and hat? I think you are no pilgrim but a lying rogue, and so good day to you.'

The lad was secretly afraid as he rode on, for it was a lonely spot and this false pilgrim might have both weapons and hidden accomplices. To encourage himself, he began to sing loudly Sir John Ball's now famous song about the

Miller; but he had not got further than the second line when a voice from behind hailed him.

'Where learnt you that, young sir?'

'From those who, like myself, would away with bondage.' The man came running after him and stood in his path, but seeing that it was in no threatening attitude, Hubert could not resist boasting: 'Sir John Ball writ to me from prison; time it is, said he, to make a good end to what has been begun. If you like, I'll show you his very hand.'

When the crumpled note found inside a new purse had been duly produced and admired, Hubert's companion exclaimed:

'Certes, you are well met! You are young and your horse is fleet, and you must be my deputy.' He lowered his voice, despite the solitude of their surroundings. 'I bear a message, but not in writing, and have ridden with it all the way from Colchester. It is short, and you must learn it by rote. Harkee: "Jack Straw greeteth well Wat Tyler, and would have him know that sixty thousand of his Essex friends march brisk to London, where they purpose to encamp in the fields about Mile End." '

'Sixty thousand!' Hubert echoed incredulously.

'No less, and more come in upon their march. Now do you repeat the message that I may hear you have it right.'

It was late afternoon when Hubert saw the great twin towers of St Thomas of Canterbury dominating the landscape, and heard their vast bells ring backward. But as he drew nearer, this alarm signal ceased or at least was drowned in a confused roar. He had been here on pilgrimage with his father and was accustomed to see every road and field-path leading to the town thronged with pilgrim bands, each behind a leader who shouted its gathering-cry as he shepherded his flock to the many hospices outside the walls. Here this evening was a very different multitude.

In place of scrip and bourdon they had weapons, chiefly pruning-knives, pitchforks and sickles; they were chanting, not the Rosary on the Litanies, but 'John the Miller', that jingle as inflammatory as drums of war. Many had got themselves a white hood and red liripipe similar to that affected by Sir John Ball, an idea borrowed by him from the Flemings who had come to be nicknamed White Hoods in their rebellion against the Count of Flanders. The faces turned on Hubert as he tried to edge his horse through the press made him afraid; they were not the homely sunburnt countenances of peasants, but queerly impersonal and mask-like. It was as though each man here had ceased to be an individual with a will of his own, and had become instead but one of a herd, moved by a common impulse, frightening in its blind ferocity.

Thinking it prudent to leave his horse at a nearby hospice, Hubert was carried with them through the gates of Canterbury, along the neat, wide streets between tall houses, whence terrified citizens peeped through the shutters, and so to the conduit at the junction of two ways. Here they halted, and a dead silence fell. Craning between the necks in front, Hubert could see a single figure sitting by the conduit on a blinkered horse, and his heart leapt with excitement and awe. Sir John Ball had been released from jail by twenty thousand of his admirers, just as he had prophesied.

It was plain that his stay in prison had replenished his fund of eloquence. Ever original in his texts, he began now in the famous bellow:

'All rich men are like the pig, profitable only in death.'

This put the crowd into a merry humour, but when the laughter had died, Sir John grew solemn. Hitherto his list of villains had been long and varied, from noble to manor bailiff; his incarceration in a clerical jail had most enormously increased his bile against prelates, and today he concentrated upon these.

'Bishops are to be found more readily in the stable than in the choir; they run swifter to the cookhouse than to Mass; they care more for a roast pasty than for Christ's Passion, more for boiled lamb than Christ crucified; they study more in salmon than in Solomon. Soon ye are to seek your Archbishop in London, good folk, and how d'ye expect to find him?'

'Us'll find un right enough, Sir Priest, never fear!' yelled a man, shaking his fist at the absent Sudbury. But this had not been Ball's meaning, and he waved aside the interruption.

'With no house of his own, like Christ? With no title of worldly lordship? With but twelve simple men as his servants? Nay!' thundered Sir John, the veins starting out upon his brow with hate. 'Ye will find him with the title of Lord Chancellor, in a house as splendid as the King's palace, arrayed in as costly garments, served by a multitude of knights, squires and pages, his clerks riding about him in gilt harness, and he himself upon a palfrey, with jewelled housings as rich as if it were an holy horse. Whereas Christ had but an ass saddled with His disciples' garments. Doth John Ball lie? If ye doubt me, go see for yourselves what manner of house the Archbishop keep here, of whom God in His mercy make soon an end!'

The crowd were not slow to accept such an open invitation to violence. They made a concerted rush towards the archiepiscopal palace; Hubert carried along with them. For a dreadful moment he feared there might be sacrilege, for as they passed the cathedral, some entered by the south porch. But they did not attempt to go further, and automatically they dipped a finger in the holy water vat and signed themselves. In the choir the canons were singing Compline; birettaed heads turned fearfully towards the mob in the porch, and the Precentor dropped his baton from a nerveless hand. In the silence a voice from among the insurgents shouted:

'Sir Priests, you'll soon have to elect a new Primate, for Archbishop Sudbury is a traitor to King Richard and the commons, and we're for London to give him a traitor's death.' And then to the rest: 'Come, boys, let's ding down his crow's nest here!'

At this point Hubert at last managed to extricate himself from the crush. He was full of the message given him by the bogus pilgrim, and he must find Wat Tyler without further delay. In the market-place he came upon the Mayor and bailiffs looking on helplessly while another crowd flung vast quantities of documents upon a bonfire by the cross, chanting, 'Away with the learning of lawyers! Away with it!' On enquiry, he was told that Wat had 'taken up his inn', as the phrase went, at the house of an honest burgess in Saddlers Street, where were shops whose trades overlapped, spurriers and bridlesmiths besides saddlers. Beneath their unglazed arches they showed sign of violent entry, the counter-shutter broken down and the perches behind stripped of their wares. At the foot of the short outside stair of one house, a man in a white hood stood on guard; yes, he said, Wat Tyler lodged above, but the stranger must be searched for secret weapons before he was allowed to go up.

An honest burgess Wat's host might be; at the moment he was certainly a terrified one. He stood in the entrance to the kitchen, as though protecting his wife and children who huddled there, while he kept assuring his uninvited guest that he had already disclosed the whereabouts of his savings, that he had no more, and that as for his wares, they had just been stolen.

72

'Stolen, you dog?' roared Wat. 'They were taken for the service of King Richard and the commons, because a disloyal wretch would not render them willingly.'

Very different now looked Wat Tyler from the outlaw who had skulked in fen and forest. He wore the cuirbouilli, a tunic of leather impressed when soft with ornamental devices, and a sword-belt proper only for knights fell horizontally over his hips. As he straddled before the hearth-place, he played with a very handsome sword, running his thumb up and down the blade.

'And who might you be, my gallant?' he demanded, his green eyes appraising the newcomer.

Hubert hesitated. This man did not at all resemble the romantic mental pictures he had formed of Robin Hood, nor were his followers in the least like the Merry Men of Sherwood Forest. Then he said with what he hoped was a wise air:

'Sir John Ball in his messages to the commons calls them after their separate crafts, as John the Miller or Dick the Carter. And so, if you please, I will be Hubert the squire.'

'You've a head on your shoulders for one so young,' approved Wat, 'and I hope a loyal heart in your bosom. You see this sword? I've sworn by St Sebastian I'll never sheathe it till I've slain the traitors about our young King, I who was of his father's archers of the guard when Richard was born at Bordeaux.'

Somewhat reassured by such words, Hubert delivered the message he had learned by heart upon his ride.

'Sixty thousand, eh?' mused Wat. 'I suspect this Straw of being a braggart, but by God's bones I shall have that number and more when I march on London. We'll encamp on Blackheath, and with the Essex men at Mile End, we'll hold the Tower between us like a nut in a pair of crackers.'

Over a late supper, Wat entertained his new recruit with stories of the French wars which took away the boy's appetite. He was in the midst of a particularly grisly description of King Edward's treatment of what he termed the 'useless mouths' of Calais, by which he meant women and children and the old, when he stopped and listened with his one ear cocked. The crackle of flames which had marked the destruction of Sudbury's palace, and the confused uproar in the streets, alike had begun to die down, so that the gallopade of a single horse was plainly audible, mingled with a voice shouting authoritatively:

'Way! Way in the name of our lord the King!'

'I'll wager my shooting-arm that's a royal messenger,' muttered Wat. 'Only such ride by night as well as by day and can requisition fresh horses from whom they please. Bring a torch, squire, and we'll discover what message the King sends to Canterbury.'

As soon as they came into the High Street, they saw the messenger, easily identified by King Richard's badge, the white hart couchant, painted on an escutcheon which hung round his neck from a chain. He was still on horseback, surrounded by a group of rioters, who seemed to be giving him directions.

'There's our brave captain!' cried one, pointing to Wat.

The messenger addressed him sternly. Was he indeed the chief of those who were making stirs in his Highness' county of Kent? He was the captain chosen by the King's Kentish commons, haughtily replied Wat Tyler.

'Then conduct me forthwith to your lodging, for I am the bearer of a letter to you from our lord the King.'

When they had regained the house in Saddlers Street, Wat took Hubert aside. His Court-French had grown somewhat rusty, he admitted, so let his young friend inform him of the letter's contents. Despite his sneering remark to his brother on Ralph's last visit home, Hubert was perfectly well able both to read and to speak French, but for a moment he was too awed to do as Wat bade him.

It was the King himself, and not some clerk, who had written this brief missive; though the hand was elegant, there was a dash about it which made him sure that its penman was young and impulsive like himself. But as he began to read, his awe gave place to something approaching incredulity.

'Richard, King of England and France. We desire to know why you our commons are behaving in this fashion, and for what cause you are making insurrection in our realm. We bid you cease from violence out of reverence to us, and we will make, according to your will, reasonable amendment of all that is ill done in our kingdom.'

At the foot was a seal, impressed with Richard's privy signet. There could be no doubt that this letter, astounding though it was in its mildness, had been written by the King.

Wat's amazement was mingled with a vast contempt. Either this royal lad was even younger than his years, or his Council were timid almost past belief. But contempt gave place to glee, as vague visions of power danced before Wat's eyes. Already he was the acknowledged leader of a mob who had learnt to respect his ruthlessness, and who had gone too far in sedition to draw back; but now who knew to what heights he might rise? *He* had not the slightest intention of ceasing from violence however many rustic grievances were redressed. And if in the end Richard proved troublesome, well, it was not so very long since Edward II, his great-grandfather, had been put out of the way in secret. Meanwhile he must be flattered.

'You shall be my scribe, squire,' said Wat, 'and write my answer to our lord the King in your best French. Inform him with all reverence that we have risen only that we may free him from the tutelage of his Council, he being now of good discretion and fine stature (aye, lay that on thick, squire!), and to crave of him, our liege lord, amendment of our wrongs.'

For the benefit of the messenger who stood by, Wat kissed King Richard's letter in what seemed a fervour of loyalty, though he could scarcely keep a straight face. God's bones, what a windfall it was! The majority of his mob could not read, but all were familiar with that cognizance of the white hart couchant, crowned and chained. Thus he could impose upon these simple rustics by showing them the letter and pretending to read it aloud to them, inventing such words as would make it seem that Richard was entirely on their side.

(v)

The Princess Joan had set out in May on an extensive pilgrimage, the weather being fine and her boredom extreme. A visit to the many shrines of Kent would afford distraction under the guise of piety.

Canterbury was first upon her list. At the shrine of St Thomas, the most splendid in England, she offered three gold nobles, and another at the Point of the Sword, the reliquary containing a bit of the weapon which had killed St Thomas. She pretended interest in a grisly description of his martyrdom, and feigned to admire a too-realistic portrayal of it in a painted window, which showed the saint's brains spilled upon the floor.

Then she must kneel for a decent interval at the tomb of her third husband, over which hung his famous black armour. How grim was the face on his effigy below, long moustaches drooping over the steel gorget. As she said a *De Profundis* for his soul, she marvelled all over again how she had ever come to fall in love with him.

She bought a number of little Canterbury-bells, the pilgrim sign peculiar to St Thomas, to give to her future daughter-in-law, who had been about to start on her long, slow journey to England when the Council wrote urging delay. With riots breaking out both in Kent and Essex, it would be imprudent to allow their future Queen to come until all was quiet again. Poor Richard was dreadfully impatient; he is like me, reflected the Princess, of a very amorous disposition. One could only hope that he was not in for the same rude awakening as she had suffered after she caught his father.

In southern Kent she found no rioting, though there were disturbing rumours at the religious hospices where she chose to stay. Now she was turning homewards to be in time for the great feast of Corpus Christi and its processions. She had visited many famous roods and images and a number of holy wells, and felt that even Brother Dominic would be pleased with her. He had been left behind at Berkhamsted, for he would have expected her at the very least to wear a plain and unbecoming attire and to walk barefoot when approaching a shrine. As it was, she had travelled in gay clothes and in the greatest possible comfort, slung high above the ruts in a litter, while her ladies, poor things, followed in a whirlicote, facing one another and thrown together when the vehicle came down into hollows with a thud that jarred the spine.

Her barge awaited her at Gravesend to bear her in even greater comfort to Westminster, but she was in no hurry, for there were yet two days before the feast. Dining at an Augustinian abbey near West Malling, she found her hosts so pleasant that she decided to stay the night in their hospice. They were Canons Regular, the least ascetic of the monastic orders, jovial, bearded men who talked at table and ate and drank what they pleased. Ordering her escutcheon to be hung on the gate so that messengers might be able to locate her, she settled down to listen to the prior, a much travelled man, who regaled her with a description of his journey to the Holy Land.

He was telling her about the dogs that kept night watch at the castle of Rhodes, and that knew exactly how to distinguish the Christian from the Infidel, when there came an interruption. One of her son's knights had arrived with an urgent message from Richard. The riots in Kent and Essex had now assumed the most alarming proportions; both Colchester and Rochester had fallen to the mob without resistance; the Archbishop's palace at Canterbury had been burnt to the ground; and the latest news was that both the Kent and Essex contingents, each numbering some sixty thousand, were executing a rapid march upon the capital.

'Our lord King was at Windsor when I left, madam, but intended setting out at once for the Tower, whither he begs you to hasten. I have brought a party of his archers to protect you on your way.'

The Princess was not easily alarmed. She had spent a large part of her life in a France where rival armies clashed continually, and the dreaded Free Companies slew and plundered without respect of persons. So she was less afraid than vexed in the present crisis; speed being essential, she must exchange her litter for a horse, and ride astride, an attitude not only unbecoming but uncomfortable for so well fleshed a lady. The greater part of her retinue would have to follow with the carts and pack-beasts at a slower pace.

On a lonely stretch of heath, some distance from London, Richard's knight, who had been riding ahead of the party, came galloping back to report that he had noticed a thick cloud of smoke issuing from a secluded manor house. They were well out of the route of the insurgents, but there might be stragglers, and they must turn aside. But there was no time. Across some fields, wantonly trampling the hay, a considerable mob advanced rapidly towards them, some laden with spoil, others hallooing and flourishing an assortment of weapons, while one held aloft on a pitchfork what looked like documents. Behind them, in the manner of a sheepdog rounding up strays, came a man on horseback, driving them forward with cracks of a many-thonged whip.

The archers of the guard hesitated to bend their bows; they were hopelessly outnumbered, and resistance might result in a massacre. The knight in charge drew his sword and stood *en garde;* with his other hand he gestured to the badge of the white hart on the escutcheons of his little party, sternly shouting:

'This lady is the Princess of Wales, mother of our lord the King. Molest her not on pain of treason!'

It appeared that the man with the whip was well able to control his ruffians. He halted them at a short distance from the cavalcade and rode forward alone. Any alarm the Princess had experienced was immediately dispelled by her admiration for what she deemed a proper man, let him be noble or churl. The muscular figure that now approached, the insolent green eyes, the suggestion of power and recklessness, all had for her an instant appeal. She simpered, and extended her hand, palm downwards, for his kiss.

Wat Tyler looked at the hand; then he looked at the face with its sensual lips and fluttering eyelids; and lastly he looked at his followers. And he saw himself as fortune's darling. First that invaluable letter from the King; now the chance to show his mob on what terms he was with the King's mother.

'You are well met, Fair Maid of Kent,' cried Wat jovially, 'and you shall ride on your way without harm. But as captain of the King's loyal commons, I claim this privilege.'

Making sure he had the full attention of all present, he leant from his saddle, grabbed the Princess round her ample waist, and kissed her full and lingeringly upon the mouth.

'God's bones!' chortled Wat. 'Now I know why you never lacked for husbands. God speed you, most amorous of ladies!'

Chapter Three

London Betrayed

(i)

Mayor Walworth stood at a window of his house overlooking Billingsgate-dock. It had always been his favourite view, downriver to the newly built Custom House and Tower-stairs, upstream to the Bridge, across to Southwark with its many inns and the disreputable district called the Bankside. He loved the busy scene upon the waterway; wherries ferrying folk from stair to stair; long, low galleys with two banks of oars; great carracks and merchant cogs, his own ships, carrying his merchandise. Especially did he love to point out to admirers the quay below where he, a poor 'prentice, had once gutted herring, his hands raw with cold.

But on this afternoon of Wednesday 12 June, the Vigil of Corpus Christi, he regarded his view with different eyes. The highway of the Thames had become the main defence of London from a vast and hostile mob.

Since an early hour he had been up and about the City, seeing for himself that her other defences were well guarded. He had posted watchmen on top of the Barbican, outside the Cripple Gate, whence could be viewed three

81

counties. Each of the five gates was to be kept closed till further notice; at the last stroke of curfew, the wickets on either side of them were to be shut, and no foot-passengers allowed in or out except by special leave of the Mayor. Posts and chains were fastened across Fish Street-hill into which the Bridge led at its northern end; guards were doubled at the several bars, Smithfield, Whitechapel, Holborn and the Temple; shipping had been directed to congregate either in the pool or in the docks on the City banks. At a threat of French invasion on the death of King Edward III, breastworks had been thrown up along the quays, and these still remained. Walworth manned them with archers; and as a final precaution he commanded the raising of the drawbridge which formed the thirteenth arch of London Bridge.

Yes, he had done all he could as guardian of the King's peace, but he was exceedingly worried. Assembling his aldermen of the twenty-six wards at Guildhall this morning, he found that even in such a crisis, they indulged their bitter little private feuds. Far worse than this, there was a clique among them who were downright insubordinate. Despite the fact that the Essex rebels, who seemed to be led by a fellow named Jack Straw, had already reached Mile End, the aldermen in whose wards were the Ald Gate and the Bishop's Gate refused to undertake the defence of these vital entrances, on the petty excuse that King Edward had transferred such charge to the foreign merchants he favoured. Both aldermen added insult to injury by reminding Master Mayor of his public boast last winter that there would be no riots in London during his term of office.

Swallowing his wrath, Walworth retorted that there *were* no riots in London; she was threatened by insurgents from the country. Bitterly did he regret, not for the first time, an ordinance made in 1354 whereby aldermen could not be removed from office without some special cause. Here indeed was cause enough, but there was no time for electing others. All he could do was positively to order Alderman Farringdon and his colleague to guard their respective gates.

Meanwhile the advent of rebels from Kent was hourly expected, and standing here at his window, Walworth was seeking assurance from the aldermen of Bridge Within and Bridge Without that he had taken every possible precaution on the south. Yes, they agreed, any hostile force would have to go all the way round by the bridge at Kingston if they would cross the river. But they spoke without enthusiasm. They had been among the majority at Guildhall earlier who had resisted the Mayor's wish to call out the London militia, arguing that among such citizens were many who for a long time had been waiting for a chance to riot, and reminding him of the very serious threat of last November which had prevented Parliament from sitting at Westminster. And now, while professing themselves equal to defending their respective strong points, both Alderman Horne and Alderman Sibley were for parleying with the rebels.

'You don't want to go and aggravate 'em, Master Mayor,' said Horne. 'you told us yourself that our lord King sent a messenger to 'em at Canterbury, saying he was ready to listen to their grumbles, if they would go home.'

'Which they didn't do,' snapped Walworth.

'They ought to be given another chance,' chimed in Sibley. Though according to reports there was no man of standing among them, some of them must be reasonable folk, and he dared say harmless enough. What he proposed was that he and his colleague venture across by boat, with a trumpeter and a royal standard, and bid them retire in the King's name. If they did so, well and good; if they refused, no harm would have been done, and presently, after they had eaten up the surrounding neighbourhood, they would disperse of their own accord, since Master Mayor had made it impossible for them to cross the river.

'An empty stomach,' added the alderman sagely, 'takes the fire out of any man.'

At this point a breathless messenger arrived. The vanguard of the Kentish rebels had been seen on Blackheath, and some of the bolder appeared to be pushing on towards Southwark. Very unwillingly, the Mayor gave in to his aldermen's suggestion, and offered his own barge. As for himself, he was expecting a summons to the Tower, where the young King and his Council had been in conference since early morning.

(ii)

In the vast West Chamber on the second storey of the White Tower, Richard sat in his chair of estate, one long leg crossed over the other, jerking up and down with exasperation. It was incredible to him that these veteran soldiers and statesmen could be so effete in a crisis.

Instead of suggesting what could be done, they lamented what could not. Neither aid nor advice could be expected from any of the King's uncles. The truce between England and Scotland was running out, and Sir John de Ghent had gone to the Border to negotiate a new one. (Suppose, exclaimed someone, that those wily Scots, who undoubtedly would have heard of the rebellion, thought it a heaven-sent chance to invade!) Sir Thomas de Woodstock was in so disgruntled a mood since his failure to capture St Malo that he had retired into Wales where he possessed vast estates in right of his wife. There was even a hasty rumour that he was encouraging the rebels underhand. As for Sir Edmund de Langley, he had gone off to Plymouth with five hundred lances, as many archers, and the more energetic barons and knights, *en route to* Portugal,

England's latest ally against France. An attempt to recall him had only made him up-anchor, for he aimed at marrying his son John to the King of Portugal's daughter, and would by no means allow his voyage to be interrupted.

Others of the Council were in a fidget lest the mob gained entrance into London, especially Lord Arundel, who was detested by his villeins for the harsh jurisdiction he exercised at his shire-court over the Rapes of Arundel and Chichester. Then there were the hostages many of them held for ransom, either here in the Tower or in their respective houses. Supposing the mob, in their hatred of foreigners, killed such valuable gentlemen, some of whom were worth as much as 40,000 francs! Apart from all this, the Council displayed something approaching genius in avoiding a decision as to what was to be done. Every now and then they almost reached agreement, when one or other would think of an entirely new objection, and the whole matter must be thrashed out again from the beginning. At intervals the Earl of Warwick could be heard repeating his conviction that these rebels were in the pay of France.

Their faces grew red while they bickered; they started little fresh feuds among themselves. Once or twice Richard offered a proposal; they listened with token respect, and then resumed their squabbling. He might be King, but he was just a boy of fourteen who, with his looks and fastidiousness, ought to have been born a girl.

He gave it up after a while and lapsed into his own thoughts. One could expect no decision from this unwieldy body. During the last parliament, the Nether House had petitioned that he might have only the five great Officers of State to advise him, but the Council clung on to their power like leeches. He fled for refuge to the thought of Anne. Here in this very Tower, at this very moment, she ought to be awaiting her coronation.

Preparations for it were evident in the shape of tapestries worked with the arms of the Empire, Bohemia, Pomerania and Poland, the regal houses from which she sprang. Closing his eyes, he evoked her image; today he saw her as the Lady Venus in the illustrations of the *Roman de la Rose,* riding in a chariot drawn by doves.

When next he attended, the Council had got into an argument as to whether or not the Tower itself was safe. Combined, the Essex and Kent rebels were said to number more than one hundred thousand, while in the Tower were but six hundred men-at-arms,. They glowered at Richard when he reminded them that at Poitiers his father had but eight thousand to France's sixty; and Chancellor Sudbury wailed:

'Again I beg leave to resign the Great Seal. My Lord Prior here and I are become so detested, because we are held responsible for the poll-tax, that maybe if I retired from public life the commons would be satisfied.'

For at least the third time since he had joined the conference, Mayor Walworth begged an order from the King to call out those citizens who by law kept arms ready in the dwellings for just such an emergency as this. Before Richard could reply, Lord Salisbury growled:

'They are not to be trusted. Your aldermen tell me that full thirty thousand are of like mind with these clowns. What you *ought* to have done, Master Mayor, was to forbid your citizens of the better sort to take refuge here in the Tower. How, may I ask, do you expect us to feed them, if we have to stand a siege?'

'Feed them!' echoed Arundel, aghast. 'Is the Tower then not well provisioned?'

It was very typical of the Council as a whole that instead of conferring on this practical question, they united in a verbal attack upon the Mayor. The Tower was outside his jurisdiction, and how dared he permit folk to encumber it who would eat provisions needed by the defenders. Salisbury was just beginning, 'I remember well at the siege of Calais,' when King Richard, unable to bear any more, crisply interrupted him.

'Would it be too much to ask you, Sir William de Montacute, just what you propose that we should do at present?'

To so direct a question, Salisbury gave a surprisingly direct answer.

'Nothing, sire. It is impossible for this rabble to enter either the City or the Tower, and presently they'll go home with their tail between their legs.'

Richard sighed sharply. It was clear that not a man among them, except the Mayor, was ready to take the responsibility for action, and he found it infuriating that those who spent their time breathing fire against the French should become demoralized in the face of an assault by peasants. Ten days had passed since the original riot at Brentwood, and by this time the Council could have summoned the *posse comitatus* from the Midlands and the West.

There were footsteps on the stone staircase, built within the circular turret on the north-east and communicating with all the floors of the White Tower. Glad of any diversion, Richard turned to greet his squire, Ralph Standyche, who whispered that Sir John Newton, a hostage of the rebels, had been sent by them across the river under a flag of truce and with a message he was to disclose to no one but the King. Richard leapt up with animation, and motioning the rest to remain where they were, took Ralph by the sleeve and drew him to the staircase.

'No knight goes to an encounter such as this without his faithful squire,' said he gaily. 'You shall be a witness to what your future father-in-law has to say to me.'

Sir John Newton was in a pitiable state when they found him at the water-stair under St Thomas's Tower. Nothing could be got from him until he had explained over and over again the conditions in which he had been obliged to yield up Rochester Castle to the rebels and, with his two young sons, to travel about with them ever since. For some reason, the sight of Ralph seemed to add to his embarrassment, and it was long before he could stammer out his message, simple though it was. The Kentish mob wished to speak personally with King Richard on the shore below Blackheath.

'By St Mary, so they shall!' cried Richard, clapping his hands. 'Do you know what King Edward I said in a time of great peril? "I wish that all should know the truth of my estate and of my kingdom for what concerns all must be approved by all." I too would have no secrets from my commons, and it is my wish that they have none from me.'

'But it is not to be thought of!' Newton wailed in horror. 'A party of these ruffians are at this very moment engaged in breaking open the prisons of the Marshalsea and the King's Bench in Southwark, and releasing the felons. Thus a criminal element will be added to their ranks, and if you should venture your person – '

'Tell me truly,' interrupted Richard. 'What is the watchword of these insurgents?'

' "King Richard and the commons", but in my opinion that is but show. I heard one say they intended to march on two miles when they had emptied the prisons, and fire the Archbishop's palace at Lambeth, as they did at Canterbury. I have been carried about with them perforce throughout their march, and can testify that there is no man, however exalted, safe from maltreatment at their hands.'

Richard was not listening, for he was rapt away from this sordid world to the dreamland of chivalry, his true home.

Perhaps one day men would write of him as had the chroniclers of old of King Arthur: 'All men of worship said it was merry to live under such a chieftain, that would put his person in adventure as other poor knights did.' Here indeed was an adventure such as Arthur would have relished; and the Princess Anne would hear of it. She, the heroine of all his legends, would know that, as a true knight, he had proved his hardihood alone and so was not unworthy of her love.

'Carry this message back to my commons, Sir John. I will meet them on the shore below Blackheath and listen to their grievances tomorrow at the hour of Prime. And now I'll leave you to give news of your daughter to my good squire here, while I go tell the Council what I have decided.' He hugged himself in a sort of childish ecstasy. 'I can just see their faces, those feeble poltroons!'

His laughter echoed in the vaulted passages as he ran off. Ralph, turning to smile at Sir John, went suddenly cold, his brow and upper lip prickling with apprehension. The knight looked so stricken, that Ralph feared the worst. But when he spoke Barbara's name; the older man, with a sickly smile, reassured him that the maid was safe.

'Yet there is someone else dear to you, lad, of whom I have ill tidings. Your brother is in the ranks of the insurgents.'

After the first shock Ralph blamed himself. Their father being so over-indulgent, it had been up to him as elder brother to correct and chastise. He had intended a lecture the last time he was home, but had neglected to administer it. There was no real harm in Hubert, only a tendency to daydream and to dramatize himself...

At this point in his musings, Ralph had to put away as disloyal the thought that Hubert shared such defects with King Richard.

(iii)

Hubert awoke from a dream in which he was at home again, and for a moment wondered sleepily why his bed-sack had become so hard. Then someone snored almost in his ear, and he remembered that, in company with some sixty thousand other insurgents, he was bivouacking on Blackheath. He sat up, thinking that it must be day, but he saw that the sun had not yet risen, and that what lit the scene was something sinister and ugly. Far away in Lambeth, the Archbishop's palace glowed and winked through a pall of smoke; nearer at hand, flames still shot up from the ruins of John Imworth's house, he who was Warden of the Marshalsea.

Hubert felt ill with misery and homesickness. Disillusionment had begun to set in even before he left Canterbury; far from being an initiate, as he had believed, he was between two worlds, accepted by neither. Because he sympathized with their grievances, he had expected at least his father's villeins to look upon him as their natural leader, once the die of rebellion was cast. Instead, they seemed half suspicious, half reproachful; while as for his own class, Sir John Newton, without mincing words, had castigated him as a renegade and a betrayer. Nor could Hubert cling any longer to his simple belief that this revolt was a sort of crusade, and that the motive of those taking part in it was of the purest. At Canterbury, and along the route, he had seen murder and rapine committed. It was all very well for Sir John Ball to boast that he had authority in the name of the Holy See to absolve from such crimes; peasants might swallow such a monstrous assertion, Hubert could not. He was caught up in something evil, and for two pins would have slipped off home again, but for his fear of Wat Tyler.

He had pictured Wat as another Robin Hood; a few days' acquaintance had been long enough to dispel that delusion. Wat did not rob the rich to give to the poor; he robbed indiscriminately and gave nothing away. Even in the midst of his exploits, Robin Hood had always found time to hear Mass; Wat was worse than a pagan, scarcely opening his mouth without blaspheming, as cruel as the Turk, hunting down deserters and hanging them on the nearest tree. And he was a liar. Hubert had heard him pretend to read aloud that letter he had received from King Richard, deceiving his simple followers into a belief that the King was wholly on their side.

They were hungry this morning, for they had already stripped bare all the villages near the south bank of the Thames. But they were cheerful and excited; the King had promised to visit them in person and listen to their grievances, and at least a large minority of them asked no more than that. Meanwhile they shared out the last of the beef they had stolen, drained the remaining barrels of ale, and repeated to each other Sir John Ball's latest message. It was intended as a hint that they must give blind obedience to Wat Tyler, who had brought them all the way from Canterbury in under two days. 'Look that ye shape to one head and no more, and in the name of the Trinity stand together manfully with John Trueman and all his fellows.'

'*Vous est triste, mon vieux,*' Wat rallied Hubert in his execrable French, flinging himself down on the trampled grass beside the boy. '*Allors,* I'll tell you a secret will cure your gloom. We have friends in the enemy camp, powerful friends, no less than aldermen. One spoke with Jack Straw from the top of the Ald Gate; two others came across river to parley with me, but not in the way Master Mayor intended.' Wat rocked to and fro with glee. 'Their message was this-wise. Let Straw demonstrate against the Ald Gate, while my brave boys do the same against the Bridge, and we'll all find entry.'

Far from feeling cheered, Hubert became yet more uneasy.

'But since the King is coming to listen to our complaints, why must you force entry into London?'

'*Mon enfant!*' mocked Wat, ruffling the lad's hair. 'Are you in very truth so simple? D'you think I'd let a ripe plum like London hang on the tree when it's ready to fall into my hand? Have we not sworn to punish the great traitors, the chief of whom are within those walls? As for the King, we shall need him anon when we march through the shires, driving off the manor-lords and sharing out their estates. Then when there are none greater or stronger than ourselves, we'll make such laws as please us. But first we must have London, where there is loot such as even I have not seen in all my campaigns,' concluded Wat, smacking his lips at the thought.

It was now dawn, and a familiar figure in white hood and red liripipe was seen walking his blinkered horse from one section of the encampment to another, giving out his text for a sermon. They had heard it many times during their lives, for it was a favourite one, thought to have been composed by the holy hermit, Richard Rolle of Hampole. 'When Adam delved and Eve span, who was then a gentleman?' But the lesson Rolle had intended was not that preached by Sir John Ball.

'Good people,' bellowed Sir John, 'it is the tyranny of rich men which has caused servitude to arise in spite of God's law. For if God had willed that there should be distinction, He would have said at the Creation, "Let there be lords; let there be serfs." Why should we be kept in bondage, seeing we be all come from one father and mother?'

His hearers were as quiet as mice, falling at once under his spell. Full two-thirds of them knew not what they wanted nor what thy sought; they followed one another like sheep, and could not distinguish the true shepherd from the hireling. Some said it was only to have the poll-tax abolished; others to protest against the ruinous French war; others again had their own private grudges. But Ball could unite them; when he harped upon the string that nothing could go well in England until everything was held in common and all distinctions levelled, they felt that he articulated their own sentiments, and they murmured, 'Sir John Ball saith troth.'

When next he came within earshot of Hubert, he had reverted to his favourite word-painting of the Last Judgement. So vivid was his description that hands shaded eyes to stare up into the dawn sky; surely they could see God up there, seated among the cherubim; it was His voice and not Sir John's that thundered to the goats on His left hand, lords, prelates, sheriffs, bailiffs, lawyers:

'Depart from me, ye wicked, into everlasting fire! Ye false stinking hounds, because of the stench of the money for which ye ran in this world, ye are cast out from my feast. Ye high prelates, who are like the money-changers in the Temple; ye questmongers who, for a good dinner, will spare a thief and damn an honest man; ye cunning lawyers whose justice is that of the Jews at my Passion; ye serve your master Pilate, and so shall ye in hell eternally!'

Then the eyes of the congregation grew moist as Sir John voiced the complaint of the sheep, all poor men like themselves, gathered on the right hand of the Lord.

'O just God, mighty Judge, avenge us on those whose tournaments were our torments because at our expense they jousted. O just Lord, their minstrels and their jesters received from them food and robes when they cried

"Largesse!" But when we begged for our fair wage they set us in the stocks!...'

From London came the sound of many church bells pealing joyfully, and there was a certain wistfulness in the faces of some of those who listened. One of the greatest of all feasts, and yet they could not hear Mass. Hubert had a woundingly clear vision of other feasts of Corpus Christi, the procession round the village green at home, the clouds of incense, maidens clad in white strewing flowers in the path of the Blessed Sacrament, the rich canopy lovingly embroidered by the women of a parish guild, the glorious hymn of St Thomas Aquinas sung with such fervour, every man sinking to his knees at the passing of the Host.

Ball had moved on again, and from the ribald laughter seemed to be telling one of the jests with which he loved to spice his sermons. Now there were growls and shaken fists, as he insisted that they must not wait till Judgement Day, but anticipate the Lord's vengeance.

'Harvest time is come,' Hubert heard him bawl, 'and we must be like the wise husbandman of Scripture who gathered the wheat into his barn, but uprooted and burned the tares that had half choked the good grain. We will be doing the rich a charity in cutting short their lives ere they can work more evil, and first we must begin with that false shepherd, the Chancellor-Archbishop, and pluck up and make away with him wherever he may be seized.'

Savage howls responded, interspersed with promises to make Sir John Ball the new Archbishop, for he alone was worthy of that office. When the uproar died, Sir John led them in singing his oddly rousing jingle of 'John the Miller', inventing a few more lines on the spur of the moment:

'And do well and better and flee sin,
And seek peace and hold therein,
And so biddeth John Trueman and all his fellows.'

This had the effect of making the mob feel pleased with themselves. Though they were prevented from hearing Mass today, they were good Christians, they desired to flee sin, and all they asked from the authorities was a just and righteous peace.

'And now,' concluded Sir John, 'let us make ready to receive our lord King. He is young, and knows not under what servitude we lie.'

(iv)

It lacked a quarter of an hour before the bells would ring for Prime, when Richard entered his barge.

He had wished to go to the rendezvous attended only by his chamber knights and squires; the commons had asked to speak with him, and not with his Council. But in this he had been overruled. Four other barges followed his, containing the Earls of Salisbury and Warwick with a number of their retainers, all with harness concealed under their tunics; and at Richard's feet sat his elder half-brother, the Earl of Kent. The tide had just turned, and the ebb carried them swiftly past huddled shipping and round the loops of a river deserted save for the swans.

Richard had chosen to come to this strange conference in some state. He had the artist's eye, and well he knew how folk loved spectacles. The sun was his ally, its early beams breaking forth to turn the gilding of the great carved figurehead into dazzling gold, flashing in the few fine jewels he wore and making the oars, ten on either side, strew diamonds as they swept in and out with rhythmic throb. All was sparkle and colour and pride of heraldry; the leopards in the royal standard streaming out behind seemed to ramp and paw like living creatures; a breeze swayed the tassels of the rich canopy and the hangings on the two trumpets in the bows. Their music rang clear through the early summer morning, announcing the advent of a king.

What he had expected to find at the rendezvous, Richard scarcely knew. What he saw, when the last loop was rounded, was the sloping southern bank entirely occupied by men. Kent, who had served briefly in France, drew a whistling breath of apprehension, for it was plain that this mob had a leader with military experience. They were drawn up into rough 'battles' under two great banners, each bearing a St George's cross, and these flags were fixed in the middle of thick thorn bushes, the common practice in conflict, for it added to the difficulty of capturing them. And though the majority had but makeshift weapons, the front ranks were composed of bowmen. Civilians they might be, but this was a weapon even servants and labourers could handle with skill. Ever since the beginning of the French wars, statutes had compelled all able-bodied men to practise archery.

As Richard's barge drew in to land, the insurgents, hitherto silent, erupted into a cacophony of loyal cheers, demonic shrieks, and demands for the heads of the Chancellor and Treasurer. Even Richard saw it was impossible for him to step ashore into this frantic mob, and he bade the watermen lie on their oars twenty yards from the bank. Then he stood up; his voice had not yet broken, and his boyish treble rang out touchingly through cupped hands:

'Sirs, what do you want? Tell me, now that I have come to talk with you.'

There was a confused buzz, as men conferred or argued with their neighbours. Then the cheers broke out, this time dominant. Who would resist the attraction of this lad, combining the grace of childhood with the dignity of his rank, whose thick fair hair was like a golden cap, and who made so simple and forthright an appeal? But a single voice overtopped the acclamations, aggressive and with an undertone of insolence:

'Lord King, you must needs disembark. These honest folk have many things to say to you which cannot be said at a distance.'

'Very well, I will land,' replied Richard coolly, seeing himself as all the heroes in his books of romance.

But this was too much for his half-brother.

'Sire, will you go upon your death?' Kent muttered. 'As a member of your Council and your near kin, it is my duty to save you from such madness. Pull away!' he snapped at the oarsmen, 'and make all speed back to the Tower.'

Richard had turned red with rage, and his fury increased when he saw that he was helpless. The watermen needed no second bidding; frantically their oars dug the river as they brought the barge about. As soon as the multitude on the bank realized what was happening, there were savage roars of 'Treachery!', and the archers, feet astride, turned sideways and nocked their arrows. For several minutes it seemed as though Kent's decision had put the King into greater peril than if he had landed. For he would be within range of the longbows for two hundred yards, nor had he the slightest protection from them.

But as the moments went by, and not a shaft was loosed, exultation mingled with Richard's anger. He had been right! These peasants were loyal to his person; their watchword was no empty one. His heart warmed to them; already he had been flattered by Wat Tyler's reply from Canterbury to his letter; he *was* of good discretion and fine stature; he, like them, was in subjection, and if he redressed their grievances, he would have all the commons of England behind him when he dissolved the Continuous Council and asserted his regality.

'Don't you ever give orders to my servants again,' he raged at Kent, 'or by Christ's Passion, I'll have your head for it, my half-brother though you are! All you have done today is to turn honest men desperate; but if God spares me, before I am much older I will speak with my commons and hear what they have to say.'

(v)

As Richard's barge disappeared behind the Isle of Dogs, Wat sent after it a blistering curse. So nearly had he got the royal lad into his clutches, and now the trap was empty. What next to do? He had a bewildered, angry, famished mob to manage: he must give them both food and action, otherwise they would begin to straggle homewards. So hungry were they that some had broken into the Lock, an isolated leper-house, devouring whatever they could find there, though it might be tainted with the dread disease.

He went among them, and with a confidence not entirely genuine, he swore he had friends in London ready to admit them if they made a show of strength at the Bridgefoot. Privately he doubted whether the traitor aldermen would be able to implement their promises; supine though the authorities had shown themselves so far, they would be roused if there was an attempt to enter London. But the first thing was to fill empty bellies.

'To Southwark, my brave boys!' Wat ordered them. 'It's but a mile or two across the marshes, and it's famous for its ale. You shall eat and drink your fill, and then to action!'

The mob applauded him. They had not the vaguest idea what to do now that the King had failed in his promise to speak with them. They were as wax, therefore, in the hands of a man like Wat, who always seemed to know precisely what he wanted and how to achieve it; and his influence over them had enormously increased since that encounter with the Princess Joan. The tale of it had spread; their captain had kissed the King's mother in public, and very willing she had seemed for the salute.

When Southwark was reached, he let them forage as they chose. Many of the inhabitants had fled at their approach, and those who remained tried to placate this terrible mob by pressing meat and drink upon them. While some broke into the inns of the Bishops of Winchester and Rochester, intent on pillage, others gorged themselves at the great pilgrim inns, the Christopher, the Tabard and the George. Wat, devouring a roast capon as he strolled, cheered them by explaining the use of a roughly enclosed space.

'That's what they call a tenter-ground, where weavers strain and stretch their cloth into what shape they please by means of hooks. I'll warrant, *camarades*, the great ones in London are on tenterhooks at this moment, knowing their last hour is near!'

At the Bridgefoot he encountered Hubert, who was staring in awe at the airy marvel which seemed as though it could never have been built by the hand of man. It was now low tide, but even so the river roared through the narrow arches, making a continuous thunder and foam round the massive wooden starlings on which their piers rested.

'Look,' said Hubert wistfully, pointing to the Stone Gate which guarded the southern end, 'they have put up boughs and garlands in honour of Corpus Christi.'

'We'll put up something else, squire,' replied Wat, with a grim chuckle. 'The heads of the Chancellor and Treasurer.'

Hubert scarcely heard him. In common with all, he had a great reverence for bridges, to build and maintain which was considered a major work of charity; and London Bridge was the pride of England, a national wonder. Miracles had marked its erection nearly two hundred years before; on the middle pier rose the beautiful chapel of St Thomas of Canterbury, containing relics of that favourite saint. What must it be like, thought Hubert, to live and work in one of those tall houses, detached, as it were, from the earth.

Wat, meanwhile, had gone to round up his mob, whom he found augmented by the rougher elements in Southwark, bear-wards, watermen and keepers of the stews. He had still no precise plan in mind as he massed them at the Bridgefoot; if his allies, the two aldermen, failed to keep tryst with him, he might have to attempt a crossing by water. There was a large wharf near by, where stone and timber were landed for the repair of the bridge, and he had seen some barges moored there; it would be an extreme risk, for he would be exposed to archers undoubtedly stationed on the northern quays.

As he thus cogitated, a wicket in the Stone Gate suddenly opened, and someone flourishing a royal standard strode boldly towards him. It was Alderman Horne.

With a wink at Wat Tyler, he harangued the mob. King Richard had confided to him his bitter chagrin in being prevented by the traitors in his Council from landing below Blackheath earlier this morning. His Highness yearned to converse with his good commons, and as a pledge that he was on their side in this quarrel, he had given John Horne his standard, with secret orders to admit them to the bridge. Let them press on and fear no further obstacle; his colleague, Alderman Sibley, was in command of the drawbridge, while another ally, Alderman Farringdon, was at this very moment opening the Ald Gate to their Essex comrades.

A large proportion of the rioters had not understood what he said, knowing only their own Kentish dialect. But that he was a friend was obvious from his tone and expression, and they greeted his speech with a roar of applause. When it died, Wat issued crisp orders; in all military attacks, said he, a war-cry was shouted, 'God and St George' by the English, 'God and St Denis' by the French. His brave lads must yell at the very tops of their voices 'King Richard and the commons', said the cunning Wat; he knew that this would sound innocent to the citizens at large, and might well persuade many to join him.

Formidable as leviathan, the mob began to move, the more intelligent among them covering their heads with makeshift shields lest there be cross-bowmen on the turrets of the gate. But not a bolt was shot, and as if of their own accord the huge central doors opened to receive them. Bellowing their war-cry, they jostled along the narrow way between the houses, then came to a sudden halt.

Rearing high in the air was the drawbridge which formed the thirteenth arch, and between it and the insurgents was a giddy drop, with the river swirling and foaming far below. Thus thwarted on the threshold of their goal, the rioters turned upon Horne, threatening to pitch him over into the Thames. But he, all merry and confident, begged them to have patience.

'I told you Alderman Sibley is in charge here,' he shouted, 'and he is even now acting a little droll. When the burgesses of his ward of Bridge Within come to offer him aid, as assuredly some of them will do, he is to bid them mind their own business and leave him to his duty with his constables. To these he is to lament that further resistance is useless, seeing you have already gained the southern portion of the bridge.'

Even as he spoke, the huge platform rearing up on end seemed to tremble, and above the tumult of the river could be heard a clang of chains. Then, slowly and jerkily, the monster began to move downwards; it had not yet quite made contact with the opposite arch when the front rank of rioters leapt upon it, scattering the terrified constables of the ward. The bulk of the mob surged on behind them, as irresistible as the river itself.

By noon of that Thursday, 13 June 1381, London had fallen without one blow struck in her defence.

Chapter Four

Gale Havoc

(i)

Wat's quick wits were busy as he marched at the head of his mob up Fish Street-hill. Hitherto he had been able to make this human tide ebb and flow at his pleasure; now he had allies without whose aid he could never have entered London. It was unknown terrain to him, and he would need these traitor aldermen as guides; but he had not the smallest intention of sharing his command, and from the first he must assert himself as captain of the commons.

He was relieved to hear that there would be no rivalry by Jack Straw, at least for the moment. The Essex rioter had straightway been led by Alderman Farringdon to sack the great priory of St John at Clerkenwell. It was the headquarters of the Knights Hospitallers in England, and therefore the official abode of Treasurer Hales. And now that they had succeeded in their treachery, Sibley and Horne were for using the Kentish mob on similar ploys. They had a list of clerical victims: Sir John Fordham, bishop-elect of Durham and Clerk of the Privy Seal, was lodged with the Bishop of Chester at the latter's inn, and thus two birds could be killed with one stone. Then there were all the foreigners, who kept trade secrets, forestalled the market, and threw Englishmen out of work. Wat listened in silent contempt; if you imagine I have marched from Kent in order to settle your private scores for you, thought he, you are very much mistaken.

The streets were deserted. Many citizens had fled into the fields outside the walls, others had sought sanctuary in the churches, others again cowered behind closed shutters. By the time his guides had conducted him into broad Westcheap, Wat had made up his mind as to how to assert himself. Leaping up the steps of the Standard, a market-cross, he flung out his arms for silence.

'You came here, brothers,' he bawled, 'to lay your wrongs before King Richard; you saw this morning how the traitors about his person would not let him speak with you. They are safe in the Tower for the moment, yet you shall take vengeance on them, never fear. Meantime, we'll make an example. There is another great oppressor who is at present on the Scottish Border, but who perforce left his house and goods behind him. I speak of Sir John de Ghent, Duke of Lancaster.'

There was one deafening howl of execration at that name, for Ghent was indeed the most hated man in England, and not the most ignorant peasant but had heard of his misdeeds. A new rumour had it that he was making a secret treaty with the Scots and was to invade England in their company and seize the throne.

'We'll burn this wasp's nest as a warning to others of the swarm,' shouted Wat. 'But you have heard the good Sir John Ball tell you many a time that you are come to execute justice, not to seek profit. By God's bones I swear I'll hang any man I catch looting until I give the word for it. And now, aldermen, guide us to Ghent's house.'

The huge shadow of St Paul's engulfed them as they streamed westward, the four Jesus bells in its high clochard vainly summoning the citizens to resist. Another, very different, procession had passed along here earlier, leaving behind it bushels of flower petals which had been strewn in the path of the Blessed Sacrament; feet slipped now and again in pools of grease spilled by candles. The gates in the wall enclosing the churchyard were shut now, and Paul's Chain was drawn across on the south; the rioters made no attempt at molestation, rustic eyes gazing up in wonder at the wooden spire, soaring 260 feet above the belfry, its ball, containing precious relics, dazzling gold against the cloudless sky. From the west end of the churchyard a short street, Bowyers-row, tempted them to plunder, for here were the booths of those who made longbows; but they remembered Wat's threat and refrained.

Conspicuous on his blinkered horse, Sir John Ball led them in his catchy jingle. The Londoners among them were ignorant of this song, but they picked up the tune, fitting to it any ribaldry or nonsense that occurred to them. Thus they reached the Lud Gate.

The leaves were bolted to their central brass pillar, and there had been an attempt to barricade the entries for foot passengers on either side. While such obstacles went down like matchwood before the sheer weight of numbers, Alderman Horne and his friend broke into the watchhouse of the gate, and with whoops of glee purloined the watchmen's fire-pots, explaining to their rustic comrades how a rope soaked in pitch and resin was coiled about a spike in the centre of each pot. Sir John de Ghent should not lack for fire upon his hearthstone, they gloated, be the weather never so scorching.

Down short, steep Ludgate-hill they cascaded to Fleet-bridge, where a forest of masts peeped at them through its spiked parapet. On the south side of Fleet Street the bell of little St Bride's rang somewhat jerkily for Vespers, as though the ringer's hand trembled; further on, the deep-toned bells of the White Friars took up the summons. There were shouts of greeting from the mob to their friends the friars, changing into howls of execration as the great round church of the Temple came in sight in the midst of its monastic buildings, leased since the suppression of the Knights Templars to students of the Common Law. All lawyers were on the commons' black list; it was their cursed sheepskin charters that bound villeins and artisans alike in chains. They would pay the Temple students a visit on their return, they swore; and a wag among them pointed to the sign of the Devil tavern near by, where St Dunstan nipped old Satan's nose with red-hot pincers.

Jostling through the narrow Straits of St Clement's on either side of that venerable church, their pace quickened, for beyond several episcopal inns lay their goal. The Strand was marshy here and the highway was carried over a bridge; once across that, and there was Ghent's house of the Savoy, said to be the fairest manor in all England, shuttered now and silent, its caretakers fled.

Wat, at his most professional, inspected the gates carved with Ghent's portcullis and three barbed arrows, the token rent paid by its builder, Peter of Savoy, to King Henry III. They must improvise a ram, said Wat, and eager hands pointed to the Convent Garden, enclosed by a wall, on the other side of the Strand, where the Black Monks of Westminster grew fruit and vegetables for public sale. There were many trees in the garden, and soon a group came dragging a stout log. Wat taught them how to swing it against a weak point in the gates; all that was needed, said he, was a breach large enough for one man to squeeze through, who could then open them from the inside.

When a sufficient number had got into the forecourt, he began to bark out orders. Some were sent to collect all torches, prickets and candles the house contained; others to find whatever implements could be used for demolition.

A third party must fling out of the windows every moveable; presently these would be piled in the courtyard and burned under his own eyes. He repeated his threat to hang any man he caught secreting loot.

The mob scattered; where they found an obstacle in the shape of a stout door, there were yells for assistance, and by united force it went crashing inwards. At each of these forced points the rioters poured in like water, whirling axes and hammers above their heads, and fell to work, ripping up floors, smashing furniture, hewing away the beautiful ceilings with their images of angels holding shields of arms. Glazed windows were splintered into fragments, and through these apertures came hurtling the spoil captured by Ghent in France, arras, furs, jewels, silken coverlets, mazers and ewers of finest gold. They glittered and shimmered in an untidy heap, and by it straddled Wat. It was not to be fired until he gave the word; there was stuff here that would not burn. The jewels must be smashed into fragments and flung into the river, along with the gold and silver plate.

All the while he was on the lookout for something he knew must happen sooner or later; he wanted it to happen, for it would give him a chance to prove once and for all who was master of this mob, both countrymen and Londoners alike.

'You in the leather apron!' he suddenly barked. 'Come here.'

The man he addressed sheepishly obeyed, his arms hugged across his chest. Wat ripped them apart, and a silver goblet secreted there rolled upon the pavement.

'So you'd disobey my orders, would you, dog?' snarled Wat.

A terrified silence fell, men a moment before so busy, pausing in their work of destruction to stare from Wat to the shivering artisan who stood before him. Leisurely inspecting the scene, and making sure that the two aldermen were present to witness what he was about to do, Wat shouted for a rope.

'Fling one end over that broken arch and make a noose in the other. I'll need an execution party; you, and you, and you; I had some trouble with you on the march, and it's time you were taught a lesson.'

The thief attempted defiance. He was a freeman of Dowgate Ward, he stuttered, a journeyman brazier; if he had done wrong, he had the right to be tried at Guildhall, and he appealed to the two aldermen. Finding no help there, he fell on his knees before Wat, sobbing and pleading; he might as well have supplicated the flagstones. He was frogmarched to the makeshift gallows and strung up; not a voice was raised in protest as he danced in air, slowly choking. Wat let them stare their fill at the object-lesson, then turned back to business, very well satisfied. Henceforth his ascendancy would be unquestioned.

When the vast heap in the courtyard was ignited, an ugly excitement swept through the mob. Some danced about it like children; others, fascinated by this means of destruction, ran with their torches through the great building. Little whiffs of smoke writhed through cracks in the walls; then flames poked groping yellow fingers. Paint bubbled and blistered; an acrid stink made men retch. There was no wind, and the smoke rose sluggish, a growing pall, spitting out a multitude of sparks.

Screams from rioters trapped inside were quickly drowned in the steady roar of flames; figures were glimpsed for an instant clinging to the window mullions until they were sucked into the raging inferno within. Turrets and chimneys seemed to nod before crumbling; beams took on the appearance of grey feathers, spraying down on to the heads below. The rioters there, smoke-blackened, some with their clothes on fire, seemed like veritable demons, chanting Sir John Ball's jingle, yelling curses, leaping up and down from pain or sheer madness.

Then two of them came staggering to Wat with a couple of small barrels they had discovered in a cellar where some of their comrades were drinking themselves stupid. The barrels did not sound as if they contained liquor, said they; maybe they were the strong-boxes of Sir John de Ghent. Pleased with these followers who had learnt their lesson from the figure that still writhed in air in the archway, Wat swore that though the barrels were full of gold pieces, they must go on to the bonfire with the rest.

It was his one mistake. There was a blinding flash and an explosion that lifted men off their feet, killing some outright, badly injuring others. The barrels had contained not money, but powder of saltpetre.

Like a herd of maddened cattle, the rioters stampeded into the Strand, the Londoners among them rushing to wallow in the pond in Convent Garden. Wat let these go; he had overheard the two aldermen resolve to take their portion of the mob to Westminster and wreck the house of Sir John de Butterwyk, Sub-Sheriff of Middlesex. His business was to round up his Kentish followers and see them encamped. He had work for them tomorrow, far more weighty work than the destruction of empty manors, and he knew the tendency of all mobs to scatter beyond hope of future rallying. He might not know his way about London, but from the Surrey shore he had seen and fixed upon his camp.

Bawling the watchword, 'King Richard and the commons', Wat brought his contingent into some sort of order, dispatching Sir John Ball to look for strays. The sun had now set, but London remained as bright as noon, lit by the glowing mass of the Savoy and northward by another great conflagration where Jack Straw had been at work. It seemed as if the very Thames was burning, red with the reflection of flames.

But, Wat gloated to himself, far more ominous to the authorities in the Tower would be the watch-fires he intended to light on his chosen camping-ground. For it was right under their noses, on the open spaces of Tower Hill, on St Katherine's Wharf, and on the grassy slopes of East Smithfield beyond the City wall.

(ii)

A hardened campaigner, Wat felt no fatigue after his exertions of the day. Having seen his men encamped, the next thing was to feed them. They were in a tetchy mood, some badly burnt from their exploit at the Savoy, some grumbling because they had been denied plunder, all famished and dead-beat. He sent out foraging parties; traders were to be asked to supply food and drink; only if they refused were these commodities to be taken by force. It was not in Wat's interests to antagonize the citizens, only to show them he was master.

These arrangements completed, and his own head-quarters chosen, Wat decided to make a reconnaissance of the Tower, and 'Hubert the Squire' should accompany him. Before they left Kent, Wat had made it his business to discover the lad's surname and family background. Since then he had not missed a certain disillusionment, even revulsion, in this romantic boy, who had a brother at Court. Hubert must be implicated so deeply that no hope of pardon or reward would tempt him to betray his captain into the hands of the authorities; he must be marked on every possible occasion at Wat Tyler's side in the role of henchman.

Tonight, Wat was the knowledgeable old soldier, fascinating his companion with his comments and reminiscences. He had seen famous strongholds during his military career, said he, but not one that could compare with the Tower of London.

'Some of my poor boys are bragging they'll storm it tomorrow. God's bones, they talk like infants!'

True enough, he remembered many a castle in France which had seemed impregnable. But all the while the miners of the besieging force were sapping away with their picks, shoring up the foundations with great wooden beams, until the moment arrived when they beat a hasty retreat, flung in their torches, and behold! The apparently solid pile became a heap of rubble. But for a tactic like that you must have skilled miners, and in any case the Tower would defy such a stratagem.

It was built, he pointed out to Hubert, in the form of two irregular squares, one within the other, its curtain wall rising sheer from the moat on every side, defended at intervals by towers, as was the far higher ballium wall enclosing the Inner Ward. Even were one portion to be taken by storm, it could be isolated by closing the passage through the towers; and mark the wall coping, how it was finished with a roll to prevent arrows which had struck the lower part from glancing over the parapet.

In the midst of all soared La Tour Blanche, the heart of the fortress, whitewashed so that its height of ninety feet stood out in sharp relief against the fortifications which surrounded it. From the leaden roof of this White Tower, four turrets rose a further sixteen feet, ornamented with exceedingly elaborate wrought-iron pinnacles in the shape of fleurs-de-lis. Their rich gilding flashed in the glare of the watch-fires below.

Cocking a snook at some men-at-arms whom he could see prowling along the wall-walk, Wat coolly inspected the approaches. From land there was but one, the Bulwark-gate upon the west, connected by a fortified causeway and then by drawbridges, with a whole series of outworks which guarded the Warding-gate in the Outer Ward. He returned to the wharf, slowly pacing its twelve hundred feet among his sleeping followers. At one point a small inlet ran from the Thames into the Wharf, and moored at a stair was the identical barge, canopied and gilded, in which King Richard had paid his interrupted visit to the shore below Blackheath. Evidently its watermen had fled, leaving it as a prize for whoever cared to take it. Further east, St Thomas's Tower straddled the moat, windowless except in its high turrets; under it ran a canal, disappearing beneath the wharf, wide enough for the passage of great barges, strongly guarded on its landward side by a water-gate with a double portcullis.

Wat pondered. According to his London friends, flocks of the better sort among the citizens had sought refuge in the Tower, which meant that in no long time there might be shortage of provisions, for since he had possession of the wharf, barges would not be able to bring supplies by the water-gate.

'There are dainty bellies in there,' he remarked to his companion, 'would cause their owners to hang out the white flag ere they'd condescend to digest rats and cats. If they were wise, they'd drive out all useless mouths; if they did, by God's bones I'd let these women and brats starve in the sight of the garrison, as King Edward did at Calais.'

On the other hand, his was not the sort of army that could be kept together for the long, dull business of a siege. If only he had some 'gyns', he could catapult decomposed carcases over the walls. One lucky shot with these had poisoned the only well in the castle of Villefranche, he remembered. As it was, he would have to invent a ruse to lure King Richard out of the Tower; for the custody of the royal lad's person remained his prime objective.

Dismissing Hubert to his rest, Wat betook himself to a
lodging he had chosen for his headquarters, the Ram's
Head, an inn halfway down a long alley from Tower Hill to
the river, called Petty Wales from a tradition that the native
Princes of Wales had stayed here before the subjection of
that principality by King Edward I. He had an appointment
to meet Jack Straw and the London leaders at his inn, and
came late on purpose to emphasize the fact that he was
captain-general of the whole uprising.

They were boasting of the havoc they had wrought that
day. The priory of St John of Jerusalem, bragged Straw, was
still burning, for he had left men posted to see that no one
attempted to quench the flames. His friend, Alderman
Farringdon, had dragged from its hospice a party of
Flemings who had sought sanctuary there, instantly
dispatching them; a few Englishmen had the bad luck to
perish with them, Straw's lads not being able to tell who
was a foreigner, since the London dialect sounded to them
an alien tongue.

Aldermen Horne and Sibley took up the tale. Having
wrecked Sir John de Butterwyk's house at Westminster,
they had purposed to do the like with the inn of the Bishop
of Chester near St Mary-le-Strand; but both he and the
bishop-elect of Durham had fled, and the aldermen's
followers being by this time exceedingly thirsty, they had
contented themselves with rolling tuns of wine from the
cellars and got roaring drunk. However, enough were sober
to sack the Temple, where they burnt vast quantities of
rolls and charters; further east they opened the Fleet jail
and released all native prisoners, summarily executing the
foreign ones.

Last but by no means least, they had plucked from
the sanctuary of St Martin-le-Grand one Roger Legett,
beheading him in St Martin's-lane. He was one of the hated

questmongers, whose business and profit it was to set on
foot judicial enquiries which often led to arrests.

Wat listened to all this braggadocio in contempt. He had
long summed up Straw as a mere rabble-rouser; as for these
aldermen, their only ambition seemed to be the paying-off
of private scores, and they now began to argue as to who
should be next on their list of victims. Wat let them bicker
while he ate a belated supper of leg-of-mutton pie. When
he judged the moment ripe, he rapped sharply on the
board with his knife-handle.

'Brothers,' said he, 'my lads of Kent rose against the poll-
tax and their serfdom. There are two great oppressors
whose heads they demand as an example to the rest, the
Chancellor and Treasurer; and may I never draw clothyard
shaft again if these escape their just fate.'

'They're in the Tower,' objected Jack Straw, 'and how
d'you propose to crack that nut?'

'Yet since it seems there are many lesser knaves in your
city,' continued Wat, ignoring the interruption, 'I tell you
what I'll do. When my brave boys out yonder have had
their rest, I'll pick some of 'em to go forth in the manner
of heralds to the Standard in Chepe and other public
places, and there they shall invite any citizen who feels
himself wronged to come hither to me, captain-general of
King Richard's commons. He shall have his revenge, by
God's bones, but not until he has sought permission from
Wat Tyler.'

There were protests against such high-handedness, but
they lacked conviction. Something about this man
compelled others to give way to him. That he was utterly
ruthless, two of those present had witnessed at the Savoy;
and he remained the only man among them with military
experience. Though he would say nothing as to how he
proposed to capture the Chancellor and Treasurer, they
had little doubt that he would keep his vow.

Dismissing them with scant ceremony, he requisitioned from Alderman Horne the royal standard originally given to that traitor by the Mayor, and hung it out of the inn window, as knights hung their escutcheons to show where they were to be found. Then, picking the best bed in a house whence all other travellers had fled, Wat was instantly asleep.

(iii)

Within the south-east corner of the Inner Ward, bounded on the east by the Salt and on the west by the Lanthorn Tower, lay the royal apartments. They were otherwise unfortified, built by King Henry III for his own habitation, with frescoed walls, a long gallery, and a garden famous for its roses. In one of these chambers, about the time when Wat was prowling round the outside of the fortress, King Richard was taking a bath.

Painted cloths, looped together, screened the doorway; upon the floor a couch of great sponges had been arranged. On this Richard lay naked, while under the eye of his Chamberlain, one squire washed him with hot, sweet herbs before sprinkling him with rosewater, while another stood ready by the foot-sheet to dry him with warmed towels.

Richard hated the Tower, so cold, dark and barbaric; though, unlike the rest of it, the royal lodgings had fair large windows, they lacked other refinements he deemed necessary for gracious living. It was upon this subject that he chattered to his squires while they bathed him, particularly on his plans for transforming the manor of Sheen, where he intended to take Anne after their marriage. St Edward the Confessor had given it that name, a Saxon word signifying all that was bright and beautiful; *he* was going to make it into a fairy-tale palace, fit for his

115

Daughter of the Caesars. On St Neyt, an islet in the river near-by, he would build a little house just for himself and his Queen; there they would enjoy a privacy unknown to any previous royal persons.

'Of course it shall include a bath-house,' he prattled. 'There will be a gigantic oven under the floor for the heating of the water, and taps of the finest bronze. It will be lined with two thousand tiles, each with a different design; and besides this bath-house I shall have a spicery, a saucery, a special closet for my books, as many latrines as there are rooms, and a dancing-chamber which shall have in place of wall-paintings, arras depicting the Siege of the Castle of Love. The Queen – '

He broke off as the squire who kept the door announced the Earl of Salisbury. That nobleman paused in outraged astonishment before asking whether his Highness was aware that a mob, numbering over one hundred thousand, was at this moment blockading the Tower. Richard coolly assenting, Salisbury went on to say that the Council was in conference with the Lieutenant of the Tower, the Keeper of the Armoury, and Master Mayor. They lacked the presence of his Highness, and had presumed that he was indisposed. Naturally it had not entered their heads that in such a crisis, his Highness would be engaged in making his toilette.

'And have you come to a decision as to what is to be done?' asked Richard evenly.

'We have not, sire.'

'Then, by your leave, I cannot see that taking a bath in this hot weather is any more a waste of time than fruitless debate. Yet, though they never listen to any of my proposals, pray tell the Council I will be with them as soon as I am dressed.'

When Salisbury rejoined his colleagues in the White Tower, he found that belatedly it had occurred to them

116

that the fortress was also an arsenal. On the north of the Inner Ward stood the Bowyer Tower, built by the late King for the storing of long- and cross-bows with their arrows and bolts. Within La Tour Blanche, occupying one entire floor, was the Armoury, excellently stocked with every kind of offensive and defensive arms. Finally, on the extreme north was the Bastion, eighty feet in diameter, containing many of the 'gyns' used in the French wars, catapults of various construction, bombards with their heavy stone balls, and a supply of the deadly Greek-fire. The blockaders being but peasants and artisans, a taste of artillery would soon make them take to their heels in panic. When this happened, archers and billmen could sally from the fortress and strike them down.

Gay chatter approached up the wall-stair, and the assembly rose to greet King Richard, fresh from his bath. His thick fair hair, turned under in a roll at the nape, was a little damp from steam; he exuded a fragrance of herbs; his pourpoint, of one of the clear heraldic colours he loved, set off to perfection his broad shoulders and narrow waist; and in one hand he twirled a rose, just picked from the garden. He gave the impression of acting a part, and in one sense this was true. But he was no *poseur*. In dress, in speech, in deed, he earnestly endeavoured to model himself upon the chivalrous heroes of his legends.

'Fair, sweet councillors,' said he, 'how fare you in your debates?'

But when their decision was made known to him, his fair skin flushed, and he said with finality:

'I forbid it. You do not kill the worst criminals without hearing what they have to say.'

'I think, sire,' snorted Lord Arundel, 'you cannot have heard what these wretches have been at today. At least a score of innocent men have died at their hands, not to speak of the wanton destruction they have wrought and the breaking of your peace.'

'Because they grew desperate when I was prevented from listening to their grievances on the shore below Blackheath. I have sworn to hear what they have to say, and I shall keep my vow by God's grace.'

Salisbury raised his eyebrows at such childish obstinacy, before voicing his own objection to the latest proposal of his colleagues. There were, he reminded them, but six hundred men-at-arms in the Tower; once let these sally, and the sheer weight of the mob would overwhelm them.

'If we begin what we cannot carry through, we shall never be able to repair matters. It will be all over with us and our heirs, and England will become a desert. Nor must we forget that our prime duty is to protect the person of our young lord the King, and that of the Princess his mother.'

Since Salisbury was looked upon as a sort of oracle in matters pertaining to the art of war, the proposal was dropped, and the Council relapsed into futile lamentations. Treasurer Hales moaned over the destruction of his priory, especially of the great bell tower, that most curious piece of workmanship, graven, gilt and enamelled, a landmark of London. The Earl of Kent relayed a hideous rumour: the mob had turned loose all the mad folk from the hospital of St Mary of Bethlehem outside the Bishop's Gate. The Chancellor wailed that if only they had know that traitors would admit the insurgents into London, they could have taken both the King and his Mother safely to Windsor by this time.

This mention of the traitor aldermen recovered for Walworth his power of speech. Ever since he had received word of their treachery, he had been in a state of shock; as Mayor he felt involved in their disgraceful behaviour, and the very stones of his beloved London seemed to cry out against him. Somehow he must redeem the good name of the City; and first begging leave to speak in English, since his French was too imperfect for him to express what he felt in that courtly tongue, he burst out:

'Me lords, you didn't oughter judge the cits by a 'andful of Judases, and I'll take orf me chain of office if thousands of stout freemen don't rally round me for the protection of our lord the King. Just you let me get outer this 'ere Tower, I care not 'ow, and you'll soon see a citizen army wot will put these rogues to flight.'

'The citizens have had plenty of time to offer resistance,' Kent retorted acidly. 'Not one came to the aid of my servants when my house of Cole Harbour was attacked by the mob.'

Before anyone else could speak, Richard held up a hand for silence. His anger had vanished, and he was cool and firm.

'Master Mayor, you are a brave man, but I will have no force used until a parley had been tried. I do not deny that since the jails were broken open, there are felons among the rioters, yet for the most part they remain the peasants whose purpose in marching to London was to confide to me their wrongs. Now since they are encamped as it were upon our doorstep, I propose to go out to them by way of the postern in the Warding-gate and speak with those encamped on the wharf. I will have none accompany me; they have ever been consistent in their assertions of loyalty to my person, and had they wished to harm me, they could have riddled my barge with arrows from the shore below Blackheath.'

Some of the Council exclaimed in horror, others smiled at such boyish bravado, all were surprised, the general opinion being that Richard was a milksop. But that tough old soldier, Sir Robert Knolles, took Lord Salisbury aside. It was plain, said he, that the most pressing necessity was to disperse this vast horde; if that could be done by parley, the immediate threat would be removed, and once the blockade was lifted it ought to be possible to capture a ringleader and strike terror in the rest by his public execution. But there was no need, Knolles added with a wink, to disclose this latter part of the plan to King Richard. Salisbury agreeing with enthusiasm, it was arranged that Knolles himself should appear at the postern and say that his Highness was willing to consider grievances if these were set down in writing and presented by a deputation; but on the strict condition that the rest at once betook themselves to their several homes.

The many bells of London announced the hour of two in the morning as Knolles went off upon his errand. Many of the Council had fallen asleep from sheer exhaustion, others paced restlessly, Mayor Walworth sweated in his gown of budge-fur, for night had brought no abatement of the heat. Only Richard appeared fresh and relaxed, concealing his chagrin in being once again overruled, biding his time. Knolles was gone but a short while, and looked as grim as a goose on his return.

'The rogues would have heard me but for that leader of theirs, Wat Tyler. I know him, for he was an archer of the Prince's guard, and was well thrashed by his captain for insubordination before being drummed out of the army. He had the impudence to tell me just now that all I said was but trifling. His mob will not be gone, he swore, until they have spoken with the King.'

There was a stunned silence, which Richard took care not to break until the message from Wat Tyler had had time to sink home. Then he said with cheerful decision:

'Sir Robert Knolles, you will please to go out to the postern once again and carry a message from me personally. You will tell my commons that if they will assemble in the fields about Mile End, I will meet them there this morning at seven of the bell. There they shall be free to tell me their grievances.'

Forgetting his manners, Kent burst into a loud guffaw.

'Your Highness speaks as though arranging a *joute à plasisance!*'

'No, brother,' replied Richard gravely, 'I think it may well prove a *joute à l'outrance*, yet am I resolved to perform it.'

Knolles returned from this second errand to report success; the King's offer had been accepted with enthusiasm. Richard clapped his hands, his eyes dancing.

'Am I not outrageous?' he demanded gleefully. 'Is this not an adventure such as Sir Degrevant himself would have loved, whose boast was his audacity?'

'Such legendary knights,' sneered Kent, *sotto voce*, 'can never have outgrown childhood.'

When Richard left the Council chamber, Lord Salisbury stilled a chorus of shocked protest by pointing out that his Highness' decision, preposterously foolhardy though it was, had possibilities. It would draw the insurgents away from both the Tower and the City; once they were outside the walls, the Chancellor and Treasurer could seek safe sanctuary. And all being fair in war, such simple rustics could be tricked into dispersing if the king promised them all that they asked. When they had so dispersed would be the time to punish them under martial law.

'Master Mayor,' concluded Salisbury, 'you have pledged your word that many thousand citizens are ready to protect the person of our lord the King. I need not tell you that this madcap adventure on which his heart is set will place him in the gravest peril. Therefore, as soon as it is possible for you to leave the Tower, do you order all your loyal aldermen to have cried in their wards that every man between sixteen and sixty, each with his proper arms and harness, assemble on Tower Hill half an hour after Prime, on pain of life and limb, thence to escort the King to Mile End.'

In common with the rest of those in the beleaguered fortress, Richard had not slept but, keyed up to the highest pitch of excitement, he scouted the suggestion of taking some repose. With his bosom friend, Sir Robert de Vere, he walked along the ballium wall, at intervals calling the password to the sentries. From the Julius Caesar, Flint, Brick and Martin Towers upon the north, they had an excellent view of Tower Hill, where already camp-fires were having to compete with the first dim light of dawn.

'Oh see!' cried Richard, leaning over the parapet. 'My commons begin to set out for Mile End. I knew I was right! They trust me as their justiciar, who am bound by the sacred laws of chivalry, no less than by my office, to succour the oppressed. Was it not King Henry III who deemed it unworthy of his regality that any man should depart from him either sad or lacking his heart's desire? Alack, poor souls, I'll swear the most of them know not why they have marched all this way from their homes, any more than the common soldiers on a battlefield know for what cause they must die. Who is this man who calls himself their captain?'

'A tiler of houses, I suppose, from his name,' replied de Vere indifferently. And then, overwhelmed by the sheer romance of the situation, he went off into flights of fancy even exceeding Richard's own. 'Do you remember how King John of France proposed to solve the problem of the Free Companies by enlisting them for a crusade? What if you could persuade these insurgents to put on the red cross! As for me, I wish I could ride ahead of you to Mile End like Tailefer, the minstrel warrior, who sang the Song of Roland before the army of Duke William at Hastings. But at least I shall set down in verse your exploit for the benefit of posterity. It will excel even the feats of Arthur and his Table Round!'

So they prattle, these two children; for de Vere, though four years older, inhabited the same cloudy dreamland as his friend. What should he wear? pondered Richard. Perhaps his houppelande, the first of its kind his Master Tailor had made for him; but no, its high, enclosing collar would make him sweat in this heat. He must look absolutely unwarlike, that was essential; but on the other hand he must emphasize his kingship. Then suddenly his blue eyes swam with tears.

'I know, Robert,' he said solemnly, 'as I told my brother Kent there are some out yonder may choose to remove the coronals from the lances and fight *à l'outrance*. These are they who clamour for the blood of innocent men, and this I may not give them. But with Sir Gawaine, for myself I do not value death at two cherries! If I fail to return from Mile End, I charge you tell the Princess Anne of what I endeavoured to achieve, and how it was she who inspired me to this knightly enterprise.'

(iv)

Irritable from lack of sleep, Lord Salisbury prowled the battlements in his turn. But when, by half-past six, there was no sign of the citizens whom Walworth had slipped out to summon, Salisbury gave them up and sought the King.

He found him in the garden-house among the roses, just returned from Mass in the chapel of St John. The old man's exasperation increased. Richard was dressed as if for some stately summer excursion, and his demeanour matched his costume. Except for the ornamental baselard at his girdle, he was unarmed; his low-necked, close-fitting pourpoint of thin silk was such that no harness could be concealed under it. The liripipe of his hood was twisted round the crown in an elaborate turban and fastened with a brooch of ivory and rubies in the design of his white hart. His long slim legs were encased in parti-coloured hose, one gules, one argent, and his feet in the piked shoes he was trying to make fashionable. The finishing touch was put to Salisbury's disgust, when the King beckoned to one of his squires for the handcoverchiefs he had introduced, little pieces of material for the wiping of his nose. Good God, thought Salisbury, could effeminacy go further! Aloud he said, without wasting words:

'I have to inform you, sire, that the citizens I ordered to escort you to Mile End have failed to appear. Therefore you will be unable to go.'

'You had no right,' said Richard, with a touch of sharpness, 'to give any such order, Sir William de Montacute. This is my enterprise and it is for me to say whom I will have for escort. It would make my commons think I did not trust them if they saw me come in the midst of an armed band.'

'You are not seriously proposing,' gasped Salisbury, 'to ride on this mad venture with but your chamber knights and squires?'

'It were fit,' solemnly replied the boy, 'I proved my hardihood alone, as all true knights should do. Yet I am willing that those of my Council who please, accompany me.'

Not daring to trust himself to speak, Salisbury bowed and withdrew. Most certainly *he* was not going to witness the son of that great soldier, the Prince of Wales, being torn in pieces by a sweaty multitude. Richard, meanwhile, happily made his own arrangements. For very shame, his two half-brothers volunteered and were graciously accepted; Sir Robert de Vere, as Great Chamberlain, must bear the Sword of State before his master. The rest of the small escort consisted of such chamber knights and squires as happened to be on duty, including young Ralph Standyche. Into their care Richard committed two banners of the white hart for a certain purpose he had in mind. The little procession, thus formed, was ready to start, when Sir Robert Knolles appeared with a dozen archers and insisted on coming too. Richard scowled at the grim veteran, but there was no time to argue with him, or they would be late at Mile End.

As they rode under the arch formed by the Hall and Garden Towers and emerged into Water-lane, the strip of ground between the ballium and curtain walls, they found Mayor Walworth, still in his budge gown, his face beetroot-red from heat and mortification.

'Them base curs!' he raged. 'If any man 'ad told me the cits of London would – ' Words failed him; he swallowed noisily, and prepared to shame his fellow citizens by riding without them to what might be an ugly death.

After they had passed through the Warding-gate and along the drawbridge which connected this gatehouse with its guardian towers, Ralph Standyche glanced back, and saw the sentries hesitating whether or no to close these defences behind King Richard. It was evident that the incredible lack of decision among their betters had infected such simple men. Ralph's fears for his headstrong master increased, reaching their climax when, having crossed a walled causeway over the moat, the cavalcade issued through the Bulwark-gate on to the open spaces of Tower Hill.

For some eighty of the insurgents had not gone with their comrades to Mile End. Armed with an assortment of weapons, they prowled about the hill, shading their eyes now and then to stare up at the Tower and swearing they would storm it. This, Ralph tried to assure himself, was mere empty bravado, yet they looked ugly customers, and he could not but remember the hesitation of the guards at the several gates. There was no attempt to molest the little cavalcade, but just before the Ald Gate was reached, a man ran up and seized Richard's rein, shouting:

'Avenge me on that false traitor, Prior Hales, who has robbed me of my tenements by force! Do me right and justice, for if you will not, I am strong enough to take the law into my own hands,' and he flourished a battle-axe.

It was a major test of the King's courage, but he did not flinch. He answered temperately yet firmly:

'Sir, you and all my subjects shall have justice, my royal word on that.'

His accoster dropped the rein and stepped back, muttering. Walworth glared at him, for he was one of the traitor aldermen, Thomas Farringdon; while the fright proved too much for Richard's half-brothers. Once outside the Ald Gate they fell behind, and as the procession passed along narrow Hog-lane towards Whitechapel, a hamlet taking its name from a chapel of ease built of wattles and white plaster, the two Hollands edged their horses on to the marshy ground northwards, dry in this weather, whence they fled over the fields.

Topping a rise in the lane, Richard beheld a vast crowd occupying all the pastures about the Roman milestone which marked Mile End.

Their aspect was entirely different from that which they had worn on the shore yesterday; there was no belligerent flourishing of weapons, no hostile shrieks, no ranks of bowmen. They knelt as one man, shouting a welcome to their lord King Richard, and swearing they would have no other lord but he. Some pressed forward to kiss his hand, some merely gaped in admiration of his youth and beauty, some dared a kick from his horse by jostling to stroke its housings, resplendent with the leopards and the lilies, many fervently repeated their old watchword, 'King

Richard and the commons.' He for his part waved back his small escort and rode alone into the midst of the multitude, thus ostentatiously expressing his confidence in their good-will.

At any other moment his refinement would have been offended by their stench. But now, his dream of knightly deeds become reality, he felt he loved them, stink and all. There was something timeless about their appearance; they might have been the Saxon house carles who, in the margin of his Book of Hours, were carried captive with their master Lot in just such tunics coloured with the few country dyes, russet-brown or kendal-green, mostly of sackcloth, shapeless, ragged, patched. Many had their wide-brimmed straw hats slung on their shoulders, for the sun was not yet fierce; some wore long drawers from waist to ankle and nothing else. Their chests, bare arms and feet were tanned by weather; their careful craftsmen's hands fidgeted as though missing the familiar implements of husbandry. More than one shepherd had brought his crook and bagpipes, as loth to be separated from them as a housewife from her distaff.

Yet Richard was not unaware of another element present in the crowd, though it was much in the minority. It centred round a sharp-faced, under-sized man who, every now and then, started to recite a catalogue of grievances before his voice was drowned in the far louder acclamations. The King supposed him to be Wat Tyler, whom he had not yet seen; encouraged by the very slight influence he appeared to have over the insurgents, Richard ignored him, raised a hand for silence, and spoke with the utmost simplicity.

'My good people, I am your King. What do you want, and what do you wish to say to me?'

There was a pause. Such direct language took them by surprise. He was indeed their Sovereign Lord, anointed with the sacred oil; on those young brows had rested the crown of St Edward the Confessor. Yet he addressed them almost as if he were their intimate friend. Even Jack Straw was silent; then several voices began to speak at once, in so strong a dialect that Richard could understand but a phrase here and there, yet he caught enough to know that they were asking to have the poll-tax abolished, and that they wished to be no longer serfs. About the poll-tax he knew he could do nothing for the moment, since it had been imposed by Parliament; but he had come prepared to deal with their other grievance.

'You have done well,' he said, when the voices petered out, 'to make your complaints known to me, your King. Yet you have done ill to come to London in a hostile manner, breaking my peace and committing many outrages.' He paused to let that sink home. 'I am, however, willing to believe that you were led astray by certain evil men among you, and if you will go quietly home, I will issue a general pardon for all crimes committed so far.'

'We will by no means go home,' shouted Jack Straw, 'until you take and deal with all the traitors whom we have sworn to punish!'

The group about Straw echoed his defiance; but once again the King ignored them and continued to address the well-meaning majority.

'I have taken you under my protection, and from henceforth I alone will be your lord. All holders in villeinage who honestly desire it shall become free tenants, paying fourpence an acre in lieu of servile work. But this is on condition that you go home peaceably forthwith; and you must leave behind you two or three from each bailiwick to whom I will give charters, sealed with my privy signet, releasing you from serfdom.'

An instant of open-mouthed astonishment, and then the mob went wild with joy, men hugging their neighbours, flinging up their straw hats, capering like children. It was incredible! On the simple condition that they went home (and how much they longed for their homes!) they had obtained in one moment their demands. Richard, his own heart bursting with pride, watched them for a while in silence. He, and he alone, had quelled a very dangerous rebellion, and that without bloodshed; by nightfall all these poor misguided men would have dispersed, secure in the protection of their King. His voice unsteady with emotion, he said at length:

'You, my good people of Kent, shall have one of my banners of the white hart, which I have brought hither with me for the purpose; and you, my good commons of Essex, shall have another. These shall serve as your protection on your homeward way, that you may not be arrested by my officers. Now do you choose from among you those you would have receive the charters I have promised, and when I return to London, I will set thirty clerks to work copying the same.'

As the multitude became busy selecting their representatives, some pressing forward to receive the banners, the King beckoned to Ralph Standyche.

'Ride back to the Tower, squire, and inform the Council that I have satisfied my commons, who are content to return quietly to their homes. Say further that I am dictating in their presence a general pardon to be published for all manner of felonies done up to this hour.'

He was trying to speak gravely, but his eyes danced with mischief. Let the Council dare despise him for a dreamer after this!

(v)

As soon as Richard and his little escort had issued from the Bulwark-gate, the captain of the guard hurried to seek

JANE LANE

orders from the lieutenant, in command in the absence of
the constable, whose post was a mere sinecure. A vital
question must be answered: Were the portcullises to be
lowered and the draw-bridges raised during King Richard's
absence?

The lieutenant, pacing up and down among the trees on
Tower-green in front of his lodging, was infected by the
paralysis which had made the whole Council supine
during this emergency. First he said yes, and then he said
no; a way of retreat must be kept open for the King on his
return from Mile End, if, indeed, he ever did return from so
rash a venture.

'But let no man enter unless he has the password,' added
the lieutenant, trying to sound firm.

He groaned in spirit; whatever he did he would be
blamed. He might even lose his post, as already, in
consequence of these wicked riots, he had lost some of his
most precious perquisites. While such disorders lasted,
there would be no pilgrims sailing downstream on their
way to Compostella, on whom he was entitled to levy a tax
of half a groat per person.

The captain of the guard, hopelessly confused, went
round his sentries, passing on his superior's decision, if
such it could be called. He had reached the Bulwark-gate
when he was aghast to see approaching it over Tower Hill
that small but particularly truculent portion of the mob
who had not gone to Mile End with their fellows. Their
pace was rapid, their demeanour purposeful, and at their
head marched a dangerous-looking ruffian who lacked one
ear.

The luckless captain had now to act upon his own
initiative; he must choose on the instant between
admitting these rioters or offering resistance. If the latter, it
would provoke an affray, he was hopelessly outnumbered,
and there was no time to summon assistance. Moreover he

130

remembered that King Richard was completely at the mercy of the bulk of the insurgents at Mile End; if this one-eared rogue who appeared to be their leader chanced to get killed in a scuffle, the King might be lynched.

'I bid you stand and give the password,' the captain shouted, horribly aware of the feebleness of his demand.

Wat Tyler and his band of picked desperadoes were already thrusting themselves forward through the open gates, but not, apparently, with any hostile intent. On the contrary, they shook hands with the Tower guards, stroked their beards with uncouth familiarity, and informed them that in future all common men were brothers. While this was in progress, Wat made a grab at the keys, deftly snatching them from the captain's girdle. Whirling them above his head in triumph, he yelled:

'Now, boys, the Tower is ours, and the chief traitors in it!'

When he had accepted Richard's invitation to a conference at Mile End, it had seemed a heaven-sent opportunity for capturing the King's person, but on second thoughts Wat had decided that this could wait. For the moment it was more important to gain possession of the Tower and complete the demoralization of the authorities by executing, in as public a manner as possible, those two victims who headed the insurgents' blacklist, Chancellor Sudbury and Treasurer Hales.

As soon as the wharf was vacated early that morning, the pair had sought to escape by boat, only to find that a certain number had been left on guard here as on Tower Hill. Pelted with stones and refuse, Sudbury and Hales were forced to make a hasty retreat by the water-gate from which they had just emerged. Since then, they had accepted their inevitable doom; neither was of the stuff of which martyrs are made – one was weak, the other worldly. But in this dread hour, both turned instinctively to their duties as Christians and clerics; they must prepare their souls for death, praying for grace to meet it in such a manner as would not disgrace their priesthood.

Instead of a huge, impregnable fortress, the Tower of London had become in the space of twenty-four hours a kind of rabbit warren. Members of the Council, refugee citizens, the Gentlemen Gaoler and his yeomen warders, keepers of the Mint and Jewel Houses, canons, chaplains, clerks, and singing-men attached to the tow chapels, all had bolted underground, cowering in the towers of the Inner Ward. Like a plague, the shameful panic of superiors had spread to the very scullions; even the servants of the two doomed men had deserted them, so that each must serve the other's Mass.

On the second storey of the White Tower was the royal chapel of St John, with its crypt on the floor below. That great embellisher, King Henry III, had beautified it with stained glass and carvings; a choir of angel minstrels, holding dulcimer, lute, lyre, gittern and psaltery, appeared to play in the vaulted roof; sunlight, steaming through the windows, cast patches of vivid colour on the two victims in their vestments, solitary in the chancel beyond the glorious roodscreen. When each had said his Mass, by common though silent consent they knelt before the high alter, recited together the seven penitential psalms, the *commendacione* and the *dirige*, and began the long Litany of the Saints. In that high empty chapel their voices were pitifully thin.

During the past half-hour they had been aware of ominous sounds from outside, now near, now distant, now again approaching. They were the sounds as of some beast seeking prey, savage, pertinacious, snuffing for the scent. Footsteps thudded up and down stone passages, muffled by the tremendous thickness of the walls; the shrill scream of women arose and was as suddenly cut off. Meaningless laughter made the blood run cold; there was a whoop of glee as the Mint was discovered, with its gold discs already struck into coins of the realm; and again when a key was found to open the Jewel House where the regalia was kept.

But this beast was not out for either loot or women. It wanted blood.

Sudbury's voice faltered in the list of martyrs in the Litany, and his friend gently prompted him, 'Sancti Fabiane et Sebastiane, orate pro nobis.' The Archbishop, ashamed, recovered himself and went on, but while his lips articulated the familiar words, his poor frightened mind darted hither and thither like a squirrel in a cage. He tried to comfort himself; it had been clear from the beginning that the rioters had no quarrel with any cleric as a cleric, but only as a manorial lord; and except for dragging victims out of sanctuary, they had respected the rights of the Church. They were no heretics or pagans. Incited by the mad Ball, they had indeed sacked the archiepiscopal palaces, yet that they would lay violent hands on the Archbishop's person, here in the presence of the Blessed Sacrament in the pyx above the altar, was surely unthinkable.

' "From sudden and unprovided death," ' he recited; but this time it was Hales who failed to make the response.

For the hunt was near; from the very crypt below came the eager growls of a beast certain it has tracked down the hiding-place of its quarry. It seemed to cast to and fro at fault, snarling with frustration. A moment's silence as though it conferred with itself. Then feet pounded up the spiral stair in the fifteen-foot wall, a door was flung violently open, and between the great round pillars faces peered this way and that.

Stiff from kneeling for so long, Sudbury stumbled a little as he rose, his friend's hand assisting him. Though his mouth was bone dry, he managed to speak articulately, even with dignity, in answer to a roar of voices denouncing him as a traitor.

'Here am I, no traitor, but your Archbishop. And here is the Most Reverend Father in God, Prior of the Knights Hospitallers, who have defended Christendom from the Infidel for near upon two centuries.'

Even as he spoke, he knew it was in vain. This was the hard core of the mob, fearing neither God nor Satan, less men than beasts slavering at the jaws for blood. It was plain that they had broken into the Armoury, each man snatching such weapons and harness as took his fancy, hideously ludicrous in a helm with the visor down and a tall crest, a silk jupon bright with armorial bearings above dirty bare legs, a lance with a knight's pennon grasped in a hand used to the plough. Masquers in some ghastly pageant they seemed, capering and hallooing as they rushed at the two victims, some to mock, some to buffet, some to tear off jewels.

In the background, grimmest of all, stood one who had found in the dungeons the execution axe. Its bright edge winked in the sunlight as it was tried by a calloused thumb.

(vi)

The porter and watchmen of the Ald Gate were huddled in a little group, talking nervously, as Ralph rode up from Mile End. When they saw the badge of the white hart on his breast, they fell silent, eyeing him askance. Realizing that something of significance must have occurred during the King's absence, Ralph reined in and demanded news.

They all began to speak at once, pointing, gesticulating, pouring out a wild and contradictory babble. The Tower had been captured by a trick and was now occupied by the rioters. No, no, they had vacated it again after murdering the garrison. The Council had surrendered it and fled, though some had been caught and executed on Tower Hill yonder. The apartments of the Princess of Wales had been invaded, and she had swooned when Wat Tyler tried to rape her. But she was safe. Her attendants had contrived to carry her to a boat and so by water to the Queen's Wardrobe near Blackfriars.

This last fact was the only one on which all agreed, and Ralph, sick with apprehension, decided that he must see the Princess and learn from her the truth of what had happened. Instead of turning south, therefore, he rode fast along Leadenhall Street and Cornhill to Cheapside.

As soon as he entered the city he was aware of an atmosphere utterly unlike that of the past few days. There was still no buying and selling, but instead of crouching behind closed shutters, folk craned from open windows in a way that was half terrified, half eager. There was something ugly in their mood; it reminded Ralph of that unholy excitement with which they flocked to a hanging. On the north side of St Marie-le-Bow, the late King had raised a permanent stone gallery whence the ladies of his Court could watch the tournaments he often held in this great broad street. Now it was filled with housewives, all talking, none listening, leaning over every now and then to stare westwards as if for the coming of some show.

Ralph would not pause to ask for what they waited, but quickening his pace he skirted St Paul's Churchyard and turned south down Paul's Wharf-hill. From here he could see already the turrets of the Queen's Wardrobe, called of old the Tower Royal, an ancient and decayed little building, bounded on the west by the Wall Brook and on the river side by Baynard's Castle.

For some moments past he had caught a confusion of sounds ahead of him, muffled by the intervening houses between him and the Thames, but growing louder. Before he could reach his goal, the first of a rowdy procession turned the corner out of Thames Street and marched straight towards him. He heeled his horse under the shadow of a penthouse and watched, growing sick with disgust.

First came a flying squadron of apprentices with shorn heads and blue frocks, yelping, laughing, some walking backwards to get a better view of what came behind. Next, like some bizarre herald, rode a man on a blinkered horse, his head encased in a white hood with a long red liripipe. His mouth was open in a sustained bellow, but because of the general uproar, Ralph could distinguish no words. Behind him marched a score or so of rioters, jigging up and down as they bawled out a song. They seemed to be staging some pageant, dressed as they were in odds and ends of knightly harness, with here a lance and there a banner flourished above their heads. One brawny ruffian carried on his shoulder a long-handled axe with a peculiarly shaped blade. Immediately after him came two who brandished poles on top of which were what Ralph, his eyes dazzled by the sun, took to be stage properties, the kind of masks worn by mummers.

But as the procession drew level, his horse shied and whinnied, and a moment later his own nostrils caught the stench of fresh blood.

Now he saw the pitiless reality. The axe's blade was dully stained, as were the hands, bare arms and dress of him who bore it. The things stuck on poles were no pasteboard masks, but human heads. Hair hung wetly round the frightful jagged edges of the severed necks, darkened ooze dripping from them; the noses were pinched in, the eyes open and showing but the whites. Upon one of these heads, fixed by a great nail driven through the skull, was an archbishop's mitre.

Even as Ralph stared, unable to withdraw his gaze, there came the final obscenity. Those who held the heads of

Sudbury and Hales placed them so that the livid lips of the Treasurer seemed to whisper his confession into the other's ear. Then the two dead mouths were pressed together in a mockery of the kiss of peace.

(vii)

The effect on Hubert of the Mile End conference was one of enormous relief, mixed with exultation. He was enchanted by King Richard, in whom he recognized a kindred spirit, a champion of the oppressed; and all his doubts about the justice of the commons' cause were dispelled by his discovery that the King really was on the same side. Now he, Hubert, could go home to the country for which he ached, away from this great overcrowded city which seemed to stifle him; and he would carry with him a royal charter pardoning all felonies and promising emancipation to his father's villeins. For to put the crowning touch upon his happiness, the inhabitants of Easter Green had chosen him as their representative.

And in future he would behave better towards his father. Of course the old gentleman would be both hurt and bewildered by this abolition of the feudal system to which he was so much attached; but when Hubert had explained to him, gently and kindly, that it was by the King's own wish, Sir Thomas would be satisfied. Meanwhile, at the first opportunity, Hubert must go to confession. Hitherto in his young life there had been certain sins like theft which he had never had to consider in his examinations of conscience; but on the march from Canterbury he would have starved had he not stolen. Lawlessness had become part of the very air he breathed, and though inevitably he had grown less shocked by it, he had never forgotten that he, and the majority of the insurgents, had not marched on London to kill and loot, but to see King Richard and tell him of their wrongs.

Thus eagerly and happily was Hubert returning to London, in company with a band of other representatives, all very self-important as became those entrusted by their fellows with so weighty a mission. He could no longer see the King who, for some reason unknown, had suddenly spurred his horse and gone galloping towards London; but Hubert was quite content to draw little pictures in his mind of that proud moment when, kneeling at his Sovereign's feet, he would receive one of the charters. He wondered if he ought to make a small speech, and began rehearsing sentences.

But as soon as he passed under the arch of the Ald Gate, it was plain to him that something had happened during the past few hours, something that had filled the citizens with relishful horror, and perhaps explained that sudden spurring forward of the King. In the enchantment of Mile End, Hubert had not noticed the absence of Wat Tyler and a number of his followers. The mood of these absentees was now disclosed to him by a terrible little incident.

A group of stall-keepers in Leadenhall-market were discussing some spectacle which, it seemed, recently had passed that way. A chandler among them disagreed with his fellows, and growing heated said in a loud voice:

'For the Chancellor and Treasurer, I say good riddance, and the same for Sir John Legge, what started this here poll-tax. But to go and chop off the head of Brother William, only because he was physician to Sir John de Ghent, that was sin and shame, for he was a right good man.'

These remarks were overheard by some of the insurgents who had remained in London. Before the chandler could defend himself or flee, he was seized and immediately throttled.

There was an interval in which men and houses seemed to whirl about Hubert in a giddy dance. When he came to himself, he was wedged into a thickening stream of rioters who appeared to be converging on a prearranged rendezvous. Drenched in sweat, sickened, terrified, he was carried forward on this human wave.

On the west of Great Eastcheap was Candlewright Street, on the south of which, opposite St Swithin's church, there stood a much-revered object called London Stone. It was a huge, time-worn boulder, fixed deep in the ground and fastened with iron bars, said to have been placed here by the Romans at a point whence they measured distances; for it marked the centre of the City. Beside this landmark, Wat Tyler sat on horseback, holding in his hand a naked sword. When all the space about him was filled with rioters, he struck London Stone with the blade and roared:

'Know ye all that I, Wat Tyler, am now master of London! I have put to death the greatest traitors, and in four days there shall be no laws in England save those that issue from my mouth. My lieutenant, Jack Straw, is away to chastise our enemies in Highbury and other villages where they lurk; and do you, lads, purge the City in like manner, aye, purge it well of traitors, great and small. And when you have done so, take what goods you please, for they are become the lawful spoil of victors. If any man resist you, bring him to me at my headquarters, and by God's bones he shall have short shrift.'

A ferocious howl greeted this speech, and the mob scattered to wholesale murder and pillage. Wat nodded, well pleased with his skill in handling them; he reckoned that only by letting them spend the rest of the day according to their fancy could he retain his control, but as the street emptied, his glance lighted on Hubert, and noting the lad's expression, he remembered that there might be danger from that quarter.

'Well met, squire!' he cried with false heartiness. 'come you with me to my inn, for I shall have need of your penmanship anon. We must draw up a memorial to King Richard, explaining what we have done, and craving his presence with us when presently we march through England, freeing villeins from their bondage.'

Though he might live to be a very old man, Hubert Standyche knew he would never forget that Friday, the 14th of June. Ironically it was the fairest day of a fine hot summer. In the great gardens of inns, both ecclesiastical and lay, in the little plot each citizen cherished behind his dwelling-house, in the fields which, on north and east, came up to the very walls of London, flowers ran riot, trees cast welcome shade. From a cloudless heaven the sun twinkled in the gilt ball and cross of St Paul's, and glittered in the Thames. It was a day for 'prentices to play truant from their masters' counters and run away to the bowling alleys and the archery butts; for housewives to gossip in the shadow of the conduits; for family parties to take boat for Islington, trailing kegs of ale to keep them cool.

But on this black Friday, the sun was a foe, stifling folk who crouched behind locked doors and barricaded windows, inflaming the passions of those who alone walked the streets of London, demons who lusted to destroy. At the sign of the Ram's Head in Petty Wales, the lord of misrule held his court, receiving reports and making his plans. He had obliged the innkeeper to take down his sign, and had commandeered the services of a master-painter to portray his own head in place of the ram's.

'I shall swing up there for future ages to admire,' bragged Wat, 'and men shall call this inn the Captain General.'

I hope you'll swing on a gallows, thought Hubert venomously, loathing this brigand who kept him prisoner, mourning the new shattering of his dreams and hopes. At this very moment he ought to be kneeling at King Richard's feet, receiving a charter; if ever he knelt at those feet now it would be to receive a sentence of death. 'For all felonies committed to this hour'; so had run the promised amnesty; but only on condition that the rioters went quietly home. No king could pardon the murder of his highest officers of state; and here was Hubert, not gone quietly home, but chained to the side of the chief assassin.

He had a strong imagination, and as now one, now another, of the rioters came to Wat with tales of new outrages, he knew that these would haunt him in his dreams. He longed to stop his ears, but dared not, for Wat Tyler watched him, and he remembered that figure dancing in air at the Savoy.

The mob went about in bands, each band with a log of wood, and an axe purloined from St Nicholas' Shambles or snatched from a carpenter's booth. The logs were set up at street corners, and any citizen rash enough to be abroad had the question shot at him, 'With whom d'you hold?' If he did not know the correct reply, 'With King Richard and the commons', down went his head on the log and up went the axe. Mingling with the vain appeals of these victims, and the screams of women and children flying down alleys to avoid the gangs, was the sound most dreaded by those who cowered in their houses, the rattle of fetters on the ankles of felons released from jail.

Some of the gangs concentrated on those parts of the City inhabited by foreigners. Here men, women and even children were dragged into the street and made to pronounce the words 'Bread and cheese', their accent at once betraying them. In the Vintry, a district of vaults and wine-shops some fifty yards west of where the Wall Brook flowed into the Thames, the Merchant Vintners of Gascony had their hall and almshouses. Thirty-five of these unfortunates took refuge in the church of St Martin, their patron; but by this time the mob were quite indifferent to the rights of sanctuary, and the thirty-five were beheaded, one after another, on their own wharf. At the Bridgehead there was a whole colony of Flemings, and here a mass slaughter took place. On the other hand the Lombards, who had their bourse off Cornhill, being money-lenders offered large sums in return for their lives, and this money the mob accepted, ostensibly for Wat Tyler's war-chest, actually for their own pouches.

By late afternoon the victims were so many that it was too much trouble, especially in this heat, to fix their heads on the spikes of the various gates. They were left to roll in the gutters; and Hubert could not prevent himself from retching as one gang reported a playful game of football with these heads.

At only one point was resistance offered.

Just removed from the bustle of Cheapside stood Guildhall, enlarged forty years before but still a modest building, quite unfortified. In its spacious crypt were stored the City's muniments, and a gang, brandishing torches, marched upon it with intent to burn such records. But in the porch, called Guildhall-gate, they were confronted by Mayor Walworth and two stalwart friends of his, both ex-mayors, Nicholas Brembre and John Philipot, each wearing a mail hauberk and armed with shield and lance. So determined was the aspect of these three lone defenders that the mob slunk away, shamefacedly reporting the incident to Wat. He, immersed in plans for getting hold of the King's person, was pleased to overlook his followers' failure, while chalking up a score against the defiant Mayor.

Night came at last, mercifully concealing the horror of those once busy streets, deserted now except for drunken rioters, tipsily bawling the mad priest's jingle, chucking stones down an alley in case there might be fugitives cowering there, quarrelling over their loot. No candlelight shone through casements; no customary sound of music and singing told of hard-working people at their favourite recreation. As quiet as the dead who sprawled headless in the roadway, the citizens crouched sleepless, only the wail of a terrified child or the weeping of women betraying their presence.

Sleepless also, Hubert lay on a chest at the foot of Wat Tyler's bed, a privilege, Wat assured him, of the favourite squire. But Hubert was not deceived; he was a prisoner; and even could he escape from this inn, whither could he flee? A vision of his home came to him, woundingly clear. Until this moment he had never known how much he was a part of that little manor. He could hear his father's lame step in the hall and his voice calling a welcome; he could see the very colours in the arras worked by his mother's hand. But then as he wept in a passion of homesickness, he remembered Sir Thomas' stories about the Great Pestilence, the tales he had found so tedious. Now, suddenly, he understood the horror that had branded itself on his father as a boy.

For he too was living through a pestilence that spared neither young nor old, man nor woman, a scourge against which there was no defence.

Chapter Five

The Winning of the Spurs

(i)

Richard awoke from the healthy sleep of childhood and for a moment wondered where he was. He could hear the breathing of many others in his chamber, and someone at the bedfoot muttered and tossed as if in nightmare. Then he remembered that he was in the cramped quarters of the Queen's Wardrobe, with his mother and with such attendants who could find room or had not scattered during the terror of the past twenty-four hours. It must still be very early, for no light came through cracks in the closed shutters, though the flickering of the night-candle, burnt low in its silver basin, told him that dawn must be near.

Locking his fingers behind his neck, he made haste to recall a very vivid dream before it faded. He had seemed to be at Smithfield; there were lists and barriers set up, and first he thought they were for the grand tournament which should have been in progress here during these days in honour of his marriage. But soon he realized that it was an occasion far more solemn. It was the old chivalric ordeal, the trial by combat now fast dying out. He, Sir Richard de

Bordeaux, had accused someone of high treason; and with all the religious ritual surrounding the ordeal, the blessing of shield and spear, the swearing on the Mass-book that he wore no herb of virtue or other enchantment, the presence in the background of a pall-covered bier and a priest in black vestment, he was come to make good his accusation or die at the hands of the accused.

There was not the slightest doubt in his mind that this dream conveyed a supernatural message.

Since the shock of that moment when, riding back in triumph from Mile End, he had learned of the butchery done on Sudbury and Hales, the whole situation had changed. It was as when clear sunlight becomes the glare preceding a storm; or it was like the stealing in of a minor note which blights the character of music. Hitherto he had believed that he had to do with a multitude of simple, discontented peasants, whose isolated acts of violence could be laid at the door of the felons in their midst. Similarly, Wat Tyler had been but a name to him, the sort of ephemeral figure thrown up by all revolutions such as this.

But his cold-blooded murder of the Archbishop of Canterbury and the Treasurer of England, the cunning with which he had gained access to the Tower, the arrogance of his boast at London Stone, and the anarchy he had deliberately incited, all these things made Richard begin to see him not as a man but as a fiend in human shape.

And there was something more. The true knight of old must prove his hardihood in three separate ordeals, each more severe than the last. And this, thought Richard, was the message of his dream. On the shore below Blackhealth, and again at Mile End, his prowess had been tested; there remained a third and yet more perilous trial, and until that was accomplished, Sir Richard de Bordeaux could not be said to have won his spurs. Of its nature, he had no idea, but not for a moment did he doubt that God would reveal it to him.

There was a commotion somewhere in the house, and the knights and squires who lay in Richard's chamber woke instantly, reaching for their weapons. An attack upon the Queen's Wardrobe had been expected all yesterday and last night, and every door and window was barricaded. Even Richard had been obliged to keep reminding himself that a true knight remained cool in every crisis. But now that vivid dream had restored all his courage, and he lay where he was until the cause of the rumpus was made known to him. It seemed that Sir John Newton was trying to persuade the guards at the gate to admit him, which they refused to do; for a cloud of suspicion hung over this knight who had so tamely surrendered Rochester Castle and had been with the rebels ever since.

'Admit Sir John and bring him hither to me,' Richard ordered calmly.

The tale Newton had to tell was an ugly one. During the chaos of the night, he had contrived to slip away from Wat Tyler's inn, and had skulked about the town. Still unsated with all the blood shed yesterday, the rioters had just committed two more notable murders, the first victim, Sir Richard Lyons, dying at Wat's own hand simply because as his commanding officer, Lyons had thrashed him for insubordination during a French campaign.

'I can scarce bring myself to tell you of the other slaughter, sire,' faltered Newton. 'Sir John Imworth, Marshal of the Marshalsea jail, took refuge in the Abbey after his house in Southwark was destroyed. Within the last hour, these hell-hounds have wrenched him from the pillar to which he clung in the shrine of the Confessor, dragged him at a horse-tail all the way to the Standard in

Chepe, and there beheaded him. Jesu have pity! They are more cruel and sacrilegious than the Turk!'

There was a long silence. That ready flush had stained Richard's cheeks as he listened; now his firm lips pressed together, and his face took on an expression rapt and dedicated. At length he asked:

'Sir John, durst you venture back to the chief rebel?'

'I needs must, sire, for he holds my two sons as hostages.'

'Then say to him thus: Since it seems to King Richard that from the refusal of so many to depart with their comrades yesterday they have still further boons to crave of him, he will meet them this day at the hour of Vespers outside the Alders Gate in the open place of Smithfield. But this time, it is my positive command that Wat Tyler be there in person to confront me.'

Newton returned from his errand with speed. Tyler, he reported, was eager to meet the King, but surely it could be with no good intent. He still had some thirty thousand ruffians at his beck, and these of the most reckless kind. If both the river and the Mile End encounters had been rash, this that his Highness proposed at Smithfield was veritable suicide. Even the romantic Sir Robert de Vere objected that it could not be done.

'It must be done, therefore it can be done,' insisted the King. He looked round upon the agitated faces. 'Sweet Knights and squires, I resolve to ride to the Abbey as soon as I am dressed; I ask for volunteers to accompany me thither, and one to ride ahead to warn the Lord Abbot that I wish to receive the Holy Sacrament.' Then, summoning his Dominican confessor, he said: 'Take it not amiss, father, that for this once I seek shriving from the anchorite at Westminster rather than from you.'

He had become the boy Arthur, the child Galahad, the youthful Tristram, each of whom had proved himself by some great feat; while Wat was now the fiend who figured so prominently in his legends, sometimes in the guise of a dragon, or in the likeness of the great black horse which had tried to drown Sir Percival. Another character of romance must play his part, one of those recluses so often favoured with visions. Through such a one, God would surely speak, revealing the manner in which the fiend must be vanquished.

(ii)

The debtors in the prison above the Lud Gate stretched down their long-handled bowls for alms as Richard rode beneath them; they seemed the only familiar figures left in London. Fleet Street was a shambles; kites shrieked and hovered, rats fought, over dreadful nameless objects in the gutters. In bitter contrast, boughs and garlands, long withered by the heat, still hung on the houses, put up there for the processions of Corpus Christi. On some shutters, frightened hands had chalked as a precaution the rebels' watchword, 'King Richard and the commons'; outside the gate of the Temple a huge bonfire still smouldered, charred legal documents blown hither and thither on a gentle summer breeze. Not a living soul was encountered; even the rioters must be asleep, worn out with killing and destruction.

In the Strand it was the same. The beautiful manor of the Savoy was an unsightly heap of rubble, the episcopal inns on either side of it blackened by fire. No cowled figures were at work among the fruit and vegetables of the Convent Garden, no travellers and strings of pack-horses were to be seen in the lanes running north to St Giles and westward past the little hospital for leprous women dedicated to St James. Even the falconers had fled from the

King's Mews opposite St Martin's-in-the-Fields; there was not one left of the usual throng of beggars on the marble steps of Charing Cross.

But as Richard turned south past the ancient manor called Scotland, a procession advanced to meet him. He drew rein to await it, while the great bell, Edward of Westminster, hung within the gatehouse of the palace, ponderously hammered the hour of noon.

It was a melancholy procession. The Abbot rode his mule at the head of it, followed by his monks, the canons of St Stephen's, and the vicars and clerks of St Margaret of Antioch's, all in their choir-copes but bare-footed and with ashes on their heads, in reparation for the defilement of the Confessor's shrine. Having greeted Richard, and lamented the dreadful crime perpetrated earlier this morning, the Abbot became practical. He had taken it upon himself, he said, to make certain arrangements, sending to the royal manor of Blemundsbury near St Giles, which was used as stables for the King's stud, whence he had ordered the swiftest horses to be brought by way of the fields to Palace-yard. Thus, said he, his Highness would be able to slip away through open country to the safety of Windsor, such, no doubt, being his purpose in coming to Westminster.

'Had that been my purpose. Lord Abbot,' Richard answered reproachfully, 'I would not have failed to bring my lady mother with me. I am come here for prayer and sacrament, for today at the hour of Vespers I have a task entrusted to me by God.'

He knelt motionless before the high altar, fingers joined at the tips like a knight at his vigil, remembering how, on the eve of his coronation, he had done likewise. The prayers he said both then and now were those of a child, simple earnest, and trustful; and when signing that none was to accompany him, he sought the recluse, he was happily confident of an answer to them.

Outside the Abbey, raised upon an undercroft and clinging to the wall like a martin's nest, was an anchorage endowed by his grandfather. It had two windows; one, very small, was merely to admit light; the other was the pour-parler, closed by a shutter on the inside. Beside it hung a bell. When he had rung this, Richard was aware of movement beyond the shutter, accompanied by clinking and rustling which he identified as coming from the iron bracelets and hair shirt worn by the holy man to mortify his flesh. Presently the shutter was opened, revealing merely a black curtain with a white cross on it, behind which the anchorite seemed to be sitting on the sill. The stench from him was so nauseating that even the romantic Richard was obliged to hold his nose.

'Father,' said he, when he had made his confession and been absolved, 'Our Lord had been pleased to entrust me with a mission. Today I must confront and overpower great evil in the form of a man; unless prevented, this wickedness will destroy my realm of England, as already it has desecrated sanctuaries and slain the innocent. But it has not been revealed to me how I must accomplish my task, and from you, who spend your life in prayer and fasting, I am come to seek guidance.'

A hand, skeleton-thin, twitched aside the curtain, and he saw a pair of rheumy eyes staring at him through a tangled forest of hair. There was silence for a while; Richard waited awed but confident, prepared for mystic disclosures. At last the anchorite spoke in the odd loud voice of those who converse but seldom:

'Fair son, of all this I know nothing; it has not been shown to me. But from what you have told me in confession and I have observed as I looked into your face,

I must warn you of two snares the Devil will lay for you. One is the making of rash promises; the other is a refusal to forgive as you hope to be forgive. Beware of these.'

From the quality of Richard's silence as he and his small escort rode back from Westminster, Sir Robert de Vere guessed that something had upset him. Truly devoted to the king, and nearly five years his senior, de Vere had often feared that on the cruel material plane this boy would lose his bearings. To stage tournaments, to call each other by the names of Arthurian heroes, to ape their manners and their ideals, all this was very well so long as one did not lose touch with reality. So now, with all the tact he could command, Sir Robert insinuated his fears as he begged his friend to lay aside the Smithfield project; rashness, said he, was a sin.

Richard's face crumpled like a child's about to weep. Strung up to an acute pitch of emotion, he had just suffered a mortifying anticlimax in his visit to the anchorite. To expect guidance in so grave a crisis, and instead to be warned of personal peccadilloes! And now here was his most intimate friend hinting that he was behaving like some player in a pageant.

'If you deem me sinful,' he flashed, 'I do not wish your company at Smithfield. You may stay behind with the rest of those who laugh at me behind my back, who think me a braggart and a fantasist. I know very well I may be going to my death; I know likewise it is my regal obligation to stop this anarchy and carnage, which my greybeard councillors have made not one move to check – '

Tears choked him, and he bit his lip hard, In all his fourteen years he had never felt so utterly alone; no one believed in him, not even Robert. Ah, if only when he came to Smithfield he could raise his eyes to a window, like Sir Gareth when he fought with the Knight of the Red

Lawns, and see his lady, 'making courtesy to him by holding up both her hands.'

(iii)

From time immemorial, Smithfield, the 'Smooth Field', had been London's favourite open space, a drained expanse of that great moor which stretched northward of the city.

Every Friday there was a horse-fair, when coursers, hackneys and palfreys were put through their paces for the benefit of prospective buyers. Often the guilds staged their miracle plays here, appropriate to their several misteries, and folk came to gape at the two-storeyed pageants on wheels, a curtained dressing-room below, the stage above, the shipbuilders regaling them with Noah's Ark, the goldsmiths with the Adoration of the Magi, the vintners with the Marriage Feast at Cana. Then there was the great annual fair, the right to hold which belonged to the priory of St Bartholomew, and which packed Smithfield to suffocation on that saint's feast day, 24 August. Scarcely less popular were the hangings and burnings near the large pond which, surrounded by elms, lay on the west side. And lastly there were the tournaments held here by the late King if he deemed Cheapside too constricted for the purpose.

But in living memory there had been no such spectacle as that which was promised for today at the hour of Vespers.

With extraordinary swiftness, the tale had gone round that young King Richard had ordered Wat Tyler and his desperadoes to meet him at Smithfield at three of the clock, and only the most timid would miss such a sight. Slinking out of their refuges the citizens made for Smithfield, where they sought safe viewing-points. There was the wall of the Charter House north of Long-lane, contiguous to the ground where fifty thousand victims had been buried in the Pestilence Year; and the City wall itself, curving round from the Alders Gate eastward to the Cripple Gate. For the more nervous, there were the towers of St Zachary and St Anne-in-the-Willows in Popelane, or the huge ancient priory and hospital of St Bartholomew, its buildings forming one entire side of the Smooth Field. Even this ogre of a Wat would scarcely molest a house devoted to nursing the sick.

The rioters converged on Smithfield from two different directions. What remained of the Essex contingent under Jack Straw were seen advancing through the dense forest which bounded the northern view, laden with spoil from village and manor, full fed with beef from many a monastic pasture, well equipped with stolen weapons. In parties large or small their Kentish friends began to join them from the City, Sir John Ball conspicuous among them on his blinkered horse. And like a player bent on making a dramatic entrance, Wat Tyler came last. The spectators jostled for a better view of this monster who had cowed the government, captured the Tower, and made the streets of London run with blood.

He rode a spirited hackney, and a rumour passed from lip to lip that he had purloined it from the royal stables at Blemundsbury. He wore a knightly girdle, highly decorated, and the cote-hardie proper only for gentlemen. Behind him came his 'squires,' one bearing his sword, the other a great banner of St George. Any hopes that he had come here for a peaceful conference were dashed when he at once began drawing up his followers in battle array. Most ominous, it was seen that the two front ranks were long-bowmen, each with a quiverful in his back and two dozen arrows under the belt. Some of those who watched were reminded of another baseborn, man, Goliath of Gath, before whom the Israelites fled in the valley of Terebinth.

So they waited, rebels and spectators, for the coming of King Richard. The sun blazed down, and buildings seemed to trembled with the heat; here and there a woman fainted; dust kicked up by feet and hoofs made the eyeballs smart. John Ball roared out one of his provocative sermons, interrupted now and then by the many bells of London telling the hours. When they announced the quarter before three, every eye focused on the Alders Gate, through which the King would come.

That was the precise moment when Richard left the Queen's Wardrobe; to be punctual, neither early nor late, was part of that courtesy essential in a knight. He had overcome the mortification which had made him weep like the child he was on his way back from Westminster; though he had absolutely no idea how he was going to conquer Wat Tyler, he clung to his faith in divine guidance.

Free from interference by his Council, who had scuttled back into the Tower the moment Wat vacated it, Richard had made his own arrangements. If his tiny escort, which included Mayor Walworth and the two friends who had shared in his defiance at Guildhall yesterday, insisted on wearing harness they must conceal it under their dress. For himself, the armour he donned consisted of a crucifix which had belonged to his saintly grandmother, Queen Philippa, a tiny relic of the Confessor, and a medal with the image of his other patron, St John the Baptist. But outwardly he would appear in even fuller state than that he had assumed for his visit to the shore below Blackheath. He wore a pourpoint of cloth of gold lined with violent tartarine and embroidered with roses, a cap of maintenance, and the Order of the Garter instituted by his grandfather. Thus he set forth, this new David, with not even five smooth stones of the brook to serve as weapons.

The very route he took was appropriate, Knightrider and Gilt Spur Streets, names commemorating the many champions who had ridden to Smithfield for joust and tourney. Under his outward coolness, he tingled with excitement; he, like them, must prove his hardihood alone. He had issued strict orders that the whole conduct of affairs be left to him; his escort had permission to defend him if the rebels actually attempted to molest his person; otherwise they were to be mere witnesses.

The great twin timber frames of the Alders Gate engulfed him in shadow for a moment; he passed between them into the glare of the arena, and in fifty paces more, drew rein. White blobs of faces stared down at him from every wall; across what seemed miles of empty space he saw the massed ranks of rioters. But then for a fleeting instant his imagination painted instead the scene which ought to have been presented here this very day.

Rows of pavilions, gaily striped, each with a knight's lance and pennon planted outside it; the bustle of squires fetching and carrying for their masters, armourers with their bag of tools, coursers prancing, richly trapped, heads plumed, broad reins scalloped, the noise of minstrelsy, the riot of colour. And in a gallery he saw the heroine, slender as a lily, white as the hawthorn, her long golden hair flowing from under a chaplet of flowers. With courteous eyes and gentle glances she smiled at him, friend as well as lover, debonair and *sage*.

The vision vanished. He saw the grim reality, some thirty thousand desperate ruffians drawn up in battle array; and for a while he took cool stock of them. A tense silence had fallen: it was akin to that moment before butchers shouted the let-go to their bulldogs when a bull was to be baited. All present seemed frozen into tableaux. The jingle of a bit as a horse shook its head against the flies was startlingly loud. Then Richard licked his lips and spoke, clear and firm.

'My liegemen, I am here to ask you by the mouth of your leader why you have not observed my command to retire quietly to your homes.'

(iv)

Wat Tyler in his turn had given very strict orders to his mob. He would speak with the king; they were not to stir from where they stood until he gave them a signal, the raising of his right arm with fist clenched. Then they were to shoot down the King's escort, but Richard they were not to hurt. He was young and weak, and they could do with him what they pleased, carrying him through England with them and using his authority to punish traitors.

So now, in answer to that boyish challenge, Wat Tyler took the stage. He was in no hurry; as became the chief actor he would give his audience plenty of time to admire him as he made his horse curvet; with heavy patronage he waved now right, now left, basking in his fame. In all that vast concourse, only one pair of eyes was not fastened on him, the eyes of Ralph Standyche. For behind Wat rode his banner-bearer, and he was Ralph's younger brother.

When Wat had come within a few yards of the King, he dismounted, threw his rein to his henchman and half bent one knee, yet contrived to make the reverence mocking. Then, seizing Richard's hand, he shook it heartily.

'Brother,' he bawled, 'be of better comfort and joyful, for in the week that is to come you shall have more praise from the commons even than you have had yet, and by God's bones we shall all be good *camarades*.'

At this point he noticed Sir John Newton among the little group, and grew stern.

'Fie on you for absconding! I missed you at dinner when you should have been at table to carve my meat. Forget not that I still hold your two sons as hostages. But for your truancy, I am pleased to impose a mere forfeit in the shape of that handsome baselard on your girdle.'

Richard slightly inclined his head to Sir John as a sign that he must comply. As soon as he had the dagger, Wat began to play with it, half drawing it from its sheath, feeling the edge, making a playful stab or two, slipping it back again. The escort held their breath in anguish; standing where the ruffian did within a yard of Richard, he might decide to stab in earnest. But the King let him posture on for a while before asking in a tone of mild curiosity:

'Why will you not go back to your own country?'

As though this were the cue for which Wat Tyler had waited, he launched into a largely incoherent spate of demands and threats, misquoting statutes of the realm, gesticulating with the dagger, boasting of his power.

'Neither I nor any man under my command will budge from this spot until we have our rights. The lords of the Council are cowering in their holes like conies, but my brave lads will flush 'em out. They shall keep their heads upon their shoulders only on condition that their titles be abolished and their estates distributed among the commons. There shall be no bishopric save one, and that shall be given to Sir John Ball. As for lawyers, we will have them all away, and the same with sheriffs and bailiffs. In a word, all men henceforth shall be equal, owning no lord save the King alone...'

As he rampaged on, Ralph Standyche was observing him. The instant he had seen him at close quarters, the young man had had the feeling that they had met before. The time and place eluded him, until suddenly he saw in his mind a little picture. A lonely road in the dusk of winter, illegal undergrowth coming close on either side

157

of it, a bend and the appearance of a solitary pedestrian carrying a crude wooden cross painted red. A dangerous looking man, lacking one ear.

The King was speaking again, still cool and steady.

'I have promised before, and I renew my pledge, that the commons shall have all that in justice I can grant. I have offered an amnesty, and many have taken advantage of my pardon and gone home.' He stood up in his stirrups and appealed to that embattled host on the other side of Smithfield. 'Good people, I am still willing to believe that you have been misled into committing felonies. If you will all retire in peace forthwith, I will extend my amnesty; if not, I am powerless to save you from the punishment your crimes deserve.'

Not a man moved.

'You waste your time, brother,' exulted Wat. 'I'm captain-general of the commons and they will do as I bid them. Parbleu! the day is hot and I have made a long oration. Go, bring me hither a mug of water and a flagon of ale,' he ordered the dejected youth who held his horse.

When these requirements were brought, Wat outdid his former insolence. Aware that he had the full attention of the spectators, he rinsed his mouth, spat the water out at Richard's feet, and drank a leisurely draught of ale.

'That's better,' said he, smacking his lips. 'And now, Brother Dick, I'll return to my lads and await your answer. By God's bones I swear it had best be yes, for when they get not their demands, they are no respecters of persons.'

He turned to remount his hackney; his foot was in the stirrup, when Ralph Standyche's voice halted him.

'You swore another oath once, which you broke. When last we met, you carried the cross of a felon who had abjured the realm. The forty days allotted you to find passage overseas are long since passed. Sire, this man who calls himself captain-general of the commons is but a petty highway robber of my own county of Kent.'

A deathly hush fell. Then Wat flung his other leg across the saddle, and gathering up his reins advanced upon Ralph, wagging his head in menace.

'Come out from among the rest, you lying dog, and we'll settle the matter between the pair of us.'

Ralph was uncertain what to do. He had plenty of courage, but he remembered the King's positive command not to intervene unless a hand was actually laid upon his person. Remaining where he was, Ralph temporized.

'I spoke nothing but the truth. As for fighting you, I may not draw my weapon in the presence of my liege lord, for such would be treason. But I warn you that if I am struck, then it is lawful for me to strike back in my own defence.'

With one of his most blistering oaths, Wat unsheathed Sir John Newton's dagger and came on, the weapon poised to stab. This proved too much for the nerve of several knights and squires, who wrenched their horses round and bolted through the Alders Gate. Ralph, now solitary in the space thus vacated, felt justified in drawing his own baselard; but just in that split second before the pair met, a portly figure thrust itself between them.

'I arrest you, villain,' shouted Mayor Walworth, 'on a charge of 'igh treason, as is me dooty, and I may say me pleasure.'

Wat swung his head like an angry bull, and made to gore this obstacle, stabbing viciously at the Mayor's stomach. But under his gown of office, Walworth was wearing mail, and the stroke glanced off harmlessly. Whipping out a short cutlass, likewise concealed, this doughty citizen returned the stroke, wounding Wat in the shoulder so that he slumped forward on his horse's neck. Before he could recover, Ralph came at him, running him twice through the side with his dagger.

Though stains were darkening the rich cote-hardie, and blood and ale were dribbling from the corners of the slackened mouth, Wat had just strength enough to turn his horse and ride halfway back to his followers, croaking:

'Treason! Avenge me!'

Then he swayed, pitched sideways from the saddle, and lay still.

A confused roar burst from the mob when they saw their leader fall, as ominous as the buzz of hornets disturbed. Then the archers in the front ranks moved in unison. Every figure slewed round into profile; every left arm stretched rigid; every face seemed cut in two by the string drawn back to 'anchor' under the right ear. On the shore below Blackhealth they had looked no more formidable than village lads practicing at the butts of a summer's evening. Now they were the bowmen who had won Crécy and Poitiers, leather tabs on their fingers, bracers on their forearms, their weapons the pick of the bowyers and fletchers in London.

The exultation Ralph had felt a moment before changed to stark horror. Between them, he and Mayor Walworth had made certain that the King would never leave Smithfield alive.

But just before some file-leader shouted 'Loose!' to his fellow bowmen, Richard acted. He made two brief gestures, one to his escort to remain where they were, the other, half command, half appeal, to the mob. Then, touching his horse lightly with the spur, he cantered all alone past the body of Wat Tyler, straight towards the threatening ranks of archers. His voice, incongruously young and gay in that grim setting, held all men stupefied.

'Sirs, will you shoot your King? Only follow me into the fields without, and I will be your chief and captain!'

(v)

The bowmen hesitated. Their target was no longer anonymous, but a boy, rounded of cheek, regal of bearing, he and his mount a blaze of colour as they cantered in and out of shadows cast by the westering sun. Only in the stained glass and frescoed walls of churches had these men seen anything so appealing to the eye, and it almost seemed to them that some young saint there had come alive. The horse's housings, reaching to its fetlocks, were emblazoned with the leopards of Anjou on a field azure, quartering the lilies argent; the hanging sleeves of the rider's pourpoint flew out behind him like wings and sunlight turned his glittering cap into a halo. But that he had no shield or spear, he might have been St George himself.

The bow-strings slackened, one by one, clothyard shafts were dropped from hands nerveless with sheer incredulity. Richard for his part slowed his horse to a walk as though to emphasize his fearlessness; when he reached the massed ranks, they opened out to allow him passage. There was first a ragged then a united cheer, and with one accord they turned and streamed in his wake towards the fields. His escort, left behind, could no longer see him, except now and then a glimpse of his head, crowned with its cap of maintenance, bobbing along like a cork on a rough sea.

Now the centre of Smithfield was filled, as from walls and church towers the citizens cascaded down, all their fear forgotten, babbling of their young King's heroism, shouting congratulations to their stalwart Mayor. Walworth's pride was tempered with anxiety; he could

161

have sworn the chief rebel's wounds were mortal, yet Wat Tyler had disappeared. Either he had dragged himself into some refuge, or his followers had carried off his corpse. In either case the King's peril was extreme; if Wat were dead there would be some determined to avenge him; if he still lived he would incite the mob to further violence. And there was Richard, quite alone, in the midst of several thousand desperadoes.

For all his pomposity, Mayor Walworth could act with decision. Here was a chance to redeem the honour of the City, and at the same time to preserve it from more tumult. Spurring in through the Alders Gate, he sent messages to the loyal among his aldermen. For the second time during the past two days, the rioters had been persuaded to quit London. On this occasion the gates must be closed against their return, and well guarded, until he gave further instructions. Meantime, all men between sixteen and sixty must rendezvous with their arms and harness, at the Cross in West Chepe and at St Martin's-le-Grand.

Ever since her betrayal, London had seemed like a city of the dead. Now she arose to vigorous life again, as the tale of King Richard's feat at Smithfield was spread by eye-witnesses; scarcely less popular was the Mayor who had cut down Wat Tyler. Though the situation remained confused, two things were plain: the King at risk of his life had drawn these barbarians out of London, and he was in danger at their hands. Very well then, he must be rescued. The traitor aldermen, become fearful for their necks, went up and down, swearing they had seen King Richard slain, but no one would listen to them, and they were hissed at and pelted.

From their several quarters craftsmen came hurrying, bakers from Bread Street, fishmongers from Friday Street, butchers from St Nicholas' Shamble, wax-chandlers and pewterers, girdlers and pouch-makers, all transformed now into that citizen army who, when they exercised on summer evenings, provided London with considerable sport. But today no one laughed at the awkwardness with which they grasped axe or spear; women cheered them from window and doorway, priests blessed and censed them from church porches; from every alley leading to the river, watermen and sailors came tumbling up to swell the ranks. The very prisoners in the Tun on Cornhill, nightwalkers and other petty miscreants, thrust hands between their bars to wave encouragement.

At the rendezvous there was much officious shouting by the two sheriffs on horseback; all must be marshalled under the pennon of their respective wards. And when the vanguard of this amateur force came marching to the reopened Alders Gate, there was Mayor Walworth himself in his full pomp, budge gown and chain of office, his banner-bearer displaying the image of St Paul, and his other squires in attendance, the Sword Bearer, the Common Hunt, the Common Crier and the Water Bailiff. In fact, affectionately jested one citizen to another, Master Mayor lacked only his Fool.

Walworth's eyes grew misty with pride when he heard that when those from the most distant wards, Portsoken and Bridge Without, had come into line, he would have between six and seven thousand. Almost he was prepared to forgive them their failure to answer his summons of yesterday. Perceiving old Sir Robert Knolles in the crowd, he asked that veteran to deploy the citizens as he saw best. For himself, he said, he had a mission he would delegate to no man.

He had not for a moment forgotten Wat Tyler. That arch rebel must be found and, if alive, instantly dispatched.

(vi)

For the past three-quarters of an hour, Richard had been employing all his eloquence and charm upon the unkempt horde surrounding him. Common sense whispered that among them must be some who would not scruple to kill him if they saw the chance; but his own daring had lifted him upon a plane where common sense had no place. He was the knightly champion who, in a third ordeal, had won his spurs; and they were the oppressed whom he had rescued from a dragon. Because he sincerely believed in their helplessness, passionately trusted in their good-will, they saw themselves through his eyes.

As they listened to the young voice pleading, promising, encouraging, the evil spell cast by Wat Tyler was charmed away. Here instead was a chief and leader who made them feel ashamed of all the bloodshed and pillage of the past week, who almost caused them to forget the poll-tax, manorial servitude, statutes of labourers and other grievances which had seemed all-important. They were as frightened as cattle which had stampeded and now did not know the way back to the pasture and the byre.

But two false herdsmen remained in their midst. Jack Straw had a peculiar gift for insinuating and blowing on the embers of old grudges; and even now, when Sir John Ball opened his mouth in his famous roar, the mob seemed hypnotized by him. Thus they wavered, now swayed by Straw as he fulminated against serfdom, now held by the fiery eloquence of Ball, now touched with admiration for that other figure on horseback, defenceless for all its trappings of regality. It was while the issue still hung in balance that the banners of the wards were seen advancing into the fields.

Richard at once made up his mind. He stretched high his arm for silence, and addressed the mob.

'You all have my leave to depart to your homes. But because those of you from Kent must needs pass through the City where, because of the mischief you have wrought, you may suffer molestation, two of my chamber knights shall lead you over the bridge to Southwark, and these citizens you now see advancing shall form a guard for you. As for you of Essex, you must on no account re-enter London, but depart northward through the open country there.'

A murmur of acclamation, growing into a roar, broke from the rioters; many fell upon their knees in the trampled grass, blessing him for his clemency, others struggled to kiss his hand. While this was in progress, a little cavalcade came riding through the Bishop's Gate on the north-east; their accoutrements were such that citizens and rioters alike made respectful way for them as they approached the King. He for his part was so radiant that he could afford to smile upon these Councillors who, ever since the murder of Sudbury and Hales, had skulked in safe havens while the tempest raged.

'You are veritable strangers, my lords,' he greeted them, 'but none the less welcome.'

They were not abashed. They had behaved like sensible men; as rulers of the realm during this foolish boy's minority, it was their duty to preserve themselves. They at once resumed the reins of government. Observing how Knolles had deployed his citizen-soldiers to left and right, so as to encircle the mass of rioters, Lord Salisbury exclaimed to his colleagues:

'By'r Lady, that is well done. Now we have a God-given opportunity for crushing rebellion at one stroke, for Sir Robert has only to fall upon these curs and make an end of them, thus sparing the hangman much work.'

Richard stared at him in silence for a moment, that ready flush staining his cheeks. Then he said, so that all in the neighbourhood could hear:

'Sir William de Montacute, you disgrace the high order of knighthood. These my commons spared me when I was altogether at their mercy, and at least three-fourths of them have been seduced into riot by rabble-rousers. I will not let the innocent suffer with the guilty. You have been until of very late in hiding; therefore you did not hear me pledge my royal word that these men should depart in safety.' He turned his back on Salisbury and the rest. 'Sir Robert Knolles, form the men of Kent into a column, display my banner of the white hart at their head, and escort them with sufficient guard over the bridge to Southwark.'

Knolles ventured a protest. Pointing to a youth among the rioters he grunted:

'That young rogue was Wat Tyler's banner-bearer. Is such a rebel whelp to go unhung?'

'I said *all* have my leave to depart,' sharply retorted Richard. Child-like, he could not resist a taunt. 'It seems I must teach you a true knight's way to deal with the defeated, veteran though you are.'

There now came a diversion. With much pompous ordering of men to make room for him, Mayor Walworth rode from the direction of Smithfield to the King's side. His face empurpled with heat and triumph, his budge gown stained with blood, he held aloft by the hair the head of Wat Tyler. With pardonable conceit and much verbosity, he told his tale. By diligent enquiry he had learned how some of the chief rebel's adherents had carried him, half dead, into the hospital of St Bartholomew. Thence Walworth in person had dragged him, presiding over his execution on the very spot where the wretch had insulted King Richard at Smithfield. All Walworth asked now was his Highness' leave to stick this villainous head in place of the Chancellor's on London Bridge.

Richard knighted the jubilant Mayor, together with his two friends, Brembre and Philipot, and the chamber squire, Ralph Standyche. Then at last he could rejoin his mother who he learned had moved to the palace of Westminster.

Physical fatigue, of which he was suddenly conscious, made him light-headed; he seemed to float rather than ride along the familiar route. Sweat stiffened his face and his clothes clung to him; both hands ached from the number of times they had been seized and kissed; he had almost lost his voice after all his talking to the mob. From an unpleasant sensation in various parts of his body, he guessed that he had picked up vermin from the poor dirty multitude; and the idea of this, together with the scarecrow appearance he knew he must present, bits of his dress torn off for souvenirs, made him want to laugh hysterically.

In the gatehouse across the highway from Charing Cross, his half-brothers met him, a trifle sheepish. Glibly they explained their absence from Smithfield: they had felt it their duty, as her elder sons, to remain with the Princess of Wales. Her experience at the hands of Wat Tyler, and her anguish for the King's safety, had brought her to a state of collapse. Richard expressed conventional concern, but he was not thinking of his mother.

Life stretched before him like a flowery meadow, and he walked through it hand in hand with Anne. She would pore with him over his plans for rebuilding the Great Hall of William Rufus, making it the most magnificent in Europe; he would take her up on to the leads of that homely line of buildings beyond, the domestic quarters of the palace, and show her all London eastwards; sometimes in winter the smoke from those thousands of hearths made the spire of St Paul's seem to float without anchorage, a creature of the sky. Together they would listen to the little mysterious noises of the Thames at night; and he would tell her how Sir Launcelot once swam his horse across the river to rescue Queen Guinever from the caitiff-knight, Sir Meliagrance, who had captured her out a-maying.

Oh, how idyllic life was going to be! Single-handed he had stilled domestic strife; he would make a permanent treaty with France; he would seek honourable alliance with the Scots, and by going among them, would win the allegiance of the wild Irish. King Richard and Queen Anne would be remembered in history as the sovereigns who taught England the gracious arts of peace.

As he dismounted in Palace-yard, from the Abbey on his right a deep-toned bell began to ring for Compline; and suddenly he recalled, as it seemed in some other life, his visit to the anchorite this morning. But now his mortification was replaced by pity. The poor ascetic must be crazed by too strict fasting, so to have babbled about rash promises and a refusal to forgive.

There never were promises less rashly given than those King Richard had made to his commons at Smithfield and Mile End. There never was insurrection more readily pardoned than the peasants' revolt.

Chapter Six

The Reckoning

(i)

'The prisoner was caught red-handed, Sir Mayor,' said the Sheriff of London, 'as he was driving off the kine belonging to the Dames of St Benedict at Clerkenwell Green.'

Still in his blood-stained gown, Sir William Walworth was presiding over his mayoral court at Guildhall; despite the fatigue of that memorable day, he was resolved to waste no time in executing justice. Martial law had been proclaimed by the Council against those who were still plundering and breaking the King's peace. Now as he listened to Jack Straw who, in a desperate attempt to save his skin, was blurting out all he knew about the treason of certain aldermen, Sir William deplored the indulgence of King Richard. For a message, courteous but very firm, had come from the King. Only those caught rioting after the Smithfield amnesty might be put to death.

Examples ought to be made, Walworth considered, not least of the sheriffs who were responsible for the safe-keeping of felons in Newgate and other jails, and had failed in their trust. Had he, Sir William, not slain Wat Tyler when he did, there would have been a general rebellion, reports of peasants rising in arms coming from as far away as Yorkshire. Yet after the King's message, the worst punishment he could impose, even on those vile aldermen who had betrayed their office, was imprisonment. Had he his way, they would be taken out now along with Jack Straw and hanged at the Standard in Chepe.

Partaking of some refreshment in the mayoral sanctum later, Sir William forgot his ire. Not only was he, the parish child, the poor 'prentice, now a knight, but Richard had promised him a second signet with which to seal official documents, commemorating his slaying of Wat Tyler. And here came a royal herald to seek his approval of the design for the new seal. Solemnly Sir William studied it; except for the Pater and Ave, he did not know a word of Latin, but it would be beneath his dignity to ask for a translation of the legend encircling the images of SS Peter and Paul on the obverse, 'Sigillum Officii Majoratus Civitatis Londoni'. On the reverse was his own image, and under it was portrayed the weapon, that cutlass with which, he insisted, he had given Wat Tyler a mortal wound.

He was entitled also, the herald informed him, to a badge and a coat-of-arms, and perhaps for the former he would like some punning allusion to his name, as was the custom. Sir William, bursting with pride, rejected the idea. He was seeing in his mind's eye his family tomb in St Andrew Hubbard's. Originally it had borne merely the merchant's mark of his trade; last year he had added his insignia as Mayor; but now he would have a full-length effigy of himself, garbed as a knight, with his escutcheon, all carved by the best craftsman in London. It would be one of the sights of the City, as he would be one of the most famous of mayors.

'You'll please to make me badge a cutlass, Master 'Erald,' decided Walworth, 'and interduce this weapon into me arms. For it was that there cutlass slew Wat Tyler.'

Several times already today, Sir William had been at pains to explain to his friends that in the scuffle at Smithfield, young Ralph Standyche and his dagger had played a very minor role.

(ii)

Down the street called Long Southwark straggled the men of Kent, left to find their own way home now they were safely out of the city they had ravaged. Some continued along the Pilgrims' Way; others turned off at a fork in the direction of Dover; a few went east to Bermonds Eye to beg at the gate of the great abbey of St Saviour. Wistful glances were cast at the many inns; it had been a long, hot and exhausting day, and they had had neither food nor drink. An all-male pilgrimage, members of some parish fraternity, setting out from the Tabard with dogs wearing spiked collars to protect them from wolves during an encampment, were at once besieged for alms.

This is what we have become, thought Hubert bitterly, mere homeless beggars, we who marched up this same road less than a week ago a bannered host whom no man durst resist. He had grown to loathe Wat Tyler, but now reaction had set in, and he felt a certain admiration for that ruffian. It was Wat alone who had transformed a hugger-mugger of peasants into at least the semblance of an army, drilling them as they marched, hunting down deserters and hanging them on the highest tree he could find as an example to the rest, blaspheming one moment, jesting the next, teaching them the trade of the soldier, sparing no man hardship, himself least of all. Now he was gone, and they had disintegrated, each man an individual again.

'Think you, squire,' whined a voice at Hubert's elbow, 'that Sir Knight, your father, will take us back into his service?'

171

Hubert rounded on Adam the reeve, no longer a busy sower of strife, but empty-bellied, parch-mouthed, penniless, with fifty miles of road ahead of him and uncertainty at its end.

'Did you not take up arms to be released from such servitude? And did you not hear the lord King swear that all who desired it should become free tenants?'

'Aye, but I misdoubt whether he can grant away the rights of manor lords,' said Adam with peasant shrewdness.

'Sancte Thoma!' shouted the leader of the pilgrim band, warning his flock that he was ready to start.

Late arrivals, who had been to have scrip and bourdon blessed at St Mary Overy's at the Bridgefoot, came running at the gathering-cry. One man had hollowed out his staff into a flute, and began to play a favourite air, his fellows singing melodiously:

'Jesu Christ's mild Mother stood,
Beheld her Son on rood,
That He was impinned on.
The Son hung, the Mother stood,
And beheld her Child's blood,
Where it of His wounds ran.'

Adam regarded them with a ruminative eye. They all had victuals in the scrip slung on a cord, they were in a mood when they would be generous to the poor, and along the Pilgrims' Way there were hospices, maintained by guild or a convent, where there was free bed and board.

'For the love of St Thomas, a sup from your water-bottle, holy sir,' whined Adam, sidling up to a pilgrim so pious that he walked barefoot. In less than five minutes Adam was selling his new benefactor a couple of horsehairs, swearing they were relics from the shrine of St Withburga at Ely and came from the head of that saint.

172

Hubert sat down upon the mounting-block at the gate of St Thomas's Hospital, and let the stream flow past him. He had not an idea what he was to do or where he was to go; bitter as gall was it to remember how he had imagined his home-coming, with a royal charter pardoning all felonies and promising emancipation to his father's villeins. He had no charter; he had been caught by Wat on his way to receive one. And as for pardon, he had seen Sir Robert Knolles point him out to the King as Wat Tyler's banner-bearer; he was a marked man. At any moment a hue and cry might come after him, and whither could he flee? He could not even claim sanctuary in some church, for this was denied to those guilty of either sacrilege or treason.

A sort of sour anger overlaid his fear. All that talk about charters and amnesties, what had it been but a ruse to disperse the mob? Had Richard, still in his minority, power to issue a wholesale pardon? Surely his Council would have to concur, and was that likely after two of their most prominent members had been butchered? As for the charters, Adam the reeve was shrewd; no king, unless he was an outright tyrant, could grant away the dues of manor lords against their will. Still watching his late comrades straggle past him, Hubert included them in his anger. As he crossed London Bridge a while ago, he had seen the head of Wat Tyler impaled on a spike of the gate; some spat at it as they passed, others shook their fists. Their fickleness disgusted him, for he was too young to know that all mobs are inconstant. Ruffian though Tyler had been, he was the only person in Hubert's life to treat him like a grown man.

Then there was his brother. How cheaply, he sneered to himself, had Ralph won fame that day. He had refused Wat's challenge to come out and fight man to man; only when Mayor Walworth had disabled the commons' leader did Ralph use his baselard. But doubtless he would be knighted, and go preening down to Easter Hall to receive the praises of his father, of Master Parson, of the neighbouring manor lords. While as for Hubert, he must go in the guise of the Prodigal, nor was he by any means sure of a fatted calf at the end of it.

The late dusk of June was falling when he was hailed by a voice that sounded vaguely familiar, and pushing through the last of the wayfarers came a Chapman with his pack slung over an ass.

'You're far from home, young sir,' remarked the Chapman. Then, observing the ragged clothes and the soled hose through which one toe protruded: 'And it seems you have not prospered in your venture.'

'I have no money to buy fairings, if that is what you mean,' said Hubert grumpily.

The pedlar leaned across his beast's back and whispered:

'But still wear the purse I sold you in the churchyard of Easter Green. Was it not good-cheap? For you had not only a purse and belt, but a new song to make you of the company of John the Miller.'

Hubert stared at him through the twilight, and recognized the man who had palmed off on him one of Sir John Ball's jingles. He said with a certain wistfulness:

'It is a song no man durst sing now.'

'I heard some of the Essex men a-singing it when they marched away from London. They're uppity, as they say in those parts.' He chuckled. 'A party of 'em gave Mayor Walworth something to remember 'em by before they left, calling at his manor of Finsbury and turning loose the City's pack of hounds.'

Hubert was startled out of his gloom.

'Do you mean that Jack Straw – '

'Nay, he hangs by the neck at the Standard in Chepe, but the stout among his men keep together, for though our lord King may make promises, he is but a lad and his Council rules the roost.'

'Where may I find these men?' demanded Hubert, suddenly making up his mind. His life was forfeit anyway, and better to die fighting than at the end of a rope.

The chapman shrugged his shoulders, and taking his ass by the halter, prepared to continue on his way. But just before he did so, he gave Hubert a cunning wink, and whispered:

'The forest of Epping is large, squire, but somewhere under the greenwood tree you'll find John the Miller, John Nameless, John Trueman, and all his fellows.'

(iii)

A few days later, Sir Ralph Standyche rode home to Easter Hall.

He was now one of the King's forty chamber knights, twenty of whom must be continually at Court. Instead of sharing a bed, as he had as a squire, he lay alone; his old wage of sevenpence halfpenny a day was increased to a shilling. He ate at the knights' mess, had a squire and a page whom he must pay out of his own purse, and two servants at the expense of the Board of Green Cloth. Best of all, he was entitled to wear the knight's sword and girdle.

So much new dignity might well have turned the head of any youth of seventeen, but Ralph did not appreciate it. More than ever now he longed to be done with the Court, marry Barbara, and manage his family estate. In his opinion, Richard's whole conduct during the revolt had been so childish, headstrong and fantastical, that his service had become a burden. Oh, of course he had been extremely brave, but it was a sort of story-book courage no one was expected to display in real life; that it had succeeded was due, Ralph thought ungenerously, to a large slice of luck. Moreover, since Smithfield he had found Richard's company very tiresome. It was not that the lad bragged, or appeared swollen-headed, but rather that he lived permanently in a dreamland and expected everyone else to inhabit it with him.

The aspect of the countryside through which Ralph rode deepened his mood of criticism. On every side he saw the results of a wicked rebellion that ought to have been punished with the utmost severity, not tamely forgiven. Several hamlets appeared to be inhabited solely by women and children; weeds choked the virgates of the villeins and the demesnes of their lords. There had been no hay harvest, and untended beasts were trampling on the corn. In the wooded parts, he glimpsed scores of outlaws brazenly cooking not only game but domestic poultry. And all this, he knew, was but foretaste of what he would find on his father's manor, his inheritance.

No smoke billowed from the side openings of the louvre, its turrets peeping down at him among the trees about his home. He feared his father might be either in hiding or sick, for the central fire in the hall was never let out. But a slatternly maidservant informed him that Sir Thomas was in the solar, and as he walked thither through the hall, he wrinkled his nose at the stench from the rushes, long unchanged, upon the floor. The modest array of silver, displayed on a little court cupboard, was black with tarnish, and a fur of dust lay everywhere.

Sir Thomas was stooped over his counter-board with its black and white chequers, his money-bags beside him, his veined hands laboriously moving the counters which represented half-groats, groats and shillings. He had never been good at figures, and it was beyond him to use the mark, worth thirteen and fourpence, for accounting purposes. The grey which streaked his hair and beard had increased since Ralph's last visit, and his frame seemed to have shrunk; but his sad face lit up when he saw his elder son.

'My young knight!' cried he, clasping Ralph in a warm embrace. 'They tell me you did a braver deed at Smithfield than that which earned me my banner at Poitiers. Aye, you are a worthy servant of our hero King! You shall tell me about it as we dine; alack, it will be but poor fare. Half my livestock has been stolen, as were my bee-hives, so that I have no sweetening at all. See old Cressida there,' he rambled on, indicating his pet falcon on a perch. 'I would have lost her too when the rogues broke into my mews, but that she goes everywhere with me.'

He rang the hand-bell for a pottle of ale, muttering about how few servants he had left and how remiss they were. Ralph waited resignedly for a comparison of these bad days with those of the Pestilence Year, but instead Sir Thomas enquired if his son had leave of absence from Court.

'No, sir,' replied Ralph rather shortly. 'I am sent upon an errand by our lord King, I and nineteen others of his chamber knights. We are to ride about our native parts and persuade the manor lords to enfranchise their villeins, according to the promises given by King Richard to the insurgents.'

'I am the King's vassal,' said his father simply, 'and have sworn fealty to him. If this enfranchisement is his command, I am bound to obey it, though I confess it likes me not.'

Ralph felt profoundly irritated. He had discussed the question with other earnest young men, and they had come to the conclusion that the new system of money rents was preferable to the feudal payment in service, because the former benefited the landlord. But what his father had just said smacked of that attachment to a legendary past which he found so tiresome in King Richard. It was sentimental, and Ralph was a realist. He said loftily:

'I remember often of late an adage I was taught when I was still in the 'coats, "Make no promise save it be good". It is the common talk at Court that King Richard promised something at Mile End which he will not be able to perform. For the Soveriegn has no power to publish, without consent of Parliament, such decrees as grant away the just rights of loyal subjects before the consent of their representatives, the knights of the shire, has been obtained.'

The old man shifted uneasily on his stool, and took a draught of ale. He deemed such talk impertinent, but he could not find it in his heart to rebuke Ralph after the lad had just won his knighthood. Leaving the subject, Sir Thomas broached one of far more concern to him.

'What of the King's other promise of a general amnesty?' he asked. And then, before Ralph could reply, went plunging on. 'Every night since your brother joined the rebels, I have set a lanthorn in the gatehouse as a sign of welcome to my errant son. Poor silly child, he knew not into what treasons his wilfulness would lead him. *Mea culpa*! Well I know I am to blame for sparing the rod upon him. But then too I blame the friars. God forbid I should question the wisdom of such holy men as St Francis and St Dominic. It may be that their sons saved many a soul by wayside preaching, yet very sure I am that the friars we have in England since the Pestilence have lost the spirit of their founders. Not only do they beg for money, though their rule forbids it, but they denounce those who sit in authority, which is clean against the teaching of St Peter himself.'

While he thus tediously rambled, Sir Thomas had been screwing up his courage to ask a question the reply to which he dreaded:

'Have you any news of Hubert?'

Ralph did not answer for a moment. Though somewhat insensitive, he was not cruel. He had struggled hard with himself to be just to his brother, going so far as to confess to King Richard his relationship with Wat Tyler's banner-bearer at Smithfield, which might have lost him the royal favour, and pleading for Hubert's life. That boon was already granted, his master assured him. On the whole, Ralph decided now, it would be kinder not to add to his father's pain by mentioning the Smithfield incident; but his tone was stiff as he said:

'I saw my brother, sir, among the Kentish rebels who were escorted through London to Southwark after the King had dismissed them, and who, his Highness promised, would be safe if they went quietly home. Since then I have heard nothing of Hubert. I suppose he skulks somewhere, not having the courage to come home and face your just wrath.'

'Now by'r Lady, he knows me better,' mumbled the knight, tears upon his cheek. 'I was ever too soft with him, and am too old to change.' He dashed his sleeve across his wet cheeks, and asked anxiously: 'Is the rumour true that some are still rioting and charter-burning despite the king's most clement treatment?'

'The Mad Priest of Kent is still at large, sir, and until he is caught will incite men to mischief. And there are reports of tumults in the parts about Epping. But Essex is as a foreign land to a lad like Hubert, and I warrant he has had his bellyful of wandering,' added Ralph with some contempt.

(iv)

Hubert stood on the inside of a rough stockade, awaiting his first taste of battle. He felt no fear, only a dull depression; one after another all his illusions had been shattered and he was left with stark reality. He must kill, not for any cause, but because the alternative was the loss of his own life.

It was 28 June, the Vigil of SS Peter and Paul. By begging and stealing he had kept himself alive during the past thirteen days, and in the forest of Epping he had chanced upon some of Jack Straw's men who had guided him to the general rendezvous at Billericay. They shrugged when he enquired for Sir John Ball; that firebrand had taken to his heels after Smithfield, and was now reported to be somewhere in the Midlands. Hubert's new comrades remained unimpressed when he bragged that he had carried Wat Tyler's banner; Straw and not Tyler had been their chief. Now they were leaderless, each man for himself, without so much as their old watchword to unite them.

For from Waltham Abbey, whither he had moved, King Richard had issued a proclamation to be read at every village cross, warning his subjects against rumours that he approved of riot and pillage. His pledges of pardon at Mile End and Smithfield were given strictly on the condition that all retired home and lived peaceably; further rioting would be repressed by force.

If Hubert had feared Wat Tyler, he was infinitely more terrified of this desperate rabble. He was reminded of the tales Wat had told him about the Free Companies in France, mere packs of wolves. They had no fixed plan; they burnt, pillaged, slew, and fought among themselves over spoil. Soon after Hubert joined them, he had witnessed a dreadful little massacre when they happened on a charcoal burners' camp in the forest. His dreams were haunted by the faces of those men and women, blackened by their trade, by their screaming pleas for mercy in their own strange idiom, as their turf huts were rifled and their very infants put to death.

Among this wolf-pack were a few discharged soldiers who, when one of their scouts brought word that the King's youngest uncle, Sir Thomas de Woodstock, was marching against them with five thousand men, directed the rest in making some rough military defence. They stockaded themselves at the edge of a wood, their flanks protected by ditches; at the rear, carts were chained together in a fashion used in the French wars. They were plentifully supplied with long-bows; the stockade was formed of pointed stakes, sloping outward to form a *cheval de frise* against cavalry; and the general order was to aim at the horses under cover of these stakes.

The dullness in Hubert's mind was tinged with curiosity when the enemy came in sight over a rise; he had never seen trained soldiers at work. They were not knights who came, but footmen, formed into compact squares of men-at-arms in conical helmets with a nasal, kite-shaped shields held before their bodies, the sunlight winking in their brightly polished glaives. They marched without haste but with purpose, behind one rank of arbalesters, each man of whom was screened by a timber pavise which sheltered him while he wound up his cross-bow after a discharge.

Even more menacing than these disciplined men were the cannon wheeled along their flanks. Though scarcely larger than a plough, there was something most sinister about the iron tubes, which seemed to move of their own volition, for their mouths were framed in a mantelet, hiding the cannoneers from view. Hubert stared at them with an odd impersonal interest, wondering what form of death these bombards inflicted. Even as he so wondered, a great stone ball came hurtling towards him; he ducked instinctively, half blinded by the flash; it passed high over his head to crash harmlessly in a ditch. But almost simultaneously another cannon got its aim, and a portion of the stockade furthest from him was smashed to matchwood.

Though the rebels had no chance against trained troops, their very desperation made them formidable. Rushing through the breach in the stockade, they hewed down the mantelets and slew the cannoneers. Now the air was thick with arrows; they zinged past like swift-flying wasps, and Hubert's ears were full of the rhythmic twang of strings. But it soon transpired that the enemy had a deadlier weapon; fire-arrows, discharged from a catapult, fell upon the row of chained carts, and these, intended for protection, soon formed a blazing barrier against escape.

Then for the first time the knights made their appearance, protected by plate and mail, trampling men under their chargers' iron-shod hoofs. One of them pulled up his mount quite close to Hubert and surveyed the carnage; he was in fluted armour with a richly emblazoned jupon over it, and the visor of his helm was open on its pivots. There was something in his face which reminded the boy of King Richard; but there was nothing of King Richard in his voice as, leaning an elbow on his chair-like saddle, he shouted a command.

'There is no man here worth holding for ransom, and therefore we are not to be troubled with prisoners.'

He made some sort of signal, and leaping over the remains of the stockade came the Welsh knifemen, dreaded throughout the French wars, yelling in their own tongue as they slit the throats of captives and the wounded.

At that sight, the instinct of self-preservation reawoke in Hubert. Suddenly and frenziedly he yearned for life, even though he must spend it as an outlaw. The enemy was now occupied in collecting what pitiful spoil could be found. Hubert flung down his bow, dodged uplifted glaives and pawing horses, and weaved his way towards the forest beyond the row of blazing carts, his wits sharpened by the intensity of his desire, youth and nimbleness his allies. He ran until the dreadful din had faded to a distant murmur, and there was only the rustle of leaves about him.

Whither he could go, he had no notion, but now for a brief space he must rest. There was a stitch in his side like a sharp knife twisting, the breath whistled in his throat, and the pain of numerous minor cuts turned him faint. Collapsing in the undergrowth, he lay for a while in a swoon. His sense of hearing was the first to return; above the little noises of the wood, he heard a bell, the evening Angelus. In his light-headedness he thought it summoned him, and getting stiffly to his feet he reeled like one drunk towards the sound.

When he came through the last of the trees, he supposed he must have dreamed that tinkle of a bell, for here was no monastery, no village, no human habitation of any kind. Instead there was a scene which made him wonder whether he was dead and, his sins burned away in the fires of Purgatory, had entered Heaven.

In the middle distance a river ran in silver loops like ribbons tying posies, for within each bend the greensward was carpeted with flowers. Beyond, great noble trees threw shade, and over their heads could be glimpsed a mist of blue, suggesting far-off hills. Goats grazed upon the sward, giving a touch of homeliness to a prospect otherwise unearthly; one of them lifted its foolish bearded face to stare indifferently at Hubert, its jaws rhythmically chewing. There was no sound save running water, the clap of pigeons' wings, and the evening breeze in foliage. As Hubert still gazed fascinated, he noticed a number of conies frisking about the edges of the meadow; and then from the forest a stag and two hinds came down to the river to drink.

The peace of it all was so profound, his own fatigue so great, that Hubert would have slept, had not a very curious thing happened. Far down in a corner of the meadow rose a little cliff, all in shadow; issuing from it, as though from the heart of the rock, came a man.

Now it seemed to Hubert that this figure was but a part of his vision, so that he forgot that he was a fugitive and felt no fear. Thus it seemed to him quite natural that when this human creature passed close to them, the conies did not race for their burrows, nor the deer bound away. It was the figure of a man neither young nor old; he wore a long hooded tunic girded about the waist by a cord, from which depended a little book and a string of rosary-beads made of pebbles. His hair and beard, like his dress, were of a light brown, and his throat was tanned to the same pale russet. Wooden-soled sandals, kept in place by a strap over the instep, made a gentle clap-clap as he walked. He was all of a piece with the river and the flowered sward and the solemn tranquil woods; and as he drew near Hubert, the boy saw that his eyes were quick and merry, and that simplicity enveloped him like a cloak.

'You are welcome in God's name, my son,' said he. 'Come with me and I will dress your hurts. Our Lord warned me of your approach, and I have herbs and napkins ready.'

Emotion, the nature of which he could not identify, flickered across the surface of Hubert's mind. Whatever it was, it impelled him to tell the truth to this unearthly visitant.

'Sir Priest, I am a rebel and my life is forfeit.'

'All our lives are forfeit, son,' cheerfully replied the other, 'but we shall die only when God pleases. As for me, I am neither priest nor friar, but plain Master Anthony, such being the name I chose when I was admitted into the Order of Hermits. So far God has had compassion on my weakness, and has not permitted the fiend to appear to me in hideous shapes as he did to the first hermit of that name in the desert. I am under no vows save that of chastity, and I run little errands for Our Blessed Lord, guiding strangers over a ford when the river is swollen, entertaining wayfarers, and suchlike trifling services.'

All this was spoken in a very tranquil, matter-of-fact tone, while the hermit, his arm locked in Hubert's, assisted him towards the cliff from which he himself had emerged so mysteriously.

The bell Hubert had heard hung by a heather rope outside a cavern, the doorway of which was screened by plaited osiers. Within, the cave was of considerable size, combining the functions of oratory, kitchen and sleeping-chamber. A rocky ledge, irregular in width, ran round the sides, supporting some rudely carved images, and a few cups and platters made of earthenware; while at the far end was a plain stone altar, with tapers upon it and a roughly sculpted crucifix in bold relief above. In a sort of recess stood a charcoal brazier, the smoke from which disappeared in what seemed a natural chimney; an iron pot hung over it, and the odour of food made Hubert realize how ravenous he was.

Deftly dressing his hurts while he supped, the hermit talked to him. His voice, as soothing as the murmur of the brook outside, seemed to Hubert now near, now distant, so great was the lad's fatigue. He had dug, said the hermit, a garden-bed near the cave, in which he grew beans and other vegetables in their seasons, for these, with nuts and roots he found in the forest, and goats' milk, formed his diet. Then, still courteously putting Hubert at his ease, he went on to speak of his work at the riverside, describing the art of finding a ford.

'You must choose a heavy stone and lob it gently into midstream. It splashes quite otherwise in four foot of water than in five or six, but this is an art acquired only by long practice. For the crossing, I have my two-handed staff, and

God gave me strong shoulders so that I may carry a woman or the infirm upon my back, like the blessed St Christopher. As for stilts, I will have none of them, for the current may cause them to slip...'

Replete with food, and lulled by the gentle voice, Hubert was nodding asleep, when a distant crashing of horses through undergrowth and confused shouting jerked him broad awake. They were hunting fugitives, and according to the order of Sir Thomas de Woodstock, none was to be spared. But before he could speak, his strange host motioned him to remain where he was, and himself left the cave in the tranquil and unhurried manner habitual with him. He was absent for some time, and when he returned, Hubert could hear the sounds of the hunt retreating.

'I spoke with Sir Thomas de Percy, brother of the Earl of Northumberland,' related the hermit, 'who knew me well in days gone by. For I must tell you that I am what they term a gentle-hermit, and such as we are much venerated because we renounced great possessions to follow Jesu Christ. Alack, those who so revere us look upon the outside and not upon the weak and sinful soul within.' He opened the Book of Hours which hung from his girdle. 'It will be light enough in the meadow for us to read Compline together; only when Our Lord sends me a guest can I have the pleasure of reciting the Divine Office in company.'

Ever since he had encountered the hermit who so mysteriously had know of his coming, Hubert had been fighting an emotion which wounded his pride. But now, suddenly, it overwhelmed him. Before he knew what he would say, he cried aloud:

'I must go home and beg my father's pardon!'

'That were a good errand,' said the hermit gently, 'but we must do nothing till the mind is quiet. A sure sign of the fiend's assault is over-eagerness, which weakens the will, the Devil, as they say, diligently fishing in troubled waters. Come, my son, let us say our prayers together, and then be you content to abide in this poor cave with me until you have regained tranquillity of soul.'

(v)

'If her sickness proves mortal, may I die in that same hour!' wailed Richard, releasing himself almost roughly from his mother's embrace.

His friend de Vere hastened to reassure him.

'The report we had from Sir Simon Burley is quite positive; the Princess Anne's ague is but mild, and her physicians are agreed there is no danger. It will mean but a few weeks' delay in her coming.'

'Which will seem a lifetime to me!'

His mother experienced sharp irritation, and because it was caused by jealousy, it made her spiteful. She decided to tell Richard something she had intended to keep to herself.

'I deem it only just you should know, dear son, a secret I wormed out of the imperial proctors who have resided with us since the marriage negotiations commenced. Several of the Lady Anne's forebears on the distaff side died of a consumption, and it is feared she may have inherited this distemper. There is thus some doubt whether she can bear strong children, and my Lord Salisbury is of the opinion that other negotiations should be set on foot privily among the royal houses of Europe to find – '

'Lord Salisbury's opinion does not interest me, madam,' Richard interrupted with most uncharacteristic rudeness.

The Princess clicked her tongue.

'Those who inherit a throne,' said she tartly, 'must be content to have their wives chosen for them for reasons of statecraft; it is not with them as with village swains. Moreover, though you have persuaded yourself you are enamoured of this damsel, she is but an image in your mind, a picture in a story-book, and when you meet her in the flesh her person may fill you with disgust, being quite unlike the maiden of your dreams.'

'Why, there is Lord Salisbury,' exclaimed de Vere, profoundly thankful for the diversion, 'dismounting in the gatehouse with others of the Council.'

'What can they want?' groaned Richard, watching, from the window of the Abbot of Waltham's chamber where he was lodged, the group now crossing the cloister-garth. With Salisbury and Arundel were Sir William Courtney, the new Chancellor and Archbishop of Canterbury, and Sir Hugh Segrave, now Treasurer. 'After this news of my bride's sickness, I am in no mood for other ill tidings.'

But when the Abbot unshered them into his presence, his visitors' look made it obvious that they had good news to impart. The Archbishop was their spokesman, and informed Richard that Sir John Ball had been caught at Coventry and tried before Sir Robert Tresilian, Lord Chief Justice.

'The wretch refused to ask pardon of your Highness, whereby, considering your Highness' known clemency, he might have saved his life, preferring what he chose to call martyrdom. He gloried in the part he played during the late revolt; one can only pray that he repented before his death. At my special request, he was given two days' respite to make his peace with God,' added Courtenay, not without complacence, for as Bishop of London he had been upon the rebels' blacklist, and he was proud of his own magnanimity.

'Thanks be to God,' said Lord Arundel, 'with the death of this mad priest and the total rout of the Essex rebels by Sir Thomas de Woodstock, all danger is past. There remains the reckoning.'

Richard was standing in the oriel, looking out at the
abbey sheep which grazed in the cloister-garth, a tinkle
from the bellwether mingling pleasantly with the plash of
the fountain near the refectory door. At Arundel's last
words, he turned sharply, sat down upon the window-seat,
and demanded:

'What mean you by the reckoning, my lord?'

'I mean, sire, that justice is equally a virtue with mercy,'
Arundel replied sententiously. 'And justice demands the
punishment of those who butchered the Chancellor and
Treasurer of England.'

'Wat Tyler paid the price of that crime,' said Richard,
trying to keep his voice steady, 'as did the wretch Starling
who played the role of executioner.'

Arundel continued as though he had not heard:

'Moreover we have seen but recently what comes of
pandering to rebels in arms. Weakly pardon them, and
they will fall to their treasons again, as they did in Essex.
The commons deem us timid; they must be taught
otherwise.'

'It is no wonder they deem us timid,' retorted Richard,
his colour rising, 'when they were allowed to enter London
and blockade the Tower without resistance.'

'I say they must be taught otherwise,' intoned Arundel.
'The Council are agreed that all who can be proved to have
taken part in the revolt must be proceeded against under
the normal processes of law, with the co-operation of a
jury. There will be no lack of witnesses against them.'

Richard stared at him for a moment as though unable to
believe his ears. Then he sprang up.

'*All*? Have you forgotten that I pledged my royal
word, both at Mile End and Smithfield, that those who
retired home and lived peaceably should be safe from
prosecution?'

'It was, sire,' the Archbishop interposed soothingly, 'a promise extorted when you were under constraint by the insurgents. As the keeper of your Highness' conscience, I do assure you that such a pledge became null and void once you were at liberty again. Many loyal subjects have suffered in life and limb and goods; your Highness may forfeit their affection if you permit such outrages to go unpunished.'

For a while Richard dared not trust himself to speak. He turned his back, staring with unseeing eyes at the almoner and his assistant, aprons over their black habits, feeding a great crowd of poor at the abbey gate from the alms-basket. At last the King said, still with his back turned:

'If I break my solemn word, I shall lose the affection of thousands of misguided commons, and withal put a stain upon my honour which can never be removed.' He drew a shuddering breath. 'You charge me with pandering to rebels. Had I not done so, none of you would be alive today.'

'Your Highness,' pleaded the Abbot, 'must not think us unadmiring of your heroic feat at Smithfield. All the world applauds your courage on that occasion. But to pardon wholesale murder, not to speak of sacrilege, is to condone such heinous crimes.' He waited for comments, and receiving none, went on with a touch of indignation: 'As for your Highness' pledges of enfranchisement, it would be impossible for me to maintain the abbey lands without the labour of my customary tenants, and for my part I will never consent of my own free will to the taking away of my rights as a manor lord.'

Salisbury spoke for the first time.

'Oh, as for the enfranchisement of serfs, that is a matter for Parliament, which must be summoned to assemble in the autumn. Fortunately his Highness gave no such pledges in writing; the charters he so rashly promised, though I believe they were written, were not able to be claimed in the hurly-burly of the black Friday.'

Richard whipped round, and now his aspect was frightening. His mother, seated in the background, gave a little gasp. She had seen that face before, as cold as the marble from which it was carved, on the effigy of her husband's tomb. Gone from Richard were his grace and charm, his careful courtliness, both in word and deed, which he cultivated even to exaggeration, as essential to the perfect knight. His resemblance to his dead father was uncanny; it was with that same cold implacable anger that the Prince had perpetrated the horror of Limoges. Richard said between his teeth:

'Those who succumb to abject fear are apt to turn merciless once their panic is past.'

The Arcbishop raised imploring eyes to heaven, the Abbot shot out a hand to restrain Arundel whose own hand had flown to his sword-hilt, the Earl of Salisbury said in a voice like ice:

'Your Highness is pleased to take advantage of your rank. There is no other man in England would call me coward, but my gage would be flung at his feet.'

'By Christ's Passion,' raged Richard, but still dead-cold, 'I do assure you, Sir William de Montacute, my rank sits heavily upon me in this hour. Were I not King, I would challenge you to mortal combat. But as for your cowardice, not I alone but all London witnessed it; you and your colleagues' *sauve-qui-peut* during the peasants' revolt will make fine songs and jests for alehouses.' His anger seemed to suffocate him, and he gasped for breath. With a wild gesture, he bade them be gone.

Left alone with his master, Sir Robert de Vere prepared to play the part of David to this distracted Saul and calm the jangled nerves. When the news of Anne's sickness arrived, Richard had been engaged in packing up his precious books for transportation from Waltham Abbey to Sheen. They lay about the chamber, some already in their travelling case, and tactfully de Vere drew attention to them by picking up the *Ars Poetica* of Horace.

'Do you remember the many scoldings I had from Sir Simon Burley when we were children because of my carelessness in handling books?' He imitated the tutor. 'No crying child should be allowed to admire the painted capitals, lest he defile the parchment with his tears. Use not straws as a book-mark, for you will forget to remove them and the book, which cannot digest them, will become distended until it bursts its strings. What's this! Eating sweetmeats over your Donatus! Having no alms-bag at hand you will leave crumbs within the pages. Such a fellow as you should have instead of a book a blacksmith's apron!'

There was no response. The King sat rigid, staring out of the window, his fists clenched on his knees.

'There is a young Dominican, John Siferwas,' his friend persevered, 'has been brought to my notice as having extraordinary skill in painting the likenesses of birds. I thought you might care to see his sketch-book in connection with the Queen's private oratory at Sheen. If one wall is to be painted to represent Eden, the imperial eagle and the ostrich of Bohemia should be prominent among its inhabitants.'

Another silence. De Vere knelt beside his master, laying an affectionate hand upon one rigid fist.

'Was it not always the custom in the days of chivalry for the knight to honour his lady by sending her the vanquished, putting these caitiffs at her grace and favour? When the Queen comes, can you not do the like with those commons who are to be tried? And when she solicits their pardon, who among the Council could be so churlish as to deny her?'

But even the mention of Anne failed to rouse Richard from his brooding. As though he had not heard a word of what his friend had said, he spoke as it were to himself.

'When I have my years, those who made me break my royal pledge shall taste my vengeance. Yea, let them be prelates or lay lords, let them be uncle or brother, they may crawl upon their knees for pardon, but they shall have it not.'

De Vere was alarmed. For he remembered the shadow which had always menaced Richard: the ambition of Ghent's son, Sir Henry de Bolingbroke, Earl of Derby. Because some maintained that the Princess Joan was still legally married to Salisbury and that therefore Richard was a bastard, Bolingbroke had been heard to boast that he alone was of pure descent from the royal house of England. Of enormous wealth, heir to estates in half a dozen counties, treated from earliest childhood as a personage, subtle, secretive, tenacious, Sir Henry de Bolingbroke had the makings of a rival to the throne.

If ever Richard were to fulfil the threat he had just uttered, he would present that rival with a party ready made.

(vi)

It will be a white Christmas, folk prophesied when, a week before Yule, there were some light flurries of snow. Certainly it would be a lean one; with both trade and agriculture disrupted during the revolt, poverty pinched and food was scarce. Many flocks and herds, always killed and salted down at Martinmas, had gone to feed the rebels; the geese, which ought to have been turned into the stubble after harvest, were but skin and bone, for there had been no harvest, which meant that there would be no sowing of winter wheat. So there was little of the usual

193

merry preparation for the twelve days of Christmas; folk huddled round their fires, anxious, bewildered and depressed.

They stay indoors to avoid the sight of me, thought Richard, just as I drive instead of ride to Dover so that I may be spared their hostile looks. Just before it was prorogued for the feast, Parliament had presented him with a bitter gift, a unanimous Nay to his plea for the abolition of servitude. With one voice they declared that the revoking by the Council of the promises made by Richard was wisely done, and the conclusion of their address had burned itself into his memory. 'And for their own parts, they would never consent of their own free will to such manumission and enfranchisement of serfs, nor would they even if they were to live and die in one day.'

And to make quite clear to the King that he was a minor, whose romantic notions they deemed dangerous and absurd, they had petitioned for the reforming of his Housefold, Lord Arundel, his *bête noire,* ousting his beloved old tutor, Sir Simon Burley.

How often had he imagined the day when for the first time he saw Anne in the flesh! It was to have been in June, and now it was the depth of winter, ruining all his cherished plans for summer flowers to be strewn in her path as she walked to the Abbey, for showing her the new turf garden he had laid down at Sheen, for the grand tournament at Smithfield. How many 'gentlemen without' could he expect when roads were either flooded or ice-bound? Everything had conspired to delay her coming; first the revolt, then her sickness, and then a threat by France to abduct her if she travelled through that country. The advisers of the boy King, Charles VI, much disliked England's alliance with the Empire; and it had taken months of diplomatic pleading by Anne's uncle, the Duke of Brabant, before they granted her safe-conduct.

Yesterday had come news of her arrival at Calais, whence she would sail without further delay, the wind being favourable. Here then went Richard to meet her, though with none of the air of a bridegroom, still less of the knight who had won his lady by proving himself in deeds of prowess. Staring glumly at the horses, one behind the other, which drew his tunnel-shaped carriage over the slushy roads, he imagined hostility in every village through which he passed, he who, so short a while ago, had been the idol of the commons, who had desired to be their champion.

'Dick Break-troth, that is what posterity will call me,' he muttered aloud.

His mother, seated opposite, sought to cheer him, though she herself was in no happy frame of mind. Her nose was about to be put out of joint by the advent of a daughter-in-law, she had found her son extremely tiresome ever since the summer, and she was physically uncomfortable. She had just adopted this odd new fashion of shaving the front hair and eyebrows, and the baring of her forehead in such cold weather had given her a headache.

'You should not give way to morbid scruples,' said she. 'In my opinion, the Council have been extremely lenient in punishing only the ringleaders under martial law, and Parliament raised no objection to your request for a general amnesty, though it is true they insisted on two hundred and eighty-seven exceptions. When one recalls that more than one hundred thousand rose in arms, not to speak of their leader's attempt to violate my person' – here she gave a dramatic shudder – 'one must admire such clemency. And I hear that many of those excepted will be allowed to buy their pardons by fines paid into the Chancellor's hanaper.'

'Because it is now impossible to levy the poll-tax, money is to be squeezed from the commons by this means,'

retorted Richard. 'But when the Queen comes, she will
solicit a free pardon for all.'

'I hope you will not induce her to do any such thing,'
said his mother sharply. 'Women should not meddle in
public affairs, as I learned to my cost at Bordeaux, where I
made myself most unpopular with the Gascons for that
very reason. Besides, dear son, you must not expect the
Lady Anne to be capable of such pleading; for the people
of Almaine in general are somewhat – um – uncouth, and
speak no language save their own.'

He bit his lip hard, and made no reply. His mother, who
could never leave well alone, enlivened the rest of the
journey by imploring him afresh not to expect Anne to
fulfil his romantic fancy of her. Even when we fall in love
with flesh and blood, sighed the Princess, how often do our
passions cool! If anyone had told her, when she married
Thomas Holland, that in two short years her affections
would have veered to Sir William de Montacute, she would
have laughed at them. But at least she had never imagined
herself enamoured of a hero who lived only within the
pages of a book.

On arrival at Dover, there were some raised eyebrows
when Richard announced his decision to await his bride's
coming in the Presence Chamber of the castle; it would
have been more in character with this ardent lad had he
insisted on pacing the sands. The excuse he gave was
plausible and even did him credit; she might well be sea-
sick, at least she would be weary and travel-stained, and
would prefer to change her dress and take some repose
before meeting her stranger husband. But the truth of
it was, he had conceived a morbid dread of his first sight
of her.

In the past few months, so many dear dreams had faded;
if his vision of Anne proved but an *ignis fatuus,* he felt his
heart would break. Their first encounter, therefore, must be

hedged about with formality; it would be like his coronation when he was ten and it was impressed on him that he must preserve a complete outward calm and stateliness, no matter what his emotions or his bodily unease. (And so he had, except that he had fainted during the banquet in Westminster Hall.) The shock of meeting an alien Anne must be cushioned with ceremony; it would be an encounter in an elaborated pageant, he and she actors and not persons, playing each a part.

Here, then, he waited, in the setting he had arranged with such forethought, his hands, slippery with sweat despite the coldness of the day, clenched upon the leopard bosses of his chair. And hour previously he had heard the boom of cannon and the mellow clash of bells announce that the bride's flotilla had been sighted; gusts of cheering from the crowds told him when she stepped ashore. Seated slightly below him, his mother patted her freshly shaven forehead, moved her shoulders so that their plump whiteness was still further exposed above her low-cut bodice, and glanced down to make sure that her train lay in the most becoming folds. She was, Richard knew, anticipating the moment when a plain German girl would be confronted with that famous beauty, the Fair Maid of Kent.

Desperately he tried to calm his nerves by running over the items of the banquet; he had spent hours with his Master Cook discussing each dish. There was a peacock, the only meat he could endure to see served whole, its feathers sewn on again after baking, jewels for its eyes; there were lampreys with belly of salmon and mussels mixed together, preserved fruits seethed in honey. The subtleties called warners, because they warned that a new course was to be brought in, were fashioned in the heraldic birds and beasts of Anne's family, of sugar and paste; the cheeses were

197

prettily coloured, red from the juice of the horse-parsley, green from that of herbs. His mother disapproved.

'All the Bohemians I have met were gross eaters,' said she, 'and know nothing of our Anglo-French cuisine.'

She had made a similar objection to the first gifts he had chosen for Anne; a fat purse of money would be more acceptable to any German, she insisted, than these costly little trifles, a Psalter bound in azure satin with crystal clasps, a silver-gilt ship with silken sails, an ivory looking-glass held in the claws of a jewelled eagle.

The doors of the anteroom stood wide open, chamber knights and squires seen there in rigid profile; he raised his eyes now and then to the empty space between them, then swiftly changed the direction of his glance. He had made a childish pact with himself; he would not look full at Anne until she approached his chair of estate upon its dais.

At least, he thought, she could not complain of her reception, Daughter of the Caesars though she was. He had chosen this chamber rather than the hall because the latter had a central fire which would have impeded her procession; here, logs blazed on a hearth with a chimney, their violet flames competing with the light of hundreds of scented wax candles held by pages. The Archbishop of Canterbury stood with the abbots and bishops, arrayed in *pontificalibus* in albs richly embroidered beneath their copes, heads mitred, pastoral staff in hand. The Lords Temporal were in their robes and coronets. The minstrels waited to play a special air composed by their king, John Camuz, in honour of the bride.

There were footsteps in the anteroom and the rustle of skirts; sick with nerves, Richard heard his Great Chamberlain, Sir Robert de Vere, deputed to meet Anne upon the quay, say something in his charming voice. He strained his ears to catch *her* voice in response, but it was so low that it eluded him. Then a procession began to advance between the doors and up the length of the chamber. Through the screen of his long lashes he half saw Ghent and Salisbury, who had escorted the bride from France, leading between them by the finger-tips a female figure; that he perceived, and no more.

Nearer she came, her heelless shoes silent on the floor rushes; now she paused, and he was aware that she sank into a deep curtsy, the ladies who carried her immensely long train dipping in unison. Now he must look at her, for she was approaching his chair. Outside, the light snow had ceased, and a shaft of sunlight fell full upon Anne of Bohemia. She stood with her hands raised and open in a gesture most profoundly touching; it greeted, but at the same time it offered, as she began a little speech in perfect French.

'*Mon seigneur et mon mari...*'

She was slender as a lily, white as the hawthorn; her hair, clasped above the brows by a silver fillet, rippled down her back in a bright cascade. She was debonair and she was gay; her glance was gentle and her eyes were courteous. She was the heroine of all his legends, come to life.

(vii)

The new year of 1382 brought open weather, so mild that snowdrops bloomed at Epiphany, and the birds sang as though it were spring. On a day soon after that feast, Sir Thomas Standyche was out with his falconer, trying a haggard, a wild-hawk caught in adult plumage. The emptying of his mews during the revolt had entailed a serious loss, for hawking was not only his favourite sport but provided much of the food for his table.

Old Cressida had been used as make-hawk today, to teach the wild one its work, but the haggard put up a very poor performance, flying at check, raking out when it should have waited on, and committing other faults which showed that it was not yet fully manned. All the way home, Sir Thomas and his falconer discussed the matter with intense interest and animation; it was not until the knight re-entered the hall of his house, and found his daughter-in-law awaiting him with a cup of mulled ale, that his spirits sank once more.

He had known Barbara from her cradle, and it had often amused him to observe the slight awe in which Sir John Newton held his daughter; now he understood why, and he was not amused. Oh she was a really excellent girl, practical, forthright, sufficiently educated by the nuns at Rochester, the mistress of every branch of housewifery, standing no nonsense from man or beast. Since her marriage to Ralph she had transformed Easter Hall. Like the Valiant Woman of Scripture, she looked well to the paths of her house and did not eat the bread of idleness.

Dust and cobwebs had disappeared, meals were well cooked and punctually served; new hangings, worked by her needle and brought with her in her dower-chest, replaced moth-eaten arras; the modest array of silver on the cupboard was polished till it shone. She had attended to the long-neglected garden, planting sour apples for verjuice and herbs for kitchen and stillroom; flowers which had no useful properties she despised. Early in the morning she was with a net and ferrets catching conies for a pie. Last thing at night she went round the house, seeing that every servant had blown out his candle and that all fires were smothered with ashes. Sir Thomas understood that there was a battle in progress between her and her maids, she refusing to allow them oil for a lamp in their sleeping-quarters. He had not the faintest doubt as to who would win.

Yes, Ralph was a lucky fellow, and seemed to appreciate his good fortune. 'My wife thinks so-and-so ought to be done, and I am of her mind,' was a phrase constantly upon his lips. The servants feared her, for though just she tolerated no fault; Master Parson held her up to his flock as the model of a Christian matron. I chose well for Ralph, Sir Thomas kept assuring himself, and it is only because I am old and too easy-going and set in my ways that I find the dame – he did not know how to express it, except that she tired him like a teasing wind.

As soon as he came into the hall this afternoon, he saw her give a certain look at Cressida on his wrist. Often, ostentatiously, she would fetch a brush and shovel to sweep up the bird's mutings, and though she was far too respectful to say so, she made it plain that in her opinion the proper place for a falcon was the mews. But this was one battle she was not going to win; Cressida was twenty years old and had gone everywhere with him, even to church, since he caught her as a nestling with a hunger-trace on her tail.

Sitting down on a stool by the fire, Sir Thomas had an absurd suspicion that even inanimate things were subject to the masterful Barbara. Nowadays the smoke, instead of wafting about the hall as of old, went dutifully through the openings in the louvre above. His daughter-in-law, having poured the ale, took her distaff from her girdle and resumed her eternal spinning. It was still strange to him not to see her toss her long, sheathed plait; when she became a wife she had braided up her hair under a coif.

'Ralph has ridden to Maidstone for a conference with a man of law,' said she, 'but will be back in time for supper.'

Sir Thomas frowned. He, no less than the villeins, resented this class of professional lawyers who had arisen at the end of the thirteenth century. The law he administered in his manor-court was fluid because based on custom; their business was the writing down of codes to regulate the holding and transfer of land, thus hardening custom in the fixed forms. He wondered uneasily why Ralph had gone to consult this particular man of law; since he had obtained his discharge from King Richard's service and had settled down at Easter Hall, Ralph had become more independent than this father thought proper, conferring with Barbara rather than with Sir Thomas upon the affairs of the estate.

At supper, which was at the country hour of four, Ralph seemed thoughtful. The servants being present, he described small sights he had seen in Maidstone, a troupe of tumblers dancing on their hands in the market-place, the setting up of stalls in the town meadow for the annual wool-fair, a leper he had encountered on the road, with warning-clapper and begging-bowl into which Ralph had flung a groat. When conserves and muscadine had been brought to the dais-chamber, Sir Thomas occupied his armchair, Ralph sat down upon the bench before the hearth, while Barbara took her usual place at an interior window, whence she could keep an eye on the servants at their duties in the hall below.

'My wife and I are agreed, sir,' Ralph began abruptly, 'that the situation on your manor is much confused. You informed King Richard by my mouth that you were willing to enfranchise your villeins, yet the few who took no part in the revolt desire to continue in the old system. Even those who have returned are in no position to pay you a groat an acre in lieu of labour, nor will they be for a long time to come. Soon the busy season will be upon us, for ploughing will start early this year. Unless the demesne is to remain half untilled, you will be obliged to employ hired labourers.'

'I like not such, nor ever have,' Sir Thomas said fretfully. 'Their faces and their ways are strange to me, and they take no pride in their work. From time beyond counting, our manorial system has been based on service in return for protection and security of tenure, and I cannot abide the hiring of labourers who are here today and gone tomorrow.'

Barbara spoke from her stool, sweetly reasonable.

'Yet since, sir, you acceded to the King's request that you enfranchise your villeins, needs must you have hired labourers in their place.'

Sir Thomas muttered something, and fidgeted in his chair. This hour after supper had always been the time for song and story, for recreation after the hard work of the day. Moreover he had the uneasy feeling that his son and daughter-in-law were in a sort of conspiracy against him. Oh, doubtless they thought it was for his own good, but the idea humiliated him, made him feel senile before his time. The worst of it was that in argument he was no match for these coldly practical young folk. He said lamely:

'In any case, I cannot afford to hire labourers, for as a result of the late stirs, my purse is much straitened.' Then a thought occurred to him, and he added with a touch of triumph: 'And you have forgotten, son, that this many a year such itinerant people demand a wage above that laid down by law.'

'It was partly on this very point, sir,' Ralph informed him, 'that I went to consult the man of law. He told me it was the common talk among those of his profession that Parliament will be fain to repeal the Statute of Labourers which forbids employers to offer or workmen to ask a wage higher than that fixed in 1349.'

'That will not help me,' grunted Sir Thomas, 'my manor being so decayed.'

'And the other matter, husband?' prompted Barbara, rethreading the needle with which she was stitching new bed-sacks.

Ralph glanced sideways at his father, and spoke with a rather forced casualness.

'Why as to that, he was doubtful. It would entail the repealing of two statutes, that of Merton in 1236 and that of Westminster some fifty years later, both of which forbade, under the severest penalties, the enclosing by a manorial lord of his waste, wood, meadow or arable. Nevertheless, he agreed with me that such repeal will have to come.'

There was silence. The old man blinked several times at the fire, looked from his son to his daughter-in-law, and at length enquired:

'What did you say?'

'I was speaking, sir,' replied Ralph, maddeningly patient, 'of enclosure. We have considered the difficulties under which you lie. Until the Statute of Labourers is repealed, you will find few willing to be hired, and if it is repealed, your straitened purse will not easily afford a higher wage. But if you could cut down a portion of your woods, clear your waste and turn your arable into pasture, why then you might raise sheep or cattle which need but a mere handful of hired men to tend them.'

'And what of my villeins?'

Ralph shrugged.

'They must live as best they can. They chose to rise in arms and put the whole realm into turmoil; let them suffer the consequences, say I. Those who absconded without your leave are no longer your concern.'

Sir Thomas crossed himself. For a moment he was too indignant to speak; then he burst out:

'God forgive you for those words! You may as well say my younger son is no longer my concern because he played truant. And by the rood, Ralph, I'll tell you this; repeal or no repeal, there will not be any enclosing on my manor. It is a thing abominable; there is no man in England owns land outright save only the lord King; we are but stewards of it, let us be lord or villein, holding it in return for customary and honourable service. I no more own this manor than I own the persons of my tenants, and I will not steal their pasture nor their arable, nor deny them their just share in waste or wood. When the time comes for you to sit in this armchair, doubtless you will do as you deem fit, but there will be no palings raised upon my manor while I am lord of it.'

'Pray God that will be for many years yet, sir,' said Ralph courteously. 'Wife, will you not fetch your lute and let us have some music?'

(viii)

In the days that followed, Sir Thomas grew yet more miserable and heavy. The revolutionary thought struck him that perhaps this living together of different generations was unwise, yet it was universal among all classes of society, an essential part of that custom to which he was so much attached. Besides, when he came to think of it, it was not the youth of his son and daughter-in-law which set him apart from them, made their company irksome; it was a certain coldly materialistic attitude towards life which they shared, but could never be his.

The longing in his heart for Hubert grew to a raging thirst. God knew the lad's wilfulness and romantic notions had caused him pain and even anger; yet if he were honest he had to admit that he had felt a secret sympathy with them. It was proper for youth to dream, to espouse causes, to risk all for an ideal, however mistaken; whereas Ralph had never reached for the stars.

There had been no news of Hubert since a rumour that he had taken part in the fight near Billericay last June, and common sense argued that he must be dead. Yet regularly, night after night, Sir Thomas took from its hook the lanthorn left for him behind the screens by an obviously disapproving but indulgent Barbara, and with something of defiance set it in a window of the little gatehouse. They may deem me an old fool if they please, thought he, but I cannot give up hope, and surely the father in the parable must have kept on the watch for his prodigal, else how did he see him when he was yet a long way off?

On the evening of 14 January, he was later than usual on his loving errand. The new Queen had been crowned that day, and at Easter Green as elsewhere throughout the realm, there were bonfires and junketings. It was said that she had gone upon her knees to the Council, begging that those excepted from the general amnesty might have their sentences commuted to fine or imprisonment, and already the populace referred to her as Good Queen Anne. Sir Thomas had feasted his villeins on beef and ale, and it was not until ten o'clock, long past his usual bedtime, that he carried his lanthorn to the gatehouse, hanging it as always in an old arrow-slot.

He was about to retire when a sound halted him, making his mouth grow dry and his heart begin to thump. For it was the gentle tap of a little mallet attached to the outside of the wicket. So incredulous was his joy that it deprived him of motion; he was certain that here was his dear prodigal returned. The tap came again, more insistent. His hands clumsy with nerves, he had to fumble at the bolts before he could withdraw them; Hubert's name was on his lips, his arms were open to embrace his son, when joy changed to bitter disappointment. The figure standing on the threshold was that of a stranger.

'You seek shelter, wayfarer?' mumbled Sir Thomas, recovering himself and remembering his obligation to offer hospitality.

'I seek Sir Thomas Standyche,' replied a very pleasant cheerful voice, 'with whom I would crave a few minutes' private talk.'

When they had sat down upon a backless bench, Sir Thomas observed, in the dim light of the lanthorn, that his visitor's garb was that ordinarily worn by hermits who, unlike anchorites, moved about the countryside at will. Nowadays there were many false hermits, who had never been admitted to this calling by their bishop, and, pretending to ecstasies and visions, preyed upon the charitable. But the mien of this man, so simple and serene, at once allayed any suspicion that he was of that company.

'For near seven months past,' began the hermit, in a tone as natural as though they had known each other all their lives, 'I have had as my companion someone very dear to you, Sir Knight. It has long been his wish to beg your pardon on his knees, but Our Lord put it strongly in my mind that I should restrain him for a space, and convince myself that his penitence was no mere passing mood. He has abided in my hermitage, ringing bells, tending herbs, doing all manner of lowly service, saying his prayers and seeking guidance from the Holy Ghost; and now, being well tested, he has received his answer.'

The hermit paused. Sir Thomas, weeping for joy and compassion, in broken words expressed his impatience to see his son and welcome him home again. But the other gently shook his head.

'We must remember,' said he with some dryness, 'the elder brother in the parable; there might fall out division in your family were your younger son to return home at this time. Moreover he has sinned against heaven as well as against his father, and Our Lord has been pleased to bestow so deep a contrition for the evil deeds committed by him during the late revolt, that he is resolved to make reparation by taking the cross.'

Sir Thomas' first reaction was one of horror and dismay. To 'take the cross' was the common term for a pilgrimage to the Holy Land, an undertaking of the direst peril, from pirates at sea, from Saracens by land, from disease and shipwreck. It would be eighteen months at least before he saw Hubert again, if ever the lad returned from so hazardous a journey. He shuddered as he thought of the corsairs who lay in wait for these overcrowded pilgrim ships, selling their passengers as slaves. And Hubert was so young! Yet even as he shrank from the prospect, he knew how typical it was of his boy. It was all of a piece with that fiery idealism which, he had been thinking only a few nights since, he missed in Ralph. Hubert had risked his home, his comfort, even his life, in a bad cause; he was humble and brave enough to dare the same in expiation.

'Where is my lad?' faltered Sir Thomas, wiping his eyes on his sleeve.

He was lodged at the parsonage, replied the hermit, and Master Parson was ready to read over him the office of pilgrims in the service-book after Mass tomorrow morning, if Sir Thomas gave consent. For a minor could not make this pilgrimage without leave of his parents. To give the father time to master his emotion, his new friend talked on tranquilly. He himself would undertake all practical arrangements, for he was not without influence, he added with a smile. Already, anticipating Sir Thomas' consent, he had provided a habit, scrip and bourdon; he would accompany Hubert to the port and see him safely on board a pilgrim vessel. There was one little detail he did not tell the knight for fear of adding to the pain of separation. Extravagant in contrition as in sin, Hubert had clamoured to have the cross branded on his flesh, and had to be reminded that this was forbidden by canon law on pain of excommunication.

It was with a youthful feeling of playing at conspirators that Sir Thomas set forth as usual for early Mass next day, thankful that his elder son and daughter-in-law were too fond of their bed at this stage of wedded life to hear Mass daily. He had now had time to grow used to the idea that Hubert had returned to him only to take farewell, and on so dangerous an errand; and pride softened his grief. Nevertheless he could not control his tears when, as he alighted at the lych-gate, a familiar voice, so long silent, begged his forgiveness and his blessing, and in the darkness he embraced his prodigal.

When the congregation had dispersed after Mass, Master Parson, somewhat nervous about performing a rite which was rare for him, locked the door, and with the hermit acting as holy water-bearer, read three psalms and three collects over Hubert, prostrate before the altar. Sir Thomas, kneeling on the chancel step, regarded that prone figure with a certain awe; Hubert was already set apart, a willing victim offering himself for sacrifice.

'In the name of the Most Holy Trinity,' read the priest, having blessed and censed the scrip, 'take this scrip, the support of your pilgrimage, that, corrected and saved, you may be worthy to reach the Holy Sepulchre, and your journey done, return to us in safety... Take this staff, the labour of your pilgrimage, that you may be able to conquer all the malice of the enemy, and come safely to the threshold of the saints.'

A habit of sackcloth was produced, two strips of white cloth, sewn on the shoulder, forming a cross, the special insignia of those who went to Jerusalem. The priest blessed and sprinkled it, praying that the banner of the sacred Cross, whose figure was signed upon him, might be to God's servant Hubert an invincible strength against the temptations of the old adversary, a defence by the way, and to them all everywhere protection.

I have a son who won his knighthood, reflected Sir Thomas, and that I deemed honour enough. But if God spares my other lad, he will return to me a palmer; he will come home and present to this our parish church his hat and scrip, sewn crosswise with palm sprigs, more honourable than any coat-of-arms.

(ix)

The morning was delicious, crisp and sparkling. A fan of trees etched their fine black lace against a sky of eggshell blue; where sun had melted the hoar-frost on the sward, dewdrops twinkled, sapphire, ruby and pure gold.

'Oh see!' cried Anne. 'Someone has scattered a whole casketful of jewels upon the grass.'

'And here is the Snow Queen come to gather them again,' said Richard, walking with her hand in his.

She was, indeed, all whiteness of velvet and fur, her face within the hood just delicately touched with colour from the cold. He feasted his eyes on her; as the most devout may question the reality of a miracle as almost too good to be true, so even now he could hardly believe that she was real.

' "Wherever they bury me," ' he quoted, ' "there I desire that they shall place the bones of Pythias." '

'But your Pythias may die before you – dear love, you are hurting my hand!'

'Do not say what you just said! Never say that again!'

His sudden gusts of anger puzzled and disturbed her, and she tried to make him laugh.

'You resemble Aristotle in that you always walk up and down when you discourse; yes, you are a peripatetic! But you are not like him to look at, for he had small eyes and thin legs and spoke with a lisp.'

The heroine of Richard's legends was lettered; Anne far surpassed that dream lady. Her father's court at Prague was one of the most cultured and cosmopolitan in Europe, and she spoke several modern languages besides Latin and Greek. She was skilful at chess, knew something of astronomy, and though she was not, like La Belle Isolde who healed Tristram's envenomed wound, 'a noble surgeon', she had some knowledge of medicine. Yet all this erudition sat lightly upon her; it was part of the dowry and wholly at her husband's service.

'I must be gone,' she sighed. 'It would be the height of discourtesy to come late to dinner with Madame la Princesse.'

But she made no move towards the barge that awaited her at the water-gate of Sheen. Glancing at him with that keen sympathy he found so precious, she noted that his black mood had not passed. So, caressing the fingers entwined within her own, she began to chatter soothingly.

'What flowers shall we plant around this new turf garden you laid down? I would have roses and lilies, marigolds and sunflowers, great flaming poppies and a hedge of honeysuckle. And when summer come again, shall we not pitch a pavilion here beside the river, and pass our time in mirth and minstrelsy, as did King Arthur and his Queen? But now for this evening, what music and poetry shall we have? Would it please you for me to continue my reading aloud of the Romance of Gui de Warewic? Or may I hear again the song Sir Robert de Vere composed upon your feat at Smithfield?'

Even before she landed in England, she knew all about his adventures during the peasants' revolt. She confessed she had wearied poor Sir Simon Burley by pestering him for details of each new development. Sir William de Pakington, Richard's elderly Keeper of the Wardrobe, was writing a chronicle, and had kept Burley supplied with information. As soon as she reached London, she must be shown the exact spot at Mile End where her husband had promised the charters; where, she demanded, was the bend in the river where his barge lay when he addressed the mob below Blackheath? So *this* was Smithfield! She had tried so hard to imagine it, but she had put St Bartholomew's upon the wrong side. She even recalled to Richard tiny details he himself had forgotten.

But this morning she could not charm away that strange, frightening blackness which fell upon him unawares, and was at the same time fierce and cold. Indeed, her mention of Smithfield seemed only to increase it.

'You will leave me alone for three mortal hours in the company of those who made me break my word,' he reproached her unreasonably.

'But dear love, were I to remain, I could not come with you into the Council Chamber.'

He ignored this, and harped upon a string which troubled her by it discordance.

'I shall taunt them. Oh I have learned just how to get under their guard! I contrive to bring in, as it were by accident, some reference to Smithfield or Mile End, and then, feigning to recollect myself, exclaim, "Certes, I forgot your lordships were hiding in the Tower on those occasions".'

'Can you not leave their cowardice to their own conscience? Can you not rest content that they granted my plea for the lives of those excepted from pardon?'

He flung round on her.

'How can *you*, who share my devotion to chivalry, ask me such a question? A true knight must keep his word at any cost. Did not Tristram renounce his beloved Isolde because he had sworn to King Mark to make her his wife? The Council have shamed me for ever in this world and maybe damned my soul in the next. Let them forgive whom they please, I shall never forgive them.' Then, seeing her distress, he softened. 'Oh hasten back to me, heart of my heart. Don't let my mother detain you. Every minute seems a year when you are not beside me.'

She reached up to kiss him. She was tall, but he was taller; he had grown fast since the summer, shooting up towards the height of his giant uncles.

'When you are dining on potage and *pâté*,' she whispered with a touch of mischief, 'spare pity for me. Madame la Princesse vows I am too thin, and stuffs me like a Michaelmas goose. There will be sucking-pig and saddle of mutton, or a great haunch of venison with red gravy dribbling from it – ugh!'

He thought for the thousandth time what a miracle she was, sharing his every taste, as fastidious as he, with his keen sense of beauty. The little personal gifts she had brought him from Bohemia showed the trouble she had taken to learn just what would appeal to him. There was a relic of St Wenceslaus, the tenth-century martyr of her family; a set of chessmen made of walrus tusk, so old that the rook was still represented as an elephant with a castle on its back; the *Divina Commedia* of Dante, of whom her grandfather had been a patron. She was his *alter ego* even in her choice of dress, delighting in the clear bright colours which symbolized the ideals of chivalry. With what grace did she now gather up her long white train, tossing it over one arm, as she moved towards the waiting barge.

He stood at the water-stairs gazing after her when she had embarked, her snowy hood and mantle conspicuous amid the riot of emblazoning painted on the side and embroidered in the trailing draperies. Her little hand, one ring flashing on the outside of her glove, made gentle loving gestures to him all the way until a loop of the river hid her from his view.

He was about to rejoin his attendant knights and squires, when the remnants of his black mood presented him with a sudden, intolerable fancy. Before Anne came to him, from the very beginning of the marriage negotiations, she had been one or other of the heroines in his legends.

But her white dress, and her going away from him in a barge, brought to mind one sad heroine he had never identified with her: Elaine la Blanche.

Superstitious dread seized him. His mother's spiteful gossip about consumption in Anne's family on the distaff side; a chance remark of Sir Robert de Vere, 'Such fragile beauty seems scarcely of this world'; a rather exaggerated solicitude among her elder ladies lest she catch cold or become over-tired; a foolish lingering doubt of which he could not rid himself that she was flesh and blood, not part of a dream from which he would awake one morning to find himself alone again; these things attacked him now like a swarm of noisome insects, poisoning him with their stings.

Elaine la Blanche, the lily maid of Astolat, clothed all in white, her bright hair streaming down, rowed by one old dumb servitor upon a barge palled through its length in blackest samite, seeming as though she lay not dead but fast asleep, for as she lay she smiled...

He spoke within his mind to Anne, threatening, blackmailing. If you should die before me, then will I prove the tyrant my Council fear I shall become. Then will I be as merciless to them as they to the poor commons. If you should die, I will burn down the house wherein you thus forsook me, yea, let it be the palace of the Confessor!

So awesome a vow both soothed and inspired him. When he sauntered across the garden to his attendant knights and squires, he was their charming Richard, as unperturbed as a landscape after sudden rain in June. But Lord Arundel, his new tutor, wondered; there lingered in the young King's eyes a threat of something more destructive than any summer storm.

Jane Lane

A Call of Trumpets

Civil war rages in England, rendering it a minefield of corruption and conflict. Town and country are besieged. Through the complex interlocking of England's turmoil with that of a king, Jane Lane brings to life some amazing characters in the court of Charles I. This is the story of Charles' adored wife, whose indiscretions prove disastrous, and of the King's nephew, Rupert, a rash, arrogant soldier whose actions lead to tragedy and his uncle's final downfall.

Conies in the Hay

1586 was the year of an unbearably hot summer when treachery came to the fore. In this scintillating drama of betrayals, Jane Lane sketches the master of espionage, Francis Walsingham, in the bright, lurid colours of the deceit for which he was renowned. Anthony Babington and his fellow conspirators are also brought to life in this vivid, tense novel, which tells of how they were duped by Walsingham into betraying the ill-fated Mary, Queen of Scots, only to be hounded to their own awful destruction.

JANE LANE

HIS FIGHT IS OURS

His Fight Is Ours follows the traumatic trials of MacIain, a Highland Chieftain of the clan Donald, as he leads his people in the second Jacobite rising on behalf of James Stuart, the Old Pretender. The battle to restore the King to his rightful throne is portrayed here in this absorbing historical escapade, which highlights all the beauty and romance of Highland life. Jane Lane presents a dazzling, picaresque story of the problems facing MacIain as leader of a proud, ancient race, and his struggles against injustice and the violent infamy of oppression.

SOW THE TEMPEST

Jane Lane gives a deft and masterful retelling of the volatile and tragic story surrounding Henry VIII, a handsome, passionate, arrogant King. England is abuzz with talk of a golden era when Henry VIII ascends to the throne. But, possessed by an immature will, Henry will stop at nothing to get what he wants and when Ann Boleyn enters his life he is determined to have her whatever the costs. Ultimately his wishes prove disastrous for a nation, its Faith, and all those who oppose the royal desire.

Jane Lane

Thunder on St Paul's Day

London is gripped by mass hysteria as Titus Oates uncovers the Popish Plot, and a gentle English family gets caught up in the terrors of trial and accusation when Oates points the finger of blame. The villainous Oates adds fuel to the fire of an angry mob with his sham plot, leaving innocents to face a bullying judge and an intimidated jury. Only one small boy may save the family in this moving tale of courage pitted against treachery.

A Wind Through the Heather

A Wind Through the Heather is a poignant, tragic story based on the Highland Clearances where thousands of farmers were driven from their homes by tyrannical and greedy landowners. Introducing the Macleods, Jane Lane recreates the shameful past suffered by an innocent family who lived to cross the Atlantic and find a new home. This wistful, historical novel focuses on the atrocities so many bravely faced and reveals how adversities were overcome.

OTHER TITLES BY JANE LANE AVAILABLE DIRECT
FROM HOUSE OF STRATUS

Quantity		£	$(US)	$(CAN)	€
	BRIDGE OF SIGHS	6.99	12.95	19.95	13.50
	A CALL OF TRUMPETS	6.99	12.95	19.95	13.50
	CAT AMONG THE PIGEONS	6.99	12.95	19.95	13.50
	COMMAND PERFORMANCE	6.99	12.95	19.95	13.50
	CONIES IN THE HAY	6.99	12.95	19.95	13.50
	COUNTESS AT WAR	6.99	12.95	19.95	13.50
	THE CROWN FOR A LIE	6.99	12.95	19.95	13.50
	DARK CONSPIRACY	6.99	12.95	19.95	13.50
	EMBER IN THE ASHES	6.99	12.95	19.95	13.50
	FAREWELL TO THE WHITE COCKADE	6.99	12.95	19.95	13.50
	FORTRESS IN THE FORTH	6.99	12.95	19.95	13.50
	HEIRS OF SQUIRE HARRY	6.99	12.95	19.95	13.50
	HIS FIGHT IS OURS	6.99	12.95	19.95	13.50

ALL HOUSE OF STRATUS BOOKS ARE AVAILABLE FROM GOOD BOOKSHOPS
OR DIRECT FROM THE PUBLISHER:

Internet: www.houseofstratus.com including synopses and features.

Email: sales@houseofstratus.com
info@houseofstratus.com
(please quote author, title and credit card details.)

OTHER TITLES BY JANE LANE AVAILABLE DIRECT
FROM HOUSE OF STRATUS

Quantity		£	$(US)	$(CAN)	€
	The Phoenix and the Laurel	6.99	12.95	19.95	13.50
	Prelude to Kingship	6.99	12.95	19.95	13.50
	Queen of the Castle	6.99	12.95	19.95	13.50
	The Sealed Knot	6.99	12.95	19.95	13.50
	A Secret Chronicle	6.99	12.95	19.95	13.50
	The Severed Crown	6.99	12.95	19.95	13.50
	Sir Devil-May-Care	6.99	12.95	19.95	13.50
	Sow the Tempest	6.99	12.95	19.95	13.50
	A State of Mind	6.99	12.95	19.95	13.50
	Thunder on St Paul's Day	6.99	12.95	19.95	13.50
	A Wind Through the Heather	6.99	12.95	19.95	13.50
	The Young and Lonely King	6.99	12.95	19.95	13.50

ALL HOUSE OF STRATUS BOOKS ARE AVAILABLE FROM GOOD BOOKSHOPS
OR DIRECT FROM THE PUBLISHER:

Tel:

Order Line
0800 169 1780 (UK)
1 800 724 1100 (USA)
International
+44 (0) 1845 527700 (UK)
+01   845 463 1100 (USA)

Fax:

+44 (0) 1845 527711 (UK)
+01   845 463 0018 (USA)
(please quote author, title and credit card details.)

Send to:

House of Stratus Sales Department
Thirsk Industrial Park
York Road, Thirsk
North Yorkshire, YO7 3BX
UK

House of Stratus Inc.
2 Neptune Road
Poughkeepsie
NY 12601
USA

PAYMENT

Please tick currency you wish to use:

☐ £ (Sterling)   ☐ $ (US)   ☐ $ (CAN)   ☐ € (Euros)

Allow for shipping costs charged per order plus an amount per book as set out in the tables below:

CURRENCY/DESTINATION

	£(Sterling)	$(US)	$(CAN)	€(Euros)
Cost per order				
UK	1.50	2.25	3.50	2.50
Europe	3.00	4.50	6.75	5.00
North America	3.00	3.50	5.25	5.00
Rest of World	3.00	4.50	6.75	5.00
Additional cost per book				
UK	0.50	0.75	1.15	0.85
Europe	1.00	1.50	2.25	1.70
North America	1.00	1.00	1.50	1.70
Rest of World	1.50	2.25	3.50	3.00

PLEASE SEND CHEQUE OR INTERNATIONAL MONEY ORDER
payable to: HOUSE OF STRATUS LTD or HOUSE OF STRATUS INC. or card payment as indicated

STERLING EXAMPLE

Cost of book(s):..................... Example: 3 x books at £6.99 each: £20.97

Cost of order: .... Example: £1.50 (Delivery to UK address)

Additional cost per book:.............. Example: 3 x £0.50: £1.50

Order total including shipping:.......... Example: £23.97

VISA, MASTERCARD, SWITCH, AMEX:

☐☐☐☐☐☐☐☐☐☐☐☐☐☐☐☐☐☐☐☐☐☐

Issue number (Switch only):

☐☐☐

Start Date: Expiry Date:

☐☐/☐☐   ☐☐/☐☐

Signature: _____

NAME: _____

ADDRESS: _____

COUNTRY: _____

ZIP/POSTCODE: _____

Please allow 28 days for delivery. Despatch normally within 48 hours.

Prices subject to change without notice.
Please tick box if you do not wish to receive any additional information. ☐

House of Stratus publishes many other titles in this genre; please check our website (www.houseofstratus.com) for more details.